Deus le volt

God wills it

Berwick Coates

Published by Berwick Coates

Publishing partner: Paragon Publishing, Rothersthorpe

© Berwick Coates 2022

ISBN 978-1-78222-893-6

Cover design Stephen Goodwin
sgssdesign.co.uk

Book design, layout and production management by Into Print
www.intoprint.net
+44 (0)1604 832149

Dedication

To Yvonne Reed

If there existed a long service and good conduct medal for loyal, meticulous, creative proof-reading over many years, I would explore all opportunities to ensure that she is awarded one.

Acknowledgements

I am happy, and relieved, to be able once again to entrust the production of this book to the people who have seen other books of mine through the obstacles of editing, preparation, and publication – Mark Webb of Paragon Publishing, and Yvonne Reed, she of Eagle Eye dot com. My son Stephen has again added sound advice, comment and help on book cover, and has indeed found somebody to make a good job of creating one – Stephen Goodwin sgssdesign.co.uk.

One

BERTRAND DE MONTCLOS halted his donkey and frowned.

If the air had not been so still, he would not have seen it – the thinnest wisp of smoke hanging like lace above the trees. Curious how you became *more* watchful, not less, as you came closer to a town. More human beings – more chance of wickedness – a lifetime of travel had taught him that.

Bertrand scratched a stubbly double chin.

Now who would light a camp fire like that so near the edge of the forest? Poachers would go deeper. So would charcoal-burners; they would have a bigger fire too. And why so near the town? Why not finish the journey? Bertrand guessed at only a few miles more, if that.

It was so close to the route too. You normally made camp well away from the highway, to avoid trouble. Unless you were with a big group. And no large company would have made do with that pathetic wraith of a fire.

No – this was the work of one person, two or three at best. Poor people too, he would wager. Yet they did not seem worried about who would come along. And they should be. Especially now – with the crowds gathering for the Council. It was bound to attract all sorts – both official and unofficial. From the holiest of abbots to the lowest of riff-raff. He caught himself smiling at the irony – even minstrels.

Odd.

'What do you think, Tristan?'

The donkey twitched his ears. It was the first remark that his rider had addressed to him since midday.

Bertrand looked back up the track. It was empty. He glanced up at the cheerless grey sky. He really should not waste time, not at this hour of a cold afternoon.

But human behaviour was the most interesting thing in the world, and he had seen precious little of that all day. It had driven him into himself. He had even run out of things to say to Tristan.

He dug his heels into the donkey's sides.

'All right, here we go. Just a quick look. But gently, now, Tristan.'

He adjusted the straps across his chest and shoulders so that he could get at the hilt of his dagger easily.

He followed the track till he reckoned it was as close as it came to the smoke. He dismounted beside a huge oak. No sense in crashing in like a frightened ox – enough to scare off anything. He tied Tristan's reins to a sapling, took off the heaviest of his bags, and hung them from the pommel of the saddle. A twitch of his belt, a caress of his knife, another glance up and down the track, a fond, absent pat on Tristan's rump, and a final pause to listen beside the trunk of the oak. Reassured, he walked round the tree and into the forest. Knees hit him in the face.

He staggered with the shock, almost choked by the sudden surge of his heart. When he looked up, the body was still swaying from his impact. On a pointless whim of mercy, he put his hands round the ankles to stop the movement.

His second instinctive reaction was to look about him. Nobody ever chose to be seen out of doors beside a recently-dead body. Bertrand looked back up again.

About a week, he would have guessed. He had seen enough in Apulia and Sicily. Not always easy, though, as now, when the birds of the forest had already been busy on the face. Humans had also been busy on the body; nothing of value had been left – belt, leather straps, boots, hat – weapons of course. His leggings hung, crushed and creased, as if he had been surprised on the privy. Bare white hairy thighs enhanced the stark indignity of violent sudden death. The killers had, naturally, taken his rings too – bands of white shone against the tan on his fingers. Slashes in material showed where they had used knives to get at his pockets. They were either very greedy or in a great hurry. Probably both, as they had just murdered a man.

Bertrand knelt and said a prayer. It was all the poor devil was going to get to see him on his way. No wife or mother was ever going to know what had happened – which was probably just as well. He looked like a soldier, even half-stripped and hanging like a child's disused puppet; there was just something about him. Bertrand had sat round camp fires and told stories to countless soldiers all over Christendom. As a soldier, the man could have come from almost anywhere; he could expect sudden death almost anywhere.

However, soldiers were not usually hanged, at any rate not in a place like this. Outside a prison, yes; in a town square, as an example to other unruly drunken looters, maybe. But why ambush a single soldier in the woods outside a town like Clermont, and then take the trouble to hang him?

And why take the trouble to hang him with the most expensive thing on the body – a long strip of rich red cloth? Cloth which, in a bale, would cost a fortune. The sort of material which only princes and bishops could afford. Bertrand made a rough calculation in his head. There must have been enough cloth there to a make a man a cloak, and they – whoever 'they' were – had cut it all up into strips, plaited and knotted it, and used it to execute a common soldier.

Bertrand shivered. Time was getting on. There was nothing he could do here. If he stopped to cut him down and bury him, it would be dark before he reached Clermont. And there was still the smoke, only thirty or forty paces away. There could be no connection with the dead man. No killer in his right mind would hang around a crime like that, not for that long, and certainly would not announce his presence with a fire, however pathetic.

Bertrand did not hesitate long. It would only be a minute, and it would take his mind off the blotched, half-eaten face of the puppet behind him.

He moved on foot towards a thicket masked by bracken, taking care to place his feet on leaf mould.

He pushed aside the ferns.

The space was barely the size of a table top, but had been cleared with great diligence. Almost as if it were a private chamber. Barely a single twig defaced the carpet of dried leaves. Bertrand could not see the fire, because a body was in the way. A single, bent body, crouched in rapt concentration over some unseen task.

Bertrand received his second surprise – it was female. But he was right about the poverty; this wretched creature was poor even by the standards of the human offscourings who crowded into the lean-to hovels up against the town walls of Clermont.

The limbs were like sticks. Hair in rats' tails. Bare feet. Caked dirt up to the calves. Torn woollen clouts about her that were quite inadequate to deal with the chill November air. Through the rents jutted ribs and lumps of bowed backbone.

He was barely breathing, but some animal intuition made her turn round.

Eyes of fire challenged his – eyes that burned holes in a white, wedge-shaped face.

And she was gone. Bertrand barely saw her move. He had to gaze at the imprint of her feet in the pressed leaves to remind himself that she had been there. The rustle was still in his ears.

He cocked his head and listened hard. He heard nothing. He looked about. She had faded like a forest elf. He thought of the times he had sat and listened in taverns, in guard rooms, round camp fires – listened and smiled and yawned while earnest raconteurs told tales of sudden sightings and mysterious apparitions and eerie vanishings – of ghosts and devils and sprites and trolls.

'As I live and breathe – may the Blessed Saints Margaret and Catherine strike me dumb if I tell a lie.'

He had told many such tales himself. But that was different – naturally.

He listened again. The girl had been real enough. Still there was nothing.

He stepped forward and looked down at the fire. It was as pitiful as the wisp of smoke.

He gazed about himself again and called out.

'You need have no fear. You can see me. Only an overweight old minstrel.' He spread his hands and span round. 'With a tired donkey.'

He said it twice – in the tongue of the north and in the tongue of the south – the Oc.

There was still no sound.

9

He examined the clearing. There was no weapon, no item of top clothing, which she might have been frightened into leaving behind. No utensil. No container.

He sniffed; it occurred to him that she might have crept into the thicket for a call of nature. Yet there was no need of fires for that.

However, another smell came to his nostrils – the smell of decay. He bent towards the embers, peered, and recoiled slightly.

Poking from the minute pile of ashes was the half-burnt body of a rat – a rat which had been dead for many days.

God and Jesus! What was this forest – a charnel house?

He sighed, and was turning to go, when he caught sight of a tiny cross stuck into the ground. Because it had been fashioned of two dry sticks, the colour of the dried-leaf carpet had masked it till now. A tie of creeper held the sticks loosely at a crazy angle. It was not only pathetic; it was incompetent.

Bertrand sighed again.

Ah, well.

Then a thought struck him: was this cross and sacrifice connected with the swinging corpse on the oak tree? Struck him so forcibly that he turned about and looked in its direction. No – surely not possible. He could think of a hundred peasants and old wives who would cross themselves and vow that 'it was witchcraft – stands to reason', and a hundred unwashed, pent-up clerics who would mutter and slaver about 'the work of Satan'.

But he, Bertrand de Montclos, had seen the world. He had looked into a thousand camp fires. He knew that if you looked at anything long enough you would start to see things. If you looked at any *two* things long enough, you would start to see connections. There was no future in that; imagination was the enemy of a quiet mind. He should know; he made his living by tapping the imagination. Like an Arab stallion, it was powerful, awesome, even magical if you like, but it was also the very devil to control. He knew that, faced with a puzzle, baffled with a problem, a man must simply do the next thing, and the next thing was usually obvious enough.

He glanced up at the fading sky. The next thing was shelter. Shelter was more important than the rotting carcases of rats or soldiers, no matter how intriguing the questions they threw up. Perhaps twenty years ago he might have pursued the mystery further. But now food, shelter, and sleep came first. Twenty – thirty years ago he was still absorbed with the dawn of things, the bursting energy of beginning, the here, the present. Now? Now he thought more and more about ends, and purposes, and finalities. Then, he set out with a thump in his chest, and great hopes of grand deeds on the way; now he spent the second half of the day wondering where he was going to lay his head. When he was twenty he could not wait to leap from his bed in the morning; now, he could not wait to fall into it at night.

And he wanted more than a blanket soaked with the dank dews of autumn, steaming in front of a lonely fire that could attract anything.

No wonder so many hermits and holy men went crazy – living like that day in day out. It was enough to drive anyone off his head. All that loneliness and depression and hunger.

As for local idiots – there was no point in following her. He could do nothing for her. She would hide, and people like that were as crafty as foxes. They were more used to people hunting them and teasing them than they were to kind souls bringing them charity.

Every forest grew its local crop of such wretches – bent in the body or soft in the head – thrust aside by their neighbours to die out of sight. It was like burying them without the trouble of a spade.

God's Will, so they said. It was on God's conscience, not theirs. God could live with that sort of thing. Think of the pains He inflicted on sane people.

Bertrand slung his bags again, took the reins, and remounted. If he wasted any more time, he was being stupid to himself. He had taken the forest track in order to steal a march on the motley crowds who would be converging from every quarter of France below the Loire – from Guienne, Gascony, Provence, the Spanish Marches.

And crowds there would certainly be.

His Holiness had been on the move throughout the region for over three months. Something was going to happen. Something big. It was impossible not to feel the excitement. Burgundy and the Auvergne were positively throbbing with speculation and rumour.

The inns would be packed.

The walls of Clermont came into view in the late autumn dusk. Bertrand paused on the edge of the trees, and scanned the countryside before him. Force of habit. Like an animal before it left cover.

Long furrows lay dark from autumn ploughing, stroked by sliding fingers of mist. Boys drove pigs, unwilling, from their heath foraging, back to the safety of the sty. Their breath hung in smoke as they shouted in high treble. Two peasants, hunched against the creeping cold, trudged along a path and parted company in front of a line of huddled thatch. Where Bertrand's track joined the road, a draper's wagon had pulled up, and his boy was preparing a meal over a small fire. They had obviously decided to stay out in some space rather than be swallowed up in the morass of tents and cabins that surged round the walls. A fat brother made his painful way on a swaying mule towards a small monastery outside the town. From the monastery belfry a solitary pealing reminded the world that the Holy Office never ceased. Always, wherever it may be, day or night, summer or winter, men were raising their voices in worship, intercession, and supplication to the Almighty. It was as regular as the sunrise. It was the heartbeat of a Christian society.

Bertrand let his shoulders rise and fall in relief. Suddenly he felt his limbs begin to ache, as they always did when food and rest became imminent. Even so, as he nudged Tristan forward, he felt his thoughts being tugged away. Not to the eyeless puppet dangling from the oak; there was nothing to be done for him, beyond the mercy of a prayer for his soul, and he had offered that. If he met the mayor, he might drop a word, so long as he did not involve himself in any way.

No – Bertrand was letting his tired thoughts dwell on something alive – well, half alive. On the elfin wraith in the woods – with her wand-like, white arms and her burning eyes. He had seen legions of paupers in his time. He had seen the coarsening of the soul brought about by poverty and want. Yet he would swear that that girl did not belong to the teeming ghetto of split logs and scruffy thatch which clung like cobwebs to the unswept walls of Clermont. She was poor, but she was, curiously, no pauper.

Idiot? Maybe. He was no expert on madness. He did not know what idiots were supposed to do. But he did know what they usually did not do: they did not usually build fires, make crosses, or offer sacrifices. And they did not usually have the means of finding and trapping a rat in a forest.

* * * * * *

Two

THE EVENING CONSTABLES were fighting a losing battle. With darkness impending, they struggled to close the gates, but the press of people was too heavy. Errands were too urgent. Dignity was being upset; patience was being exhausted.

'I have a job to do. Those are the rules.'

'To the midden with the rules. We have travelled fifteen miles today. My family is exhausted. Give us a chance, for God's sake.'

'You should have thought of that before you set out. Have you never been in a city before?'

'Call this a city? You can smell it a mile off.'

'Nobody is forcing you to stay.'

Bertrand decided to try and get a space at the first inn he found. The others would be just as crowded, and he might as well start looking straight away.

He wrinkled his nose. That harassed father was right; the smell was awful. For a moment he thought of changing his mind and going back out of the gates. The fields immediately outside the wall were littered with tents and shanties and lop-sided wagons. He had tried to charm his way into a berth in or under a dozen of them, but had failed each time. He had come closest with the draper's wagon at the join of the track and the road, but Hugh of Tournai – that was his name – had said no.

His best hope now lay in the town – a nook in a crowded loft, a shelf under a counter, a bench in an alcove.

He caught the attention of a harassed constable.

'Has His Holiness arrived yet?'

The man spat into a gutter.

'What do you think? Take a look at this lot. Mad, all of them. They will never get near him.'

He flung up his arms, turned away, and swore as he slipped in yet another cow pat.

Bertrand's spirits fell. If Pope Urban was already installed in the Bishop's palace, a tardy minstrel would be lucky to get even a corner of a stable. The sooner he started looking in earnest the better.

Almost within yards of the gateway and the swearing constable, he saw a pole jutting out across the teeming street. A crude carving of a bird of prey hung from it, already damp from the humours of the coming dark.

Bertrand grunted. The inn of *The Hawk* – a fair indication perhaps of the attitude of the owner to his customers. Odd how so many such signs – lion, hawk, fox, falcon, dragon – displayed beasts of prey. Almost by instinct he patted the waist wallet strapped to his belt, just to reassure himself.

Ah, well, beggars could not be choosers. As he moved closer, he caught sight of what was clearly the owner, in tense altercation with a trio of noisy arrivals. Arms were lifted, heads were shaken, voices were raised, oaths were flung, and flung back. Even in the bad light, Bertrand fancied he could see the innkeeper's neck becoming redder with annoyance.

Bertrand turned away, looking for another entrance. A lifetime of travel and softening his fellow man had taught him that frontal assault rarely carried the citadel. Guardians of front gates were there to keep people out. Humble servants in back yards were much more

16

approachable; after all, it was not their inn, and they were usually grateful if anyone took notice of them.

He slipped down an uncobbled alley and found what he was looking for – the entrance to the stable yard. He made sure he was not followed – he wanted nobody else sharing his good idea. Then he ducked into the gateway, so quickly that he trod on a cat. It flashed from sight with a yowl. As he stumbled to keep his balance, he bumped into a woman about to fling some slops into the alley.

He swung out of the way just in time.

'Careful, mother. I am wet enough already.'

The pleasantry died on his lips. She looked up only to see where the noise had come from. Indeed, it was not clear if she had understood him. The greying hair, which had once been black, was drawn back tightly into a piece of cloth at the nape of the neck. The dark face was expressionless, yet he could feel that the eyes took note of him. The hands which held the edge of the bowl were gnarled but still powerful.

Before he could think up something else to say, she offered the slightest shake of her head, and went back towards the inn. The cat reappeared from nowhere, and followed her, stiff-legged and purposeful.

He was about to turn away and try elsewhere when he heard the shrieking. It cut the dusk like a blade. For a moment he could barely tell if the noise were human or animal. Whatever it was, it was the cry of a creature in mortal agony. It set the hair moving on the back of his neck.

He glanced towards the woman as she disappeared into the back doorway of the inn. She must have heard it; she had heard his joke which had fallen so flat. Yet she did not stop. She did not pause in her stride. She did not look over her shoulder. Nor did the cat relax its gait.

As he stood and gaped, he caught the smell of the smoke. Not the general atmosphere of stale cooking and fireside humours and badly-tended hearths that hung over any busy town in the evening. This came from a fresh fire, and one quite near.

He peered into the deepening shadows in the stable yard. In the far wall was another opening, into an inner courtyard, where a wary innkeeper kept his supplies secluded from prying eyes and light fingers.

Edging round a midden, Bertrand moved nearer. Smoke billowed over him. As he stooped to escape the pain to his eyes, he saw the flames. He heard the crackling. He winced as he heard the shrieking, louder and fuller, from more than one throat.

For the second time that day, he saw a figure tending a fire. This one was male. It was just as intent. He stood, or rather half-crouched, and held a long pitchfork with which he poked the fire to maintain the level of flame. The ghastly noises of unspeakable pain grew louder. At each fresh stabbing wail his eyes lit up. His lips drew back to reveal grey gums and discoloured, gapped teeth.

Beside him lay a pile of sticks and other kindling, from which he tossed pieces on to the pyre. For pyre it was. Bertrand recognised the scene at once, and sighed. The man had caught some rats, and was burning them alive in their traps, so that their death agonies would frighten off other rats. It was a common enough practice in the rougher inns.

'The cat is lazy.' That was the usual excuse. 'Someone has to do something.'

The man's slit eyes glowed, but his squint was still visible. Below his eyes huge cheekbones tyrannised his face. The upward cast of shadow lit his jowls and threw into darkness the pits of his shining eyes.

Bertrand would not have called himself a superstitious man; he had travelled too many roads for that. But the screams, the charnel flames – in which the man took obvious delight – the eyes like coals, the fork to roast the victims still hotter… Bertrand found himself making the sign of the cross across his ample chest.

The man caught sight of him, scowled, and changed his grip on the pitchfork.

'What do you want?'

He stooped to pick up a burning stick, came forward, and held it high to get a good look. At once the dark shadows transferred themselves to the huge hollows below his cheekbones. He stayed slightly crouched, whether from physical deformity or from habitual furtiveness and craft it was impossible to say.

Bertrand stood his ground.

'A place to sleep.'

The man waved his fork.

'No room.'

'Not even a corner of a mattress? A nook in a stable?'

'You heard. Nothing.'

Bertrand noticed a trace of Italian accent. Squint eyes travelled over his dress, his gear, his donkey. The man let his lip curl in disfavour.

'Certainly not for a – minstrel.'

'Why? Have you room for others?'

The man lowered his awesome brow, as if wrestling with the complexity of the reply.

'Are you blind? Can you not see that we are full?'

'I have no idea how full you are. Though I can readily believe that a hostelry as well run as yours could well be very popular.'

That answer was beyond him too. He spat.

'Go round to the front.'

Bertrand shook his head.

'I have tried. The staff only argue there, and the guests only swear. Here I can see you have more sense, and I have good money to offer.'

The remark had a curious effect. The man lowered his torch a little, and Bertrand could have sworn that another sneer crossed his face, a sneer that was not directed at the fat old minstrel in front of him.

Bertrand jingled his wallet. The man held out his hand. Blackened, stubby fingers closed over three coins.

The man jabbed the air with his pitchfork.

'In there. You will have to move the chickens.'

He moved back to the fire, stuffing the coins into a fob below his belt. He glanced towards the back door of the inn, where the woman stood holding another bowl of slops.

He was able to meet her gaze only for a moment. Then he dropped his head, took up his pitchfork, walked with exaggerated purpose to the fire, and began jabbing. His lips drew back in a grimace alike of effort and cruelty.

Mercifully the noises died down; their agony was over.

Bertrand walked towards the door which the man had indicated. The woman watched him all the way. He stopped at the threshold barely a couple of paces away from her. She did not move.

Bertrand gestured vaguely.

'He said I could move the chickens.'

She nodded.

'I heard.'

As Bertrand pushed back the door, he could feel the

woman still watching him. He tied the donkey to a hook in the wall.

He had paid, and he had permission. So damn her; he was tired, and so was Tristan. And hungry.

He clapped his hands.

'Away now! Hup hup hup!'

He was able to squeeze Tristan inside with him. He saw to his donkey's needs, looped vital straps and leads over his leggings to give him warning of anybody showing interest in his bags, and settled down to the best supper he could make. He grinned to himself as he rummaged in the straw. At least he would not be short of eggs.

He heard the woman banging her empty slop bowl on the wall of the stable yard to get rid of the last of the refuse. He had heard her speak only two words, but he would judge her to be Italian too.

He made a pillow out of a satchel and a saddlecloth, and shook out a blanket. He eased off his boots and waggled his toes.

The more intrepid chickens started to creep back in their head-poking, nosy way. They edged round him and vanished into corners.

Tristan shuffled at his tether. Bertrand heaved a huge, end-of-day sigh.

'Well, at least you do not swear at me in Italian, Tristan.'

He snuggled down.

'Well, well, quite a day, eh, Tristan?'

A dead soldier, a half-naked idiot girl, a bad-tempered city ('city' they called it!), an irate innkeeper at the front, a lugubrious harridan and a hunchbacked torturer at the back. What on earth was he, Bertrand de Montclos, doing here?

21

Hoping to make some money, that was what he was doing here. Just like that draper – what was his name? – Hugh. That was it – Hugh of Tournai. And his boy was called Robert. He was making quite good progress with Robert, till Hugh stuck his head out of the wagon and asked what was going on…

'I suppose you sell nothing but the best.'

'Indeed. Nothing but the best.'

'I could tell that the moment I set eyes on your wagon. Style, I said to myself. You can tell they have style.'

'How can you tell?' Robert was caught by the flattery before he could stop himself.

Bertrand made an expansive gesture.

'Oh, you can tell these things, you know. When you have been on the road as much as I have. It is easy to tell the class from the riff-raff.'

Robert lapped it up. Bertrand ventured further.

'I daresay you are going to serve all those bishops in the Council. Plenty of customers for good quality material, I should guess.'

'That is what Hugh reckons. We have covered ground too, you know,' he could not help adding. 'Autun, Cluny, Vienne, Lyons – some of the best houses. You should see the style those abbots live in. Deny themselves nothing.'

'And now a whole council full of bishops.'

'Too good a chance to miss,' said Robert. He patted the side of the wagon. 'The best, the very best. You should see the colours. Blues, purples…'

'And reds too, I daresay,' said Bertrand innocently.

Robert nodded vigorously.

'Those are the very best – and the most expensive. Enough to make a hole even in a pope's purse.'

Robert took the spoon out of the pot and tasted the

soup. Bertrand could not stop his stomach gurgling. Robert grinned.

'You will have to ask Hugh. Not up to me. I shall get a thick ear.'

It was then that Hugh asked what Bertrand wanted.

'What any tired traveller wants at this time of the day – good company, good cheer – '

' – and a free supper and a free bed,' said Hugh. 'Yes, I know your sort. Charm your way in anywhere. And then expect us to pay you for telling hoary old stories that we have all heard before.'

Bertrand absorbed the blow with practised ease.

'We all have a trade to ply, Master Hugh.'

'How do you know my name is Hugh?'

'Never mind; it is. Robert here has been most charming and hospitable.'

Hugh turned to his boy and cuffed him.

'Then he should be more wary of strangers,' he said, turning back to Bertrand.

'I am sorry, my fat friend, but you have chosen the wrong wagon today. We met a charming man like you a fortnight ago. Talk the birds off the trees. Good company too. Even brought a flask of wine for the supper. Before I could turn round, he had whistled up his charming friends, and stolen a bale of my very best – the heaviest.'

'Red, was it?'

Robert's eyes widened in amazement. Hugh dusted his hands.

'Mind your own business. I take no more chances, especially in a place like this.'

He waved a hand towards Clermont and its encrustation of shanties.

Bertrand shrugged.

'All right, all right, I can take a hint.'

He wound Tristan's rein round his hand.

'Just one last thing. That charming man – would he have been a soldier, do you think?'

Hugh frowned.

'Yes, could be. Professional deserter, more likely. His friends too. Why?'

Bertrand shrugged innocently.

'Nothing.'

He turned towards the road, and paused again.

'He did not have a scar on his cheek, by any chance, did he?'

Robert's eyes nearly came out of their sockets.

Hugh swore.

'Go on, clear off. There are such things as constables here, you know. And they cut off long noses. I have work to do. So has Robert.'

Just to emphasise his remark, Hugh cuffed him again…

Bertrand stretched and turned over.

'I expect His Holiness has a better bed than this, eh, Tristan? I wonder why he chose Clermont.'

And why did Hugh of Tournai choose Clermont? For the reason he said? Was he coming to Clermont, or was he preparing to get away from Clermont?

As for threatening him with constables, Bertrand had travelled too. He had, as Robert had boasted, 'covered ground'. Towns did not only have constables; they had mayors. And mayors carried out investigations into sudden and unexplained deaths. When there was enough evidence. Two hours ago, there had been no evidence at all, beyond the pitiful body itself, and he had not made up his mind to seek out anybody in authority. Now… Well, we would see. In the morning, maybe…

He shut his eyes.

So this was Clermont. Great walls of Jericho – what on earth had possessed His Holiness to choose a place like this?...

Do you capture a man and plan to kill him merely for stealing a bale of cloth? And then, when you have a chance of retrieving your cloth, do you cut it up in order to hang him?

Why did Robert risk a second cuffing to come after him? ...

'Just a minute.'

He looked back over his shoulder to make sure that Hugh had gone back inside the wagon.

'I saw which direction you came from.'

'Well?'

'Did you see anybody in there?'

'The woods?'

'Yes.'

Bertrand took a breath.

'Like a soldier?'

Robert did not react, except to shake his head in impatience.

'No, no. Did you see a girl?'

Bertrand controlled his surprise.

'Thin – hungry – poorly dressed?'

Robert's face lit up.

'Yes, yes. She was the one.'

'I got a glimpse – nothing more.'

Robert's face fell.

'She came here. Hugh drove her off as well.'

Perhaps she was asking about dead soldiers too, thought Bertrand, but he said nothing.

'Why do you think he did that?'

Robert shrugged as if the answer was obvious.
'Another mouth to feed. Like you.'
It made sense.
'Why are you interested?'
Robert shook his head sadly.
'The eyes. I have never seen eyes like that.'

*   *   *   *   *   *

Three

'**WHY HERE, ARNAUD?** Why this town?'

Arnaud of Flers put down his mug and grunted with disgust.

'It is no longer a town; it has become a gigantic doss-house.' He grunted to himself. 'And some would have it called a city.'

Bertrand nodded.

'The cathedral?'

'Yes. Ha! Look at it now. Bertrand, they have turned it into a hovel. A month ago they would barely have dared to creep past the door. Now they sleep in the aisle. The crypt smells of stale piss. And worse.'

Bertrand refilled their mugs.

'His Holiness chose it. Did he expect nobody to come?'

Arnaud shook his head.

'His Holiness chose it for a council – not for a – for a mob to camp in.'

'Are you sure?'

Arnaud tapped himself on the chest.

'I am the mayor; I should know. I had the messages weeks ago. Urban has been on the move since August.'

'Before that, if what I hear is true.'

'Yes, if you reckon the Council in Piacenza as well. He has seen envoys from the Emperor Henry's son, and from the Greek Emperor. But no – I am talking of his movements in France. What goes on in Italy is none of my business.'

Bertrand smiled.

'It was once.'

Arnaud looked up prepared to argue, but changed his mind and smiled too.

'Yours too. Good times, eh?'

Bertrand made a face.

'If you call riding and looting with the Hautevilles "good times".'

'You stayed long enough.'

'Because, like you, I had little alternative.'

Arnaud laughed out loud.

'You could go where you liked, and you know it. All you did was tell stories and prise silver out of our pockets – money which we had risked our necks to put there. You can do that anywhere.'

Bertrand put on a pious expression.

'One has one's obligations.'

Arnaud leaned forward on his elbows.

'Bertrand, this is me, Arnaud, your old friend. We campaigned in Italy for over fifteen years. Do not try to blind me with clever words. You were never tied to anywhere. Come on, come on – where have you been in the last ten years?'

Bertrand wriggled.

'Here and there.'

Arnaud pushed him.

'Where?'

'Oh – Navarre, Aragon, Gascony, Provence, Burgundy.'

'Is there a town below the Loire you have not been to?'

'I have not been to Clermont before; I had no idea you were here – much less that you were the mayor.'

'Do not throw up dust. You know what I mean. And I would wager that you have been on the pilgrim road to Compostela as well. Yes?'

'Yes.' Bertrand grinned. 'Twice, actually.'

Arnaud spread his hands.

'You see?

Bertrand sighed.

'Very well. So you have made your point.'

'Not quite. The point I am making is that wherever you go, and you can choose, you can tell your stories and make a living. We soldiers have to go where the living is to be had, and the places are getting fewer and fewer. Leaders like the Hautevilles do not grow on trees. The Guiscard died ten years ago.'

'So what are you doing here – Mayor of Clermont?'

'What?'

Bertrand leaned forward himself.

'Time for you to be honest as well, my friend.'

Arnaud sat back.

'Too old. And I had made a bit. My luck would not hold for ever.'

'Why Clermont? You are a Norman.'

'I went back once. After he became King of England, the Bastard tightened his grip. England suffered. Normandy too. I was a stranger in my own land.'

'The Bastard is dead.'

'Robert rules now in Normandy, and he is hopeless. All romantic adventure and no good government. I should almost prefer to live in England – Rufus and all.'

Bertrand shuddered and pretended to cross himself.

'That fog-shotten island? Heaven forbid.'

They laughed. Bertrand looked quizzically at his friend.

'You complain when the Bastard is too firm, and you complain when his son is too lax.'

Arnaud shrugged.

'We are only human.'

Bertrand waved a hand.

'But why Clermont, Arnaud?'

'Oh – I once did a favour for the previous bishop. He needed a good soldier to keep order.'

'Set a thief to catch thieves, eh?'

'Something like that.'

They drank for a while in the sort of silence that only old friends can enjoy.

'Now it is your turn to tell me,' said Arnaud in the end.

'Tell you what?'

'Why you are in Clermont.'

Bertrand looked innocent.

'I told you – the Council.'

Arnaud laughed out loud.

'Since when have you been interested in bishops up to their ears in holy scriptures and canon law, debating pluralism, simony, and clerical marriage? I can barely pronounce them, never mind understand them.'

'Speak for yourself.'

'My friend, these are matters for scholars.'

Bertrand looked slightly aggrieved.

'Well?'

'You may have said a hundred times you wanted to become a cleric, but you never had the makings of a scholar.'

'I – I just never had the opportunity.'

'Rats and mice, Bertrand. You are a minstrel through and through. Being a mighty prince of the Church was a dream, such as we all have round the camp fire, when the flames dance and set our fancies dancing. I would wager you have never so much as learned yet to read.'

Bertrand flushed, buried his face in his mug, and drank

deeply. He lifted his head and wiped his mouth.

'How can they debate those things in a crowded cathedral?'

'Because they will do it in the Bishop's palace, as you well know. Do not change the subject. Why are you here?'

Bertrand turned his mug upside down. Arnaud turned and called out.

'Simon. Be a good lad and bring us another pot.'

A slender, pale young man set the fresh beer on the table. Arnaud punched him familiarly in the chest.

'Said your prayers today, Simon?'

Simon sniffed.

'Sir, that will cost you – '

'All right, all right, I know what it will cost. There you are.'

Arnaud tossed some coins on to the table. Simon gathered them up.

'How is your father these days?' said Arnaud.

'Well enough. If you listen, you will hear him.'

The answer was prompt, but Bertrand saw a flicker of anger cross the boy's face before he turned away.

They heard a voice raised in altercation with other customers.

Arnaud explained.

'Father has a short temper, and Simon wants to be a cleric.'

Bertrand poured.

'Like me?'

'No. You have only the desire, not the calling.'

Bertrand rode with the punch this time.

'Does this boy have the calling?'

'He thinks he has.'

'Do you?'

'No. Neither does his father.'

'Is that why they quarrel?'

'How do you know that?'

'Just guessing. Rightly, apparently.'

Arnaud poured too.

'The usual story. Sensitive son growing up, old soldier for a father. They do not see eye to eye; they just swear at each other face to face. But you are slipping away again, Bertrand. Why are you here?'

'Because something is going to happen.'

'You mean the Council?

'Something like that. And while they are waiting, people will want to be entertained.'

Arnaud sipped.

'I see.'

Bertrand laughed.

'Old friend, you were always a bad liar.'

Arnaud put on an innocent expression.

'What do you mean?'

Bertrand put a hand on his arm.

'Because you and I both know it is more than that. Much more. The difference is, I do not know why, and you do. And I expect you to tell me.'

Arnaud took a deep breath, as if preparing for a long, difficult task.

'I can tell you what has been happening. I can not tell you what is going to happen.'

Bertrand leaned against the timbers of the alcove.

'That will do for a start.'

Arnaud looked round. The innkeeper and his son were throwing out some drunken carters from the Auvergne.

'Go and piss in your own vomit. And stay out.'

The older man was fat and he was red in the face and

he was sweating, but he was still very strong. The carters did not try to come back.

The hubbub of a crowded inn resumed. Arnaud leaned on his elbows again, and looked down at the blackened cracks in his palms.

'Bertrand, men have said openly that God has deserted them. We have had drought, famine, floods, and pestilence.'

'Nothing new.'

'True. But not one after the other. And not within two years. No wonder men feel deserted. Even the robber barons have gone short, so they have treated us worse than usual. Travelling armies have been that much hungrier, and have looted all the more.'

Bertrand nodded.

'I understand. And the priests have died too. So the flocks are neglected, and they have nowhere to turn.'

'Exactly. Bishops get letters from Rome about dismissing married priests and finding celibate ones, when they are lucky if they have any priests at all in some places – single, married, or bigamists. No wonder we have clerics holding several benefices; they are not criminals; they are simply making the best of a bad job. It is the good ones who try to visit several churches to say Mass, and it is they who are branded as sinners by His Holiness.'

'Life, Arnaud. You know that.'

'If that is "Life", as you put it, men have had enough of it. I do not have the wit to explain it, but I have the instinct to sense it. It is as if – as if – ' he waved a hand in search of inspiration ' – it is like a herd stirring before a stampede. You can see nothing, but you know something is going to happen. If you can imagine a sort of great thread which binds us all together, it is the fear that this thread may suddenly snap. I do not have the words like you… '

'You put it very well, old friend,' said Bertrand.

Arnaud grunted.

'Take last week. I thought it was about to start – what I was talking about.'

'What happened?'

Bertrand suddenly jumped. The woman with the strong hands was standing at his elbow, holding a large, steaming tureen of soup and a wooden bowl. In the noise of the tavern he had not heard her approach.

Arnaud laughed. The woman served the meal without a word, and fished a thick slice of dark bread out of her apron pocket.

Bertrand looked at his friend.

'Join me?'

Arnaud shrugged.

'Why not? Another bowl, please, Livia.'

She left without a word.

'A ghost,' said Arnaud. 'You never see her come or go. But look up and she is always there. She moves like an evening mist in a forest.'

Bertrand blew on his spoon and sipped.

'It is good, though.'

'Fine cook, Livia. Buys fresh vegetables too – whenever she can.'

He chuckled.

'What?' said Bertrand.

Arnaud creased his face again.

'Livia and her great bag. It is almost as well known as she is – down to the market every day. But she does wonders with whatever she buys. Has a store of herbs too – like any apothecary. You should see her kitchen.'

Bertrand, who never missed an opportunity for a good meal, made a mental note to do so.

'That is why they all come,' continued Arnaud. 'Why they all put up with Albert's bad temper.'

Bertrand, spooning his soup, felt himself agreeing with the other customers.

'You were saying – you thought it was all about to start.'

'Yes. Last week, as I said. Soldiers. We counted fifteen in the end. Just paid off.'

Bertrand nodded.

'Roaring drunk.'

'Yes. Even when they arrived. Heaven knows where they had got it from. They bullied their way past the west gate out there just when my constables were about to shut it.'

'Which is why you have given them instructions to shut it promptly now.'

Arnaud glared.

'Would you not have done the same, if you were me?'

Bertrand waved his spoon in the air.

'No offence, my friend. Get on with the story. You digress too much; you will never make a minstrel. Keep the thread.'

Arnaud sniffed.

'Then do not interrupt. Now – where was I? Yes. This riff-raff, smelling to high heaven, burst in, as I said, at the very end of the day, and made for the first inn they could see – here.'

'And?'

'Vico turned them away.'

'Who is Vico?'

'The one who turned you away at first.'

Bertrand smiled.

'I think I am on the soldiers' side.'

Arnaud opened his mouth to argue, but Livia had arrived with his bowl and his bread.

Arnaud waited for her to withdraw, but still kept his voice down.

'Vico, for once, did the sensible thing.'

'For once?'

'Yes. Vico is not noted for his quick thinking. His name is Ludovico really, but he is Vico to everybody.'

'Ah. I thought I noticed the Italian accent.'

'Surly, stupid, and mean-tempered. But a worker. And he could see that this mob would do the house no good at all.'

'So what happened?'

'They went – to everyone's surprise.'

'How?'

Arnaud frowned.

'How what?'

'How did Vico manage it?'

'No idea. But he is very strong, and handy with a pitch-fork or an axe. All he had to do was threaten one of them. You know – "one move and this one gets it in the gut." Vico is not averse to killing most things.'

Bertrand shuddered.

'I have noticed.'

He told Arnaud about the rats. Arnaud nodded.

'Just like Vico. And he is so ugly he looks only half human. Perhaps he simply came up close and frightened them.'

Bertrand thought of the trollish brow, the gimlet squint eyes, the cavernous hollows beneath the cheekbones, the grey gums, the blackened stumps of teeth, the stoop that was almost a hunch. He remembered that he himself had felt the need to make the sign of the cross over his heart.

'So he got rid of them?'

'Yes. Quite quickly actually. One in particular went off swearing vengeance. Maybe the one he had pinned against the stable wall with the pitchfork. But the rest went quietly.'

'Lucky escape.'

'Not really. They only took off to another inn, and tore it apart.'

'There was no Vico there then.'

'No. By the time one of my constables had warned me what was happening, they had started a fire in the square, and were threatening to burn every house in sight. The cathedral itself could have gone.'

Arnaud burped.

'You see? It could have been the start of − well, I have no idea − after all that has happened, to see their house of God go up in flames, after all this work of the Devil.'

'Who says it is the Devil? Arnaud, you have travelled too far to be taken in by that.'

Arnaud licked his spoon.

'Can you say with authority that it is not? Bertrand, these poor creatures − ' he waved a hand to take in the whole inn ' − are desperate to try and find a cause, a pattern, some reason to make all these disasters intelligible. They want to know. Is it the wrath of God? Is it the evil of Satan? Is it the Jews? Is it the spells cast by a funny old woman in a lonely hovel at the foot of the wall? Right now they are prepared to believe anything.'

Bertrand wiped the remains of his bread round the bowl.

'Well, the cathedral is still there, I presume. So what did you do?'

'I went to the bishop. Told him it would cost him. A lot – either to hire a dozen extra constables, and to arm them, or to buy these animals off.'

'And he agreed?'

'Not at first. At first he complained – bitterly.'

'Mean?'

'Tight as a page's arse. I said to him, I said, "What do you want – a hole in your pocket or a burnt cathedral and a mob of distracted townsfolk looking for a scapegoat?" '

'So he paid?'

'With a bad grace, but he paid. It was a close call, Bertrand. I shudder to think what might have happened.'

'How did you manage it?'

Arnaud picked a fragment of meat from between his teeth.

'I took a leaf from the Guiscard's book.'

Bertrand smiled.

'Bribery or treachery?'

Arnaud smiled too.

'Both. You can never beat them.'

'The Guiscard was a master.'

Arnaud nodded.

'Indeed. I learned from the best. So – I dangled a bag of gold. One of them began to nibble straight away. He came to the house at dead of night. Oily creature.'

'How did he know where to come? And in the dark.'

Arnaud laughed at the irony.

'I paid Vico to bring him. Vico jumped at the idea. I think the poor fellow was still scared of him – all those dark streets, and Vico's torch lighting up his face. By the time they reached my door, I think he was afraid Vico was going to lead him into Hell itself.'

Bertrand remembered the rats in the fire, and felt

slightly sorry for him.

'I can guess the rest. You paid this man to lead his friends into a trap.'

'Yes. With my extra constables, and the dark, and the element of surprise, it was pretty straightforward. We had them disarmed before they knew what was happening. Vico enjoyed himself, I can tell you. We gave them two days to cool off in the cells, tied to a wall, and they were glad enough to get away at the end of it.'

Arnaud shook his head wryly.

'The only one to show any real fight was a fellow with a limp. You can never tell, can you? You know – what is going to happen.'

'No indeed.'

Like bumping into a body dangling from an oak on the edge of the forest.

Arnaud grunted.

'And another odd thing – he was the one who had sworn vengeance on Vico in the first place. Now he had two reasons for hating him.'

Bertrand nearly asked a question which had been growing in his mind for some time, but refrained. It was Arnaud's scene, and he, Bertrand, was only the audience. His time would come. Instead he framed another one.

'Do you think the danger has gone away?'

'No, I do not. Those drunken soldiers turned out to be nothing but – drunken soldiers. But the situation has not changed.' He grunted. 'They could even come back, when they get thirsty again.'

'What do you think will happen now?'

Arnaud spread his hands.

'Who knows which animal will be the first to start the stampede? Where will lightning strike? Take it from me,

Bertrand, there is a storm brewing – the like of which you and I have not seen in our lifetime. So I do not want you exciting one and all with your great dramas.'

Bertrand smiled.

'Rest easy, old friend. I shall tell nothing but the most moral of stories.'

Arnaud sniffed.

'Yes – well.'

He stood up.

'I must be off. Mayors, unlike minstrels, are not their own masters.'

Once again, Bertrand nearly asked a question, but changed his mind at the last moment. He even got as far as opening his mouth. Arnaud raised his eyebrows.

'Yes?'

Bertrand shook his head.

'Nothing.'

Arnaud started to grope in his pocket. Bertrand put up a hand.

'The soup is on me. I shall tell Livia you liked it.'

Arnaud picked up his leather jerkin and put it on.

'You might tell Albert to keep on watering down his beer, as he always does. I wish all the innkeepers would do the same right now. I have told my constables to turn a blind eye. The best I can do.'

After he had gone, Bertrand sipped the last of Albert's watered-down beer...

Well, we had a group of soldiers up to no good, as unemployed groups of soldiers usually were. Or deserters, if Hugh of Tournai was right; it came down to the same thing. We had a traitor, who had sold his fellows for a bag of gold. We had a dead soldier – hung. A sort of execution? Maybe. Assuming that victim and traitor were one and the same. No proof though. Unfortunately, we also had two other men with whom he may have fallen out. We had a threat of vengeance, against an ugly, vindictive creature who would think nothing of killing. And we had an irate draper, who, with his merchant's grasping instincts, would have probably jumped at the chance to square the account with a deceiver who had robbed him of his best cloth. If this was all about the same man, he had made himself amazingly unpopular with a wide range of people in a very short time. And he was supposed to be charming too!

And yet – we also had a half-starved young woman who was raising crosses and mumbling over a sacrificial fire less than fifty paces from where he hung – eyeless, half-naked, and unburied. Admittedly, a week after the event. But then the bereaved prayed over graves for years. And she did look half-mad. Had he once turned his charm on her too? If he had, his motives did not bear contemplation.

Arnaud already had his hands full. What was the best way to break the news to him – if indeed it was news? And even if it was, would Arnaud, with his present worries, want to know?

Which would he regard as the greater problem – a solitary soldier strung up in lonely woodland with a strip of red cloth, probably the fruits of his own thieving? Or the whole thread of society snapping?

*   *   *   *   *   *

Four

BERTRAND MADE A face and set down his mug.

'Anything wrong with it?'

Bertrand looked up into the blotchy features challenging him.

'Did I say there was?'

'You looked.'

'I am drinking it.'

Albert gathered up the coins.

'See that you do.'

'One thing though,' said Bertrand as Albert moved away.

'Oh?'

Bertrand looked innocently at the backs of his hands.

'Arnaud wants you to keep on what you are doing.'

Albert frowned.

'What do you mean?'

'Message from Arnaud. He does not want any trouble. Keep them peaceful. With the beer. He said you would understand.'

Albert swore.

'Slanderous bastard!'

A long word for Albert. Bertrand's regard for his intelligence rose. But not for his courtesy. So far as he could see, after many hours of watching in a corner, Albert was rude to nearly everybody. Or rather, not rude – just short-tempered. Everything annoyed him.

Bertrand included. Bertrand knew that.

'Why do you sit around so much? Why are you not out telling stories?'

'What do you keep in your sheds in the small court-yard? The one behind the midden.'

Albert hesitated, puzzled.

'Why?'

'Stores – yes?'

'Yes. Why?'

'So that, when your customers have eaten everything that is in here, you have some more to draw on?'

Albert frowned.

'Of course. Why?'

Bertrand picked up his mug again and waved towards the rest of the room.

'I sit and listen. I collect my stories here.'

Albert grunted. As he ambled away, he said, half to himself, 'Just an excuse to sit on a fat arse, if you ask me.'

Bertrand did not take offence. He shifted his ample buttocks on the hard bench. He had indeed been sitting a long time, doing nothing in particular. But then he had been on the road a long time too, and he needed the rest. He did not find it easy to switch from constant movement to steady stillness. It was as if something in him lagged behind. He had to wait for it to catch up.

Moreover, he liked to soak up a local atmosphere. He liked to get the feel of a place before he went to work. He could be as professional as the next man, and he could tell a story at the drop of a coin anywhere if need be, but, for preference, he liked to do it when the mood was on him. That mood generally came to him after a while; some instinct told him when he had absorbed enough – of the town or the village or the castle barracks or the camp site – when he was ready to turn what he had learnt into the oil which he used to lubricate his story. A story which he told in haste or in need generally rattled along, but it rattled like the chain of a drawbridge. A story which came when he was ready flowed like a great wide river, broad and smooth, enveloping and unstoppable.

He used anything to acquire this material. His eyes, naturally. His ears too. But there were other ways. His nose, for example. Even his tongue. Livia's soups and stews were a case in point. They told him a lot – about Livia, about the inn, about the customers.

Then there was his own flesh. He shifted again on the bench; it was hard and unyielding, and generous with splinters – the bench of a badly-run establishment. Were the other inns of Clermont like this? He did not know. He had never been to Clermont before – which in itself made him take longer to find what he was looking for. Arnaud was right; he had traversed Burgundy and the Auvergne more than once, but for some reason had never visited Clermont. Right now he was not regretting the fact.

Albert clearly was not a natural innkeeper. He was always being taken unawares, and consequently always getting flustered. He never seemed to have enough time for the work he set himself. Perhaps he intended to be good innkeeper, but he was no use at managing his time. Customers annoyed him. His neck would get redder, his voice would rise, his huge arms would be raised to the rafters, and the oaths would follow. He was strong, and few clients argued with him. But the order he maintained was the order of a harassed owner of a string of unruly bears – effective, but harsh, surly, loud, and late.

However, there was one customer who never seemed to provoke Albert's temper. A fat monk. He clearly had some kind of roving commission. Bertrand allowed himself a tiny grin. It was only book-blind students of the Rule who thought that monks stayed in monasteries all the time. You only had to travel a score of miles before you came across one on some errand or other – collecting rents on outlying properties, taking tax money to a local court, buying vital supplies, maintaining a distant offshoot of the parent house – some lonely cell where unkempt brothers stayed for a week or a month, according to their level of piety or the seriousness of the punishment inflicted by Father Abbot. To most of the brothers, any time outside the walls, away from the tyranny of the bell, was a welcome perk, a favour, a treat to be savoured – anything to get away from the body odour of the man in the next choir stall or the familiar cockroach under the bed.

This one seemed to have garnered for himself a sort of permanent, and very welcome chore. He had come in two or three times since Bertrand had arrived, and was treated as a regular. He was extremely well fed. Customers and staff alike shared smiles at his girth and his appetite. They even had a nickname for him.

'William the Tub.'

Simon had so far forgotten his woes as to whisper it in the ear, in answer to Bertrand's raised eyebrows and inclined head.

He looked familiar, but Bertrand could not place him at first. When Simon added 'from St. Fulbert's', he remembered. He was the one on the mule making his way to the monastery, on that first evening.

He clearly enjoyed a privileged status in *The Hawk*, and it was not all explained by his habit. He was the only customer Livia talked to, and he was the only customer that Albert never swore at.

Store it all away. Something else would happen which would help to make things clearer…

Eyes. Ears. Nose. Tongue. Skin. There was more. Bertrand used his own experience, culled from a thousand inns, a thousand bowls of soup, a thousand dogs under the table, a thousand barrel-tap bawds, a thousand drunken altercations, a thousand garrulous gossips pouring stale breath and stale beer into his ear along with their stale scandal.

All those things gave him something like a set of whiskers and hair-ends which enabled him to test the spirit and flesh of a place, its hopes and fears, its inner-most nature.

At least they usually did. But Clermont was different. For the life of him he could not make sense of it. There were enough signs – almost too many – but he could not shake the truth out of them.

There was something stirring, that was sure. Arnaud was right about that. But what was going to start the – whatever it was; what direction the stampede was going to move in; which animal was going to start it – all these things were as dark as the end of a miner's tunnel.

He had spent one whole day outside the city (he noticed that a lot of its inhabitants liked to refer to it as 'the city'), picking his way through the shambles of the shanties and wagons and sagging tents on the heath beyond the walls.

Nobody would talk. They were not abusive, nor even secretive. Just preoccupied. Everything was said with a shrug.

'What do we know?'

'That is up to His Holiness.'

'We shall hear soon enough.'

'Anybody's guess. Now, if you will excuse us, we have the children to feed... '

They did not want to talk – not really talk – and they did not want to listen. It was a waste of time even to try and gather an audience. They would have slipped away like water down a hole in the sand.

Inside the walls it was no better. Oh yes – they gossiped; they wanted to hear the news from the next valley and the next province; they shook their heads over the latest incident. In the guardroom the constables were ready to exchange dirty jokes and poke fun with him at the Bishop and the Mayor. Stallholders moaned about the latest regulations and customers complained about the latest prices. Citizens cursed the crowds of visitors. But nobody said anything really worthwhile.

In his boredom and frustration, Bertrand found himself thinking again of the girl and the dead soldier. Perhaps he could make more progress there. When he came in sight of Hugh of Tournai's wagon, he thought of a way to kill two birds with one stone.

Robert was not hard to find. Nor was he difficult to interest in a little absence without leave.

'Where is Hugh?'

'In town somewhere. The Bishop's palace. Trying to get in to sell something to the Bishop himself.'

'And to His Holiness?'

Robert continued polishing some harness.

'More than likely. I would put nothing past that man. If the world was coming to an end, and the soldiers of Antichrist himself were on the doorstep, he would get out his best bales and pitch his prices high.'

'I thought he said he has lost all his best – that soldier.'

Robert dipped a cloth-covered finger into a bowl of fat.

'Not likely. Only one bale. We have plenty more. Do you think he would come to a Church Council with only one bale of top quality? What do you take us for?'

Bertrand ignored the question.

'So he will be away for a while.'

'All morning, I should think. Maybe longer. Look what he leaves me to do.'

He nodded towards a pile of leather tack and dirty utensils.

Bertrand put on an innocent air.

'I think I may have seen that girl again. Do you fancy coming with me?'

Robert hurled the half-finished harness into the back of the wagon and went to get his jerkin, while Bertrand silently crossed himself and made a promise to unburden his soul at his next confession. But Lord – it is in a good cause.

They tramped up the slope towards the woods. By the time they had gone half-way, Bertrand was beginning to wish he had brought Tristan with him. Luckily, Robert was content to do most of the talking.

'She came from nowhere – nowhere. One minute you thought you were alone, and the next – there she was. Scared me half to death.'

'I think she is harmless enough,' said Bertrand.

'Oh yes! Poor thing – half starved. When Hugh drove her off, I could have hit him.'

'Did she speak?'

'No. That was the odd thing. She just looked. God! – those eyes.'

Bertrand had to agree with him there.

'Where did she go?'

Robert waved his arms.

'That was the funny thing. She came from nowhere. And then she – she just disappeared. Well, it seemed like that. I turned to swear at Hugh, and when I turned back, she was gone.'

'I saw her – up in the woods – up there,' said Bertrand in between breaths. 'She had a – a secret place.'

'Show me.'

The ashes were mostly scattered, of course, and the carcase had long been eaten by insects and other birds. But the crazy cross was still there, drooping and limp. Robert, transfixed with rapt interest, dropped to his knees almost as if the little clearing were a shrine.

Bertrand liked himself even less now. This was a dirty trick he was going to play, but the boy's immediate reactions were likely to be important.

'I – er – I think she went this way when she left me.'

There was slightly less of the soldier's face now. The scar was barely visible.

Robert stopped dead, stared, and dropped to his knees for the second time. To vomit.

Bertrand pretended that the whole thing was pure coincidence, and he congratulated himself on his performance of sudden horror and revulsion. He needed to keep Robert well-disposed; some intuition told him that the boy might prove useful. He delivered him back to the wagon in good time before Hugh came back.

The rest of his day was a waste of time. Arnaud's great mystery stampede remained a mystery.

There was a guardedness about everybody, as if they were in some kind of enormous secret. It was so secret that they did not know what it was themselves; all they knew was that it was indeed a secret, and that it was huge…

Vico came in with an armful of logs. He pushed

unnecessarily past Bertrand's feet and dumped the wood beside the hearth.

'You still here?'

'I pay my way.'

'See that you do.'

Albert had used exactly the same phrase.

Vico dusted his dirty hands and went over to remove an empty cask. Without effort, he rolled it on edge towards the door.

Bertrand sniffed. Vico was a worker; you had to give him that. He put in more effort than half a dozen potboys. It appeared that he had some interest in the house. His tone of voice, and his words, said that too. Albert complained about him behind his back, but rarely to his face. And Albert got cross with everybody. Odd.

Albert appeared to reserve his worst abuse for his son, Simon. Odd too.

It seemed that he would never get to the bottom of anything in this town – sorry, city.

A slight movement beside his elbow made him jump. It was Livia with his stew. He caught the garlic on her breath as she leaned down to place the bowl and the spoon. As usual she scooped a chunk of bread from her apron pocket. She inclined her head a tithe of an inch towards his empty pot. Bertrand nodded. She took it away and returned a moment later with a refill. Even though he was expecting her, she almost took him by surprise again. She did not move until he had taken a mouthful of stew, turned, and indicated his pleasure at the taste. His pleasure was quite genuine. He noticed her kneading the dishcloth in her strong hands. It was not nerves; it was habit – a sort of pulse. Not a word was spoken throughout. She did not leave; she faded away.

When she did talk, to Brother William, Bertrand could never get near enough to overhear. He caught the tone though – measured, never ingratiating, much less friendly. She saved her softest tones for the cat. She talked a lot to the cat. Vico, he noticed, could not stand being near it. It seemed to make him short of breath. He stooped over more than usual, wheezed like an old man, and went off to find some other work to do.

Bertrand blew on his spoonful of stew, and began to sip. It was good beef. Fresh from the autumn slaughtering, and well hung. None of your salt-stiff gristle and bone from the late spring and months in the barrel. There was something to be said after all for travelling in the late autumn.

It had to be the good food which attracted the customers. It was true that every hostelry in the city was full at the moment – bursting in fact. But Bertrand noticed that many of the clients at the house of *The Hawk* were regulars. They called Simon and Vico by name; they were careful to address Livia as 'Madame'; Albert often used their names when he swore at them. They were certainly not here for the comfort or the welcome.

Arnaud had filled in some details…

'They were in trouble before this Council was arranged. Albert's bad temper. People were getting fed up – it was too big a price to pay for Livia's stew.'

'Poor Albert.'

'Poor Albert indeed. Remember I said that we have had two awful years.'

'Drought, famine – '

' – flood, and pestilence. But remember I also said about the soldiers and the robber barons.'

'You told me last week.'

'No – this was before. The inn has been looted twice by small armies of riff-raff – gutted – right down to the bare boards. People began to keep away. Albert was worried to death.'

'So he panics and shouts, and loses even more customers. No wonder his temper got shorter.'

'Never rains but it pours. The local word has it that they are on the lookout for a loan.'

'Did Livia tell you?'

Arnaud roared with laughter.

'That one? Never. If you want any news here, you had better ask the cat…'

Apart from Albert's abuse, one seldom heard any of the house staff part lips to speak to a soul. Simon maintained a long-suffering silence. A pale, skinny potboy froze with nerves under Livia's cold stare. Vico, with his furtive crouch and his rat-like eyes, snarled and grunted.

It appeared that Livia was married to Albert, but she was clearly not Simon's mother. Yet Simon was Albert's son; Arnaud had said so.

Simon interested him. The boy was sensitive, and quite probably intelligent. Which made sense; his father was no fool. Not all old soldiers were stupid. Only the dead ones. Albert had survived. Which indicated a measure of prudence at the very least. For all his bad temper, he had a natural air of authority. He took it upon himself to organise, often too much – which explained why he was often over-stretched and annoyed. He clearly liked running things. Given the backing of a large organisation – like an army – Albert would have been happy. The more Bertrand thought about it, the more he thought that Albert had been a sergeant or something similar. Probably an archer. With arms like that. Big. Strong. He had also a touch of the hillman about him, and hillmen made good archers. For all his overweight now, there was still a trace of alertness there.

But he was not much good on his own. He did not have the confidence to depend on his own judgment. Simon could see this. Small wonder the boy was annoyed. And probably ashamed. To see his father bumbling and bombasting.

It added to his own problems. He was barely tolerating the life he was leading. If he could only be somewhere else…Doing something else…

Bertrand had gained of whiff of all this the previous evening…

'Father, they are doing no harm. Let them be.'

Albert turned in mid-flow. He flung an arm in the direction of a group of revellers.

'Why should I put up with scum like that − damned Gascons? Think they own the place. What are they doing here anyway?'

Simon tried to keep his voice low.

'Father. Their money is good. And we need it.'

Albert whirled on him.

'Hold your tongue. I notice you do not serve them.'

Simon sighed.

'You were standing closer.'

'You took good care to be further away when they came in. Oh, yes − I see things, you know. Too dirty for you, were they? Only good enough for an old sweat to serve? Beneath the dignity of a scholar!'

Simon sighed again.

'Father. Please.'

'And who is going to pay for your learning and your

53

books, I should like to know? Customers like them. That is who.'

'Then why do you want to throw them out?'

Albert swore.

'No son of mine comes the clever clerk with me. Get some service in, boy. Shake some of the dreaming out of you. We had no chance to dream in my day...'

And so it had continued. A series of circular arguments, which usually ended in abuse and exasperation, and got nowhere.

Simon would turn away. Albert would gaze after him, puffing. But before he resumed his normal abuse of the customers, a brief frown of pain would crease his hot face, as if he knew that the words between them had turned sour, and he was baffled to know why.

Bertrand shook his head. Poor Albert. He had no idea how to handle a son like Simon. He took it as some kind of reflection on his manhood that a son of his should prefer a life on a stool, indoors, to a life of action and adventure and travel. The sort of life *he* had had, which could lead to – who could tell? What would the boy get in the cloister but the company of a bunch of overweight, sweaty celibates crowded together in unnatural closeness – for ever?

Albert possibly possessed a small share of the truth. Simon was young, and unformed. He had seen little of the world. Granted, the lad was bright. But the world needed bright soldiers as well. The boy did not yet know his own mind. He thought constantly of a life outside the inn, because the coarseness he constantly dealt with offended him.

'You just feel sorry for yourself.'

Albert was probably right there.

Bertrand ran his fingers round the rim of the bowl and licked them. He knew all about misunderstandings between son and father...

*   *   *   *   *   *

'What are you doing here?'

'Looking for something to do.'

'I thought you told stories for a living.'

'Nobody will listen. I am bored to death.'

Arnaud laughed without mirth.

'Try my job. I have been on my feet for a week.'

He gestured towards the cathedral. People loitered and gossiped everywhere, and not just in front of the great west door where the market stalls were put up on Sundays.

'Look at them. Did you ever see such a crowd?'

No. Bertrand never had. Knots of heads were barely murmuring to each other. Dark glances were cast over shoulders at him. That mysterious secret again.

'What are they talking about, Arnaud?'

'God knows. They will not even tell me. As for the outsiders...'

Bertrand looked round the seething square. The weekly market seemed to have become a permanent one. Stallholders, wives with their cheeses, pedlars, fortune-tellers, tumblers, bear-keepers, and a host of other loud men eager to take advantage of the crowds bawled their wares above the throng. Braziers were dotted about, offering hot chestnuts and pies. The dogs had given up scavenging for fear of being trodden underfoot.

Bertrand turned back to Arnaud.

'I do not wish to add to your problems – '

'Good.'

' – but I have found a dead soldier.'

'Good. I am fed up with the live ones.'

'Should you not be told? You are the mayor.'

Arnaud continued looking about him.

'You have just told me.'

'He was hanged. He is still there. In the woods.'

'Good. Then he will be no nuisance to anybody.'

Bertrand raised his voice a little.

'Arnaud, he was put to death. Maybe murdered.'

'Oh?'

Arnaud was still not listening properly. Bertrand prompted him again.

'In very odd circumstances.'

'Then the puzzle should appeal to you.'

'I think I may have solved part of it.'

'Splendid. Then I wish you luck with the rest.'

'I can get no further without the forces of law and order. You are the forces of law and order.'

Arnaud turned back to him and gave proper attention for the first time.

'Right now, Bertrand, "the forces of law and order", as you put it, are going to be strained to the limit to make sure that a score of deaths do not take place. Maybe worse. What good can I do to that dead soldier?'

He allowed irony to creep into his voice.

'Settle the score of justice?'

'Catching the murderer – or murderers – might be a help towards that end.'

'Hmmm.'

'Arnaud, there may be clues up there.'

Arnaud pushed him gently on the elbow.

'Then go and have a look at them for me. And if you are feeling energetic, cut him down and bury him.'

'Why me?'

'You said just now that you were bored to tears. Well, now you can make yourself useful.'

'Bodies and burials are your business, not mine.'

Arnaud waved an anxious arm at the braziers in the crowded square.

'That is my business right now. If those fires get out of hand...it will only take one. With this mob. We should never contain it. The cathedral could go – and do those soldiers' work for them.'

Bertrand gave in, and changed the subject.

'What are His Holiness' plans?' said Bertrand.

'You tell me. I am only the Mayor. The Bishop has shut himself up in his palace and talks to tradesmen about redecorating his hall, would you believe. Refuses to have anything to do with any of this. Says he is too busy with the arrangements for the Church Council. If you ask me, it is only an excuse. The man is terrified.'

'What does His Holiness say? Surely he must know what is going on.'

'If he does, he gives no sign. The word is out that he is going to preach.'

'When?'

'Nobody tells me anything. All I know is I have to prepare the cathedral. The Bishop has washed his hands of it. Just look at this.'

He waved again.

'Can you see me getting them all inside there?'

Bertrand glanced at the flaking stonework of the porch, at the scored and pitted timbers of the nave, at the squat tower, with its lop-sided belfry windows. Arnaud pursued his point.

'Can you see me getting half of them in? A quarter? This is not le Puy, you know, or Vézelay.'

'And if a brazier starts a fire, and the panic reaches inside the church…?'

Arnaud nodded emphatically.

'Exactly. And whose fault will it be?'

'Then you will have to move,' said Bertrand.

'I see. Just like that.'

'Any better ideas?'

'No. But how do I get it across to His Holiness? He wants to make a big occasion of it. High Mass and everything. You should see the candles he has brought with him – specially. Yet another fire risk, if you ask me.'

Bertrand prodded a loose stone with his foot.

'He is vain – this Pope?'

Arnaud grunted.

'Show me a prince of the Church who is not.'

'This progress of his – I imagine it is part of a big plan.'

'Huge, I should think. My guess is that Urban sees himself as a great reformer, a great leader, a great shepherd of his flock. To succeed in that he needs to cut a great figure. Remember, the Emperor is his rival, not his partner. Urban needs an event, a cause, a – well – a sort of happening.'

'Like the Council?'

'Yes, maybe. But the Church has had councils before. I think Urban is after something more than that. Different. Bigger.'

'Bigger? Is that possible?'

'I am not a Pope. I am not looking for something which will make all Christendom sit up and listen.'

'Why does he think he will get it here?'

'No idea.'

Bertrand kicked his stone towards a well-trodden cow-pat.

'Well, give it to him.'

'What do you mean?'

'Tell him that Jesus aroused the greatest attention when he preached to the multitude on the hillside.'

Arnaud narrowed his eyes.

'What are you suggesting?'

Bertrand laughed.

'Come, my friend. You were not as slow as this on the trail in Apulia.'

'Get to the point.'

'Very well. What is worrying you? The crowds. The danger of a fire. The threat to law and order. Yes?'

'Go on, go on.'

'The fear of a great trampling inside the church.'

'Yes, yes.'

'Arrange the event outside the walls.'

'Outside the walls? Are you mad? What about the Mass?'

'Build a platform. You have the timber. It will keep a score of layabouts out of mischief. He can celebrate his Mass on it. A lot more will see him up there than they would inside the church. If he wants to preach as well, they can still see him.'

'They will not all hear him.'

'He will be speaking in Latin. Nobody will understand him wherever he preaches.'

Arnaud rubbed his chin. Bertrand pushed him further.

'There will be no danger of fire, no danger of a stampede. The crowds will not burst the streets round the church. You can even have your constables mounted out there – keep much better control.'

Arnaud went through a minute's fierce thinking. Then his brow cleared, and he smiled.

'Bertrand, old friend, I think you have just been brilliant.'

Bertrand shrugged.

'One of my lesser efforts. Do I get my bill paid at *The Hawk*?'

Arnaud slapped him on the shoulder as he turned away.

'Not by me. But maybe by the Bishop. Only he will never know. Now push off and bury that soldier for me. Then come and tell me all about your clues.'

* * * * * *

'I fancy there will be little profit for us here, Tristan. Nobody will stop to listen.'

Bertrand knelt by his donkey's head and fed him some straw.

'So why do I stay? Ah – a good question. Tell me the answer to that and I will steal you some onions…A pity these chickens do not lay onions too, eh?

'I remember once I was in a town square – Poitou, I think it was – and there was this magician. He was preparing his final trick – you know, all those wristy passes with his hands, and his spells, and his chantings. And I was due to leave – had a place on a cart – I knew it was at the gate and would not wait for me. But I just had to stop and see what that magician was going to do.'

He patted Tristan's nose.

'That is how I feel now. Only it is worse. I have no idea what the magic is going to be, and I am not even sure who the magician is. Or if there is one.'

Something Arnaud said came back to him…

'You know, one of the oddest things about this crowd – they have no idea what is going to happen. They have

60

no clear idea why they have come. This may sound daft, but I get the feeling that in a funny way they would like to be somewhere else, and they are only waiting for a sign. I tell you – '

He searched for a better way of putting it.

'It is like the Hautevilles. Half a dozen brothers and they must all take off from Normandy to the other end of Christendom. Anybody else would have gone raiding in Brittany or sold his sword to the Count of Champagne or whatever, but not these men. No – they ride to the end of the world in Apulia and Calabria.'

'Like Count Robert?'

'Yes, if you like. He is another one. He inherited the finest fief a son could possibly covet – Normandy. Tamed by the Bastard. Rich. Fat. But he is not content. He will be off, you wait and see. Just like the Hautevilles. I hear that the youngest, Roger, is now fighting in Sicily. Where next? Africa?

'Well, these people here are the same. There is a great unease. A gigantic sort of fidget… Oh – one other thing. You remember that soldier I told you about?'

'You mean the one *I* told *you* about – the one with the scar?'

'What scar? Oh, yes, I remember. No – he was the one who took the bag of gold. So he was the one you saw, was he? Probably served him right. His "comrades" found out then.'

'How would they have done that?'

Arnaud shrugged.

'Perhaps he was throwing his money around. Perhaps he got drunk and began boasting. Perhaps Vico gave him away to his angry "comrades". '

'Or Livia put him up to it. Can you see Vico working

it out?'

'Frankly – no. Who cares? Whichever way, it was some kind of justice, eh? Saves me trouble anyway. Did you bury him, by the way?'

'Yes. Just in time too.'

'What do you mean?'

'While there was still enough of him to bury.'

Arnaud made a gloomy face, and crossed himself.

'Yes. Well. Thank you.'

He sniffed.

'Anyway, I do not mean him. I mean the one who was swearing vengeance when we arrested them. Gave us a lot of trouble, he did. Hobbling about, swinging that stick of his.'

'Why are you telling me this?' said Bertrand.

'Because I have seen him again – in the square and round about. Keep your eyes open. Man with a limp. Badly-set leg, my guess.'

'Why should I worry? He did not threaten me.'

'I am not telling you for your benefit. For Vico's.'

'Why are you concerned for Vico?'

'I am not. But I am concerned for Albert. He does not deserve any more trouble. And this stumping little jackal may provide it. Vico knows him. So tell him to watch out. Have his pitchfork handy.'

'Why not arrest him? He probably helped to murder Scarface?'

'How many times do I have to tell you? I am too busy. I do not have enough constables. And there is no evidence. Well, not enough.'

'Thank you very much.'

'No offence, Bertrand. But you surely must see. Even if you are right. What does it mean? One grubby little bastard has been removed by another grubby little bastard. And he will no doubt be removed sooner or later by a third grubby little bastard – of whom the world is full.'

'Like Vico.'

Arnaud looked surprised.

'Now that you mention it – yes. We live in hopes, eh?…'

There was a rustle outside. Bertrand sighed.

'Go away, Vico. I have no light, so you will see no more than you saw last night.'

Footsteps shuffled off.

Vico could have his warning after breakfast. It was hard enough doing a favour to Vico at all; he was damned if he was going to put himself out to do it.

Bertrand fed Tristan some more straw.

'No wonder he stoops – peering through all those knot-holes. Probably how he got his squint as well.'

Bertrand arranged his bedding.

Vico was not the only one who heard and saw things. He would swear that Livia missed nothing. She was rather better at it than Vico. She probably did most of Vico's thinking for him. It could easily have been her idea to put the other soldiers on to Scarface.

She was certainly more clever than Albert. Bertrand had watched her beat him several times. Oh, trivial things. But her sharper wit and greater resourcefulness were clear for anyone with eyes to see. She could run rings round him, and at the same time give the impression of being a dutiful wife.

No wonder Albert was permanently cross. He had enough sense to know he was being outwitted, but he had not enough to prevent it.

Vico despised him, and his son Simon meanwhile

was a constant trial, with his moods and his airs and his pretensions. Poor Albert.

Bertrand pulled up his blanket and put his hands behind his head.

He had done his best for that soldier. Even though one of his legs had broken when Bertrand had cut him down. From what Arnaud had said, he had asked for it – greed, deceit, betrayal. No doubt showing off too. He couldn't resist parading that red cloth and boasting about his exploit in Hugh's wagon. They must have been pretty fed up with him even before they found out what he had done in Arnaud's house. So hang him with the fruits of his thieving, and share out the fruits of his treachery. Neat. And final.

It seemed to absolve Hugh. Not that Bertrand had had many suspicions in that direction. Young Robert's reaction had been genuine enough, so he obviously had not been an accomplice. It was unlikely that Hugh could have done it by himself, even if he had had the time – which seemed equally unlikely. And, as Robert had said, he had lost only one bale. A man does not commit murder because of the theft of a mere tithe of his stock. And, even if he did, he would not use the recovered stock to string up the culprit.

So there was no more mystery. He had nothing to do. Nobody wanted to hear his stories. Arnaud was too busy to be any company at all. Everybody in *The Hawk* was miserable, silent, or surly.

What a city, and what a household! Would there be any magic in the end to redeem it all?

He turned over and settled down, and knew at once he would not get to sleep. He had drunk too much. He would have to get up again. Damnation!

Better to go outside. The chicken smell was bad

64

enough, without adding to it for the night, and anyway it was difficult to do it kneeling up under this low roof.

Cursing gently, Bertrand pulled on his boots, leaving the laces undone, and shuffled across to open the door.

He reeled with the shock.

There were the same two eyes burning a hole in a livid, moonlit face. Then, just as fast as the first time, she was gone.

*   *   *   *   *   *

Five

RAISED VOICES WOKE him up in the morning.

'It is always the same; you will never *do* anything.'

'It is easy for you. All you have to do is get yourself into a mood and then tell everybody else what to do.'

'I am not in a mood.'

'I am not blind. Look at you. Face as long as a baker's shovel.'

'You are enough to depress anybody. Look at what you let her do.'

'You see? I was right. You are just feeling sorry for yourself – as always.'

'No. *I* am right. You will not answer me. You will not admit what she is doing.'

'If we are to admit everything, then admit to me that you want to leave. That you find this place beneath your precious dignity. That you are ashamed of us.'

Bertrand could recognise a family row when he heard one, and wisely lay still.

He heard Albert grunting with the effort of chopping logs and freeing the axe.

'Bring that handcart over here – if it is not too much trouble.'

Simon lowered his voice, and spoke with a different tone.

'Father – look – if I really am such a trial to you, then why should I not go?'

'To join the brothers? That would be the easy way out,

eh? Spew prayers over each other and talk about our real "Father who is in Heaven".'

Bertrand, from his bed, could feel the heavy irony.

'It is the service of God.'

'It is the service of the Order. Do you think they will let you in without payment? And who is going to provide the money – eh?'

'Ah – so that is it? Back to money again. How many times have I said that I do not want my share. Give it to Lenore. I shall manage.'

'You want it. Everyone wants their share. You would not be human if you did not. It is one of the few things I respect you for. And what would Lenore do with it?'

Simon raised his voice to reply. Albert's answer came faintly, thrown over a departing shoulder. Simon swore fiercely to himself as he hurled logs noisily into the handcart.

Tristan stirred, and Bertrand put up a hand to his nose. This was all very well, and very interesting, but Bertrand had drunk a lot of beer the previous evening. If he did not get up soon, his bladder would burst yet again.

He coughed loudly and made a great fuss about stretching and yawning. He deliberately made the chickens flutter and squawk. By the time he emerged, Simon had gone. But he had at least taken the handcart and its load of logs.

*   *   *   *   *   *

Bertrand watched the pale stream vanish into the steaming midden and sighed with contentment. A late autumn sun was warm to the back. He had slept well. All he needed now was a good breakfast. He hitched up his breeches and re-fastened his belt.

'What are you doing here?'

Vico had crept in from the inner courtyard. Bertrand guessed he had been spying for some time.

'What does it look like?'

Vico glowered, and hung about unnecessarily.

'Well, get on then. Back to your – hutch.'

Bertrand shrugged. It must be early morning bile. Mean even for a creature like Vico. Ah, well. Food was much more important than winning a trick over a sourface.

Time to exercise some charm on Livia. If such a feat were possible.

He crawled back into the chicken house and collected the morning's clutch of eggs. Carrying them delicately in his cap, he made his way to the kitchen.

'I thought I would save Vico the trouble.'

A huge iron pot was already suspended over the fire. Simon had deposited the fresh load of logs and gone off again. Livia turned from the table where she was chopping vegetables. Her bag of fresh purchases hung behind her from a huge nail. The dark face, the steady eyes, the drawn-back hair, the powerful hands, the shapeless apron with its cavernous pocket in the front – all were exactly the same. He could not imagine her doing anything so human as going to bed and getting up, much less feeling relief at having just passed water. She was simply there, as silent, as still, and as permanent as a gatepost.

Bertrand held out his capful of eggs. She nodded in acceptance, and gestured towards a wooden bowl on a side table by the wall. Bertrand tipped the eggs carefully where she had shown him. She reached up into her bag without taking her eyes off him.

He came and stood opposite her on the other side of the table, sniffed suggestively, and stretched out a hand to a half-cut onion. A knife blade was laid flat across the back of his hand as quickly and as smoothly as the darting tongue of a snake. It was the most frightening caress he had ever received. He could feel the coldness of the metal. He could see clearly the small, pale marks left on the edge by the whetstone, the tiny, clinging fragments of onion. She kept it there just long enough for him to understand, then lifted the blade and pointed with it to a side of smoked bacon hanging from a rafter. She held up three fingers.

By the time he had cut the rashers and turned back to the table, she was breaking a lump off a huge loaf with her bare hands. She put it on a platter, and pushed it towards him, along with an empty mug. Bertrand already knew where the barrel was.

'Madame is too kind. I felt this would be a generous house the moment I saw it.'

Livia offered not a flicker of reaction, which, if he were honest, scarcely surprised him. But a lifetime of dealing with landlords and their wives had taught him one invaluable piece of wisdom: you can catch more flies with honey than you can with vinegar. It was a rare person indeed who was totally impervious to all forms of flattery. Even saints were not proof against it.

The honey would continue to be laid on.

Bertrand stood by the open door, lifted up his face to the morning sun, munched and swigged – and talked.

'Have you seen the goings-on at the cathedral?'

Without waiting for an answer, because he knew he was not going to get one, he went on to relate everything he had seen and heard. A lifetime of travel had also taught him that the greatest common currency of the human race was gossip. Livia was not replying, but she was taking it all in. Bertrand could see that.

'Such crowds. My friend – my friend the Mayor – Arnaud of Flers – '

He paused to note the effect, and was gratified to note that it registered; the knife was poised momentarily in the air.

' – Arnaud says…'

Well, he thought, if a minstrel can not tell a good tale, who can?

'… so he is going to arrange a mighty platform. Just outside the west gate. And this inn is the nearest to the west gate. Imagine – His Holiness a mere arrow-shot from where we are standing. It should do a great deal for trade at *The Hawk*. My idea, you know. To have it there. You and Albert might have a lot to thank me for in a few days' time.'

The hands were wiped and kneaded in a cloth. Bertrand watched carefully. It was going in all right.

'Oh – and my friend Arnaud says one other thing. Those soldiers – remember? The ones Vico so bravely drove away. The ones he helped to arrest. Clever, that. I take my hat off to him. Well – Arnaud says that he has seen one of them again, in the city. He told me to warn you, in case he causes any trouble.'

That went in too. The knife hung in the air again, just for the blink of an eye, before she wiped off the shreds of onion. It may have been Bertrand's fancy, but he would almost have said that there was the faintest tremble. Very deliberately, the onions were tipped into the pot.

He licked the grease off his fingers. It was always sound sense to know when to stop. It was the bad story-tellers who dribbled on and repeated themselves, or who added unnecessary frills.

He had made his point. If Livia's reaction was a trifle odd, he was not going to find out anything by asking her questions, so he might as well leave it.

'That was a fine breakfast, Madame. Feast for a pope.'

Bertrand picked up a smaller pot that lay in the hearth.

'Would there be any chance of heating a spot of water, do you think?'

Half an hour later, he was propping the pot on the ruins of an old wall and squinting into his reflection in a piece of pale blue glass. He had salvaged it from a burnt abbey church years before, and always carried it with him.

It was little use in poor light, but offered just enough to enable him to shave on this fine sunny morning. He could feel the heat on his bare neck. His stomach was comfortably full. He had rested well. Vico had taken himself off somewhere – probably to the cathedral square; Bertrand had noticed him there before. Simon had disappeared. Albert was inside going about his business; his raised voice could be heard from the yard. Livia was preparing her stew for the day. Two boys were mucking out the stables, and staggering across the yard with forkfuls of waste to tip on to the midden. Those travellers who were moving on had already departed. The rest had mostly drifted down to the square.

It was all so – well, so normal. Bertrand had been there only four days, but already he had slipped into the house routine. He felt the comfort of usualness. He felt comfortable enough to allow himself the luxury of a shave. Nevertheless, he had a good look round before he took out his razor and began stropping it. It was a fine piece of steel, which he had obtained, after great trouble and expense, in Italy, and he did not care to be seen using it; the temptation to thieves was too great.

He dipped his precious piece of soap in the warm water. That was another prize of his charm, conjured out of the apron of a castle washerwoman in the Auvergne. He lathered, and bent, and squinted, and, very carefully, totally absorbed, began scraping…

So – who was the girl with the eyes? She clearly had some connection with the place, or she would not have been there. She could not have simply have wandered into a stable yard at random, down an uncobbled lane in the dark; not even idiots did that. She had a purpose. She knew the place well, or she would not have disappeared so quickly, darkness or no darkness.

Was she the girl whom Simon referred to? Lenore? He made it sound as if she were his sister. If she were, what was she doing trying to get into the chicken house late at night? For the eggs? Saints – she was thin enough. Or was it to sleep? Why did she not sleep in the main building? If it came to that, what was she doing, half-naked and half-crazed, burning dead rats as sacrifices in the middle of the woods outside Clermont? Why would Albert and Livia allow a daughter of the house to become a half-starved hermit?

Livia was content to give him free bacon and beer. Why not feed her daughter?

If she *was* her daughter. But even if she were her step-daughter, it made Livia out to be cruel beyond the normal standards of human behaviour. He had seen starving peasants abandon unwanted babies in a deep winter, and God have mercy on them all.   But this was not a crumbling cottar's hovel; it was a public building. People came and went. And letting helpless infants die was one thing; deliberately starving a grown member of the family was quite another.

The black, staring eyes came back to haunt him. He almost turned round, with his razor poised in the air, to see if she were standing behind him.

Suppose she really was connected with that soldier, the one who had paid the price for his larceny with the profits of it round his neck. Hugh of Tournai had said he was a charmer. Had be been humbugging this poor creature into an assignation in the forest? If so, it made him as bad as Vico, and he deserved hanging twice over. Worse.

Which opened up another line of possibility. If Simon was her brother, and if he had found out about this soldier, would that not give him a motive?

He delicately negotiated the skin below his nostrils.

No – the boy would not have the wherewithal – of weapons, strength, or will. And how would he have outwitted a professional soldier?

Nevertheless, she could still have been involved with him. She could still have become fascinated with him; plenty of saner girls than she had been bewitched by travelling charmers with a fancy dagger on the belt. She could still have arranged a meeting with him. She could still have been mourning him. Indeed it could have been his death which had unhinged her. Unlikely, though. Albert's remark – 'What would Lenore do with the money?' – seemed to indicate that she had been off her head for some time. And there was the sacrifice of the rat.

So – yes – she could be mad. Which could explain a lot. He had been saddened many times by the unthinking savagery with which men reacted to anything which smacked of disorder of the head. They found it baffling; therefore, frightening. It was so far removed from the set of norms which they and their forebears had struggled so long to establish. It attacked the fragile framework of their society. It was a diseased apple in a barrel of good ones, and it could rot the rest, so they felt threatened. It had to go.

For all the tolerance and wisdom that a lifetime of travel and study of human nature had given him, Bertrand himself felt something of the discomfort of his fellow-beings in the presence of anything unbalanced. Understanding of men's weaknesses did not make him proof against them.

He paused again, struck by another thought, and swished his razor in the cooling water.

Albert! If he was right, and Simon was her brother, that made Albert her father. Did Albert make no move to protect her? Was that what Simon meant when he said that Albert did nothing? Or – worse – was it Albert who was starving her and pushing her out of the house to sleep? Did this fear of the abnormal stretch even to perverting a father's natural love of his daughter?

Albert did not consider it worth leaving anything to Lenore, so he clearly regarded her as, to say the least, unusual. And if they were arguing about Simon's 'share', that meant there was something to inherit, besides the inn. Which once again came back to the fact that the family was anything but poor.

Under threat maybe – they were apparently trying to find someone to lend them some money. The abbey of St. Fulbert's. Perhaps a Jew. But not without resource – Albert might not be a good manager, but, like all old soldiers – the survivors – he had his share of low cunning. Had he in fact managed to salvage something from the wreckage of the two sackings? Did he have a bulging bag of silver in a thick box of Limousin oak behind a loose stone in his barrel-house wall? Was that why he was so suspicious of unsavoury customers?

Did Livia know? About the silver? No – it would be Albert's revenge. He could not defeat her in daily discord, but he could out-think her in long-term plotting. There was some satisfaction in that, at least. Bertrand smiled. No – Livia probably had her own box, hidden in an even better place. Bertrand would put nothing past that woman – nothing.

And where did Vico fit into all this? He behaved as if he had some interest in the house. Nobody seemed to like him though. With good reason, so far as Bertrand could see. He worked unremittingly, except when he was out collecting gossip. Brave too – look how he had seen off those soldiers. Unless it was simply bad temper and animal instincts.

Bertrand pulled faces and rubbed his chin and cheeks. They felt good. He did not peer too closely into his glass in case he saw too many wrinkles and sags. He packed his gear, and began to see to his donkey's needs. Before he had finished, Vico returned.

'Still here then?'

'Before very long you may be grateful for that, my friend,' said Bertrand, without bothering to turn round. 'Wait till the crowds come back.'

Vico grunted.

'Likely.'

Bertrand began to check Tristan's tack, and spoke without looking at Vico.

'I have a message for you from Arnaud – my friend Arnaud – the Mayor.'

He did look up then, to see the reaction. Vico had been about to stoop to pick up a pitchfork, but had paused.

'Well?'

'You know those soldiers you so bravely drove off a while ago?'

Vico's brows knotted as he worked to make sense of Bertrand's line of argument.

'Yes.'

'He says to tell you that he has seen one of them back in the city.'

Bertrand could have sworn that he saw Vico's shoulders hunch a little more. He looked over his shoulder into the corner of the yard, and wrenched them back again, as if he had made a mistake.

'Oh?'

'Yes. He says to tell you to be on your guard. He might come here again.'

Vico did retrieve the pitchfork then, and tested the two points. He grunted with satisfaction, his grey gums bared. Totally preoccupied for a moment. Then he seemed to remember Bertrand.

'You mind your own affairs. Damned minstrel. I can take care of – of things here.'

He stumped off, using the fork as a walking stick.

Bertrand completed his examination of Tristan's hooves, and fed him. He looked round the yard. There was a trough, but the water clinging to the bottom was green and still. More neglect. But Bertrand knew his inns. There would be a trough at the front as well, to cater for casual callers. He led Tristan out under the arch in the wall, down the alley, and round to the front, beneath the sign of *The Hawk*. He smiled smugly. There it was, under an open shutter.

It was the quiet time that all inns have, between the departure of the overnighters and the arrival of the midday eaters. He was content to let Tristan linger. He sat on a bench under the window, raised his head to the sun, leaned back against the wall, and shut his eyes…

He felt sorry for Simon. Not because he thought Simon was right. On the contrary; Albert had probably read his son correctly. The boy was a romantic, and did not know his own mind. He almost certainly felt sorry for himself, but did not know what to do about it. The offer to give up his portion was no more than desperate expedient, an attempt to win a point in a pointless argument. Albert was right there too.

Like most fathers, Albert was right, and that was that. Bertrand's father had been right about him too…

'Look at you!'

Every time his father said that, the words cut. Bertrand did not need to be reminded about his physique, or lack of it.

'But father, I do not want to be a soldier.'

There was the rub. What hurt his father was not so much that his son was not *cut out* to be a soldier, as that he did not want to *be* a soldier. Bertrand could never get past this deep-set disapproval. His father could not cope with the idea of a son of his not wanting to do what he had loved.

His father could see, clearly, just one thing: the only way for a boy to get on was to go for a soldier. There was no future on the land, or in a market. The one was dirty and backbreaking, and the other was demeaning. Grubby commerce. But a soldier! Now, there – there the world opened up for a young lad with enterprise. And his stupid son could not see this elemental truth.

What did the idiot want to be? A scholar. That meant being a cleric. Joining the legions of pious hypocrites who scraped a living on a patch of land beside a lop-sided wooden church, lusting after anything under thirty that came within reach.

'I do not wish to be a priest, Father. I could go into a house.'

That was worse.

'Join those black-cowled perverts and satyrs? Not while I live and breathe.'

Bertrand had seized every opportunity to try and get a glimpse of books, to try and scrape an acquaintance with letters, but in the face of his father's abuse and sarcasm, and his mother's helpless tears, it was a lost battle.

The life with the Benedictines became a tearful deprivation, then a wisp of faint hope, finally a phantom of a dream. Yet, if he were honest, there had been chances later in his life, and he had not made the most of them.

It was a familiar plight of a young man who was unhappy, or who thought he was unhappy: the further the great dream receded into limbo, the greater became the unhappiness, yet the greater too became the unanswered question – would he really have liked it? How could he know? It would always be the Heaven he had missed...

Yes, he understood Simon, but he understood Albert too. He felt sorry for Simon for the same reason that he now felt sorry for the young man he himself had once been. He knew that his father, and Albert, were honest men, according to their lights, and loved their sons in their gruff way. But they were limited. Neither understood their sons, and neither had the mental flexibility to devise a way of *trying* to understand them. Disagreement and unwillingness on the part of their sons put them, immediately and unarguably, in the wrong, and that was that. Their sons were the worst of sinners – they were dreamers. And ungrateful dreamers at that.

Bertrand had grown up with the certainty that he was a constant disappointment to his father, and he suspected that Albert felt the same about Simon…

Voices broke into his reverie.

'Where is she?'

'Gone.'

Livia's voice.

'Where?'

No answer. Livia was shrugging. Bertrand, with his eyes shut, could almost see her shrugging.

'Did you have to?'

That was Albert, beginning to raise his voice again.

'Everyone works here.'

'When he is not down in the square.'

'Ludi works harder than anybody else.'

Ludi?

'Lenore would, if you gave her a chance.'

'I give her chances all the time.'

'She is frightened of you.'

'She is frightened of work, not of me.'

'She is – not well.'

'She brings that upon herself. There is plenty of food here.'

'But she is – not like others.'

'All that praying.'

'You do your share of it. At the cathedral.'

'She prays everywhere. She talks to saints.'

'In Heaven, yes. Like all of us.'

'No – not like all of us. We go to church to pray to saints up in Heaven; she thinks they have come *down* from Heaven to talk specially to her.'

'She is – sensitive.'

'She is mad.'

Albert shouted. Bertrand knew his neck was reddening.

'She is not mad!'

'Then – she works. Like Ludi and me.'

Albert swore. Bertrand heard him slamming a door.

He opened his eyes and sat up. After a moment to make sure that Livia was no longer nearby, he leaned forward and whispered in Tristan's ear.

'This is no place for us, my friend. Wherever I sit I hear family rows. I feel like a confessor.'

He walked the donkey back to the yard, tethered him in the sun, and scrounged some loose hay for him. Vico, humping fresh bales, scowled, but said nothing.

Bertrand, smug with success, used good cheer as a weapon.

'I have lifted the eggs and taken them in to your mother. Is that not nice of me – Ludi?'

Vico swore.

Betrand chuckled to himself as he went back down the alley.

It had been a shot at a venture, but it had found its mark. It was hard to see Vico as a mother's boy, but not for one person at least.

*　*　*　*　*　*

It was only necessary to follow the crowd – workmen, apprentices lugging timber and tools, gossips and loafers, swearing foremen, constables nudging shoulders aside with their horses' flanks, beggars earning a grudging penny with scaffolding poles slung between them.

Bertrand was amazed at the progress.

'You have done wonders, my friend.'

Arnaud whirled round, ready to argue.

'Oh, you. Well, it is your idea. It had better be a good one.'

'What does His Holiness say?'

Arnaud sniffed.

'I gather he approves. So I have done something right. One of his chaplains told me it made His Holiness very thoughtful – whatever that means.'

'You know it is right, Arnaud. You have got the worst of the crowds out of the centre of the city.' He found himself saying 'city' like the inhabitants. After only four or five days. 'Now the square will not fester and smoulder.'

'We hope.'

Arnaud did not sound impressed. Bertrand reassured him.

'Of course it is better. It is like lancing a boil. You have released all the poison. Out here it will disperse.'

'Oh, yes? And where will they all go tonight? To the woods?'

'No. They will come back again. But they will have had a change, a breathing space. And so will the city. You see – I shall be right.'

'And what about tomorrow?'

'Tomorrow they will come out again. And so it will be, until – '

'Until?'

'Until we hear the will of His Holiness, and on that we must all depend.'

'Why?'

'Because it is second only to the Will of God. What choice do we have?'

Arnaud growled.

'Talking of woods,' said Bertrand.

'Who was?'

'You were. Does Albert have a daughter called Lenore?'

'Yes. Why?'

Arnaud did not take his eyes off the work in front of him.

'And is Vico Livia's son?'

'Yes.'

'And does she call him "Ludi"?'

'Yes.'

'Are you going to say anything but "yes"?'

'No. I am busy.'

'Come and eat with me later.'

'If I can get away.'

'You will get away. For Livia's cooking. Nobody is going to steal a platform as big as that. I am sure your constables have been well paid.'

Arnaud did turn round then.

'Yes, they have. But not by me.'

Bertrand grinned.

'Surely not by your bishop? You said he was as mean as – '

'No. No.'

Arnaud scratched an ear.

'By His Holiness, would you believe. There is something up, Bertrand.'

* * * * * *

Bertrand did not go straight back to the inn. He made his way through the elbows and the swearwords and the steaming gutters to the cathedral square.

The braziers were still adding their smoke to the pungent atmosphere. Two score columns rose straight in the still autumn air, like a cluster of bare pines in a burnt forest. A rumble rose too – the noise of hundreds of voices. Not furtive this time, but animated. There was something to talk about that men could see. They were coming in droves too towards the west gate to have a good look. Whatever it was, they wanted a look.

The Council could debate and argue, and gossip would have it that they were discussing matters of high moment, but they were above the heads of ordinary sinners. Most men could not even pronounce 'investiture', never mind talk about it. But a platform was for sure; it was a sight; it was a definite sign that His Holiness was going to do something.

Bertrand edged and shuffled towards the main door of the cathedral. Smoke and sweat and rotten meat and ordure assailed his nostrils. He wrinkled his nose. This was as bad as being in a pilgrim town; it reminded him of Conques and Moissac. He had not been to le Puy and Vézelay, but he suspected they were the same; Arnaud had said as much.

He recoiled from the urgency, the loudness, the sheer discomfort of crowds, the indignity. God and his saints! No wonder pilgrims wanted to escape on their holy journey. No wonder they wanted to escape the same crush in Hellfire.

He found himself in front of the great west door, gazing up at the carvings over the lintel. Why did you always have to look up to see the Divinity? Why did you never get a chance to meet Him face to face, as it were?

There, in the centre, Christ sat enthroned in majesty, on the Great Day – the Day of Judgment. In his left hand he held a huge book – the Word of God. Momentarily, and not for the first time, Bertrand found himself wishing that he could read. He looked into the face of Christ, and his heart quailed within him. The large, staring eyes bored into his very soul. Had it not been for the regular jostling around him, he would have dropped to his knees.

He wrenched his own eyes away, to the top of the great tableau, above Christ's right shoulder. There were the happy ones, the chosen of God, the blessed – in attitudes of peace, prayer, rapt worship. Still, serene. Not bowed down by a lifetime of work and hardship, like the poor mortals who constantly bumped into him. Men and women for whom life meant nothing more than finding their way to the next full plate. What it must be like to be able to enjoy an existence where such a constriction did not exist. It made him tremble even to contemplate it – like a beggar who thinks of finding a sack of gold.

He turned his gaze towards the other side – to the left, to the Devil's side. Left – *'sinister'*. It was one of the Latin words he had picked up in many searching conversations with the brothers in a score of houses. There gaped the maw of Hell. Gagging, naked wretches fell helpless into a monstrous pot, stoked and fuelled by leering devils. Swords, spears, spikes, knives, and tridents poked, slashed, gashed, gored, stabbed, and impaled livid white bare flesh. Hideous creatures, too fearsome even for the most feverish nightmare – in lurid reds and browns and greens and yellows – snapped and snarled and roared and mauled and devoured. Apes with claws, beasts with serpents' tails, fish with heads of goats! It was against every law in God's world of order. How could God be there, in such total chaos! It was proof that Hell meant separation from God.

Bertrand found himself sweating.

Frightened and furious, he tore himself away. Less than an hour before, he had been at peace with the world, clean, smooth-faced, rested, fed. Happy to watch those around him struggle to make the best of their lives, ready to feel sorry for them. He had spent most of his time since he had grown up watching his fellow-creatures. Being a traveller almost by trade, he never stayed long enough anywhere to become involved. He arrived, he ingratiated himself, he enjoyed company, he told stories, he collected his reward, and he moved on. He had not chosen such a life; it had, in a way, chosen him. There had seemed little else to do.

He was good at what he did; he knew that. It gave him a little security to know that he was not prey to the troubles of others. Indeed, by virtue of being an outsider, he could sometimes help, because he could see both sides of a question. It was lonely at times, but it also gave him a kind of strength.

Now – suddenly – he had been reminded that he was in fact like everybody else. He hated it. It was so unfamiliar. He felt the need to get back, quickly, to the role he usually played. He did not take kindly or naturally to the part of the terrified sinner. He pushed it firmly to the back of his mind.

He had to talk to somebody. Recover his confidence. Return to being the good listener, the uncommitted witness. It had never occurred to him before that, just as the penitent needed the confessor, so the priest needed the sinner.

He pushed his way down the simmering street towards *The Hawk*. He paused to throw one last look over his shoulder, as if to reassure himself that he had put space between himself and the jaws of Hell. Then he caught sight of Vico, who jumped clumsily into a doorway.

It jerked Bertrand back to everyday life. He moved on.

What was Vico doing there? He had been to the square earlier that morning. What was his second errand for?

Could it be to follow him? Why? What did Vico suspect him of doing? Was it that Vico was simply a nasty creature who habitually thought the worst of everybody? Was it that he was simply inquisitive? Had he got his stoop from peering through knotholes? Was it sheer habit? Did Livia know? Had she in fact sent her precious 'Ludi' to spy on him? If so, what did Livia suspect?

Perhaps it was Albert who had set Vico to follow him. Was Albert afraid for that box of Limousin oak hidden in the wall? With all the silver?

No. Somehow he could not see Vico doing Albert any favours. Albert was not *his* father. And Albert would certainly not tell Vico about the box of silver; it would be as good as giving it away.

Bertrand stopped again, turned round, and saw Vico dodge out of sight once more. He waited for a minute, until Vico came out from his hiding place. He smiled to himself when he saw Vico pause, gasp, and leap back again.

In better spirits, he resumed his walk back to the inn. He had been speculating too much; it was time to get some harder intelligence. Livia was a blank wall; he could hammer away at her till he was blue in the face, and get nowhere. Vico was as mean and suspicious as a tortured bear. Simon's lips were also tight – whether in secrecy or self-pity mattered not; it came down to the same thing. Lenore had run from him in terror – twice.

So it would have to be Albert.

*　*　*　*　*　*

He found Albert sweating over a new barrel. The smell of stale beer had reached him before he was half-way across the yard. At least it was healthier than the market square. Bertrand almost liked it.

Albert looked up. His face and neck were darker than ever. He was breathing heavily. But he had moved the barrel by himself. Bertrand found himself admiring those huge arms. How many arrows had they sent singing to the target? Where had Albert fought? In Germany – with or against the Emperor? In France – where? Poitou? Nevers? Burgundy? Down in Toulouse or the County of Barcelona? In the north – Normandy? Ponthieu? Flanders?

Skilled archers were valuable. Commanders would pay well for them. The Bastard had broken the shield wall at Hastings with archers, so it was said – in the depths of the taverns. Not out loud, you understand, because the knights did not want to lose the credit; after all, they were the rulers of the battlefield, as everybody knew...

Albert steadied the barrel with his thigh, and put out a hand.

'Give me that hammer.'

Bertrand put it in a palm as big as a ham. Without waiting to be told, he held the chocks while Albert knocked them into place. Talk became a series of grunts. When Albert had fixed the tap, Bertrand held out a mug for the testing. As Albert watched the beer run, Bertrand held out another. Without a word, Albert filled them both.

Bertrand gestured to a bench just outside the door. Albert grunted again, and they both subsided on to it. Albert wiped his glowing forehead with a mighty sleeve. For a while they swigged in silence and gazed into space. Thomas the cat stalked past them towards his box against a wall.

Bertrand remembered an old piece of advice from a priest...

'Get them to talk about easy things first…'

Bertrand thrust a thumb over his shoulder towards the barrel.

'Good stuff.'

Albert nodded.

'The best. Not what we serve in there. Drunken riff-raff. If you half filled it with rats' piss, they would not know the difference.'

'Thank you for the compliment.'

Albert shrugged.

Bertrand felt pleased with the progress he had made. He had come a fair distance from the day when he had passed on Arnaud's request about continuing to water the beer. 'Slanderous bastard.' 'Excuse to sit on a fat arse.' Now was the time, he felt, to push his luck while the wind was set fair. But he would have to proceed with caution.

He jerked a thumb again.

'Why kill yourself? Why not get Vico to help you?'

Albert burped.

'That ox?'

Bertrand set another lure.

'He seems to work hard. Every time I look he – '

Albert gave a short laugh.

'He is good for lifting and carrying. No more. A donkey.'

'I have seen him moving barrels.'

'Empty ones. That is all he is good for. He knows nothing about what goes inside. What do they know about beer in Calabria?'

He spat. He brooded for a moment, then turned and jabbed himself in the chest.

'Me? I am from the Vosges – from Alsace. They understand beer there.'

'Are the barrels as good?'

Albert's eyes gleamed.

'Better. A hundred times better.'

'They use good Limousin oak round here,' suggested Bertrand, laying out yet another piece of bait. 'Good for barrels – and boxes.'

Albert showed no reaction. No sign of furtiveness. Perhaps he did not have a box of silver after all. Bertrand changed back to beer.

He peered suggestively into the empty bottom of his mug.

'Good beer, that. Right from the first smell of it, I could tell. I said to myself, "Bertrand," I said – '

'Want some more?'

Bertrand leapt to his feet before Albert could change his mind.

'Here. Let me. Can I do you too?'

Albert held out his own empty mug.

Bertrand now said nothing. He could sense that the game was about to break cover. He came back, handed over the second mug, sat down, sipped, and waited.

Albert picked up a chip of wood and hurled it away.

'Monks stink.'

'Ah.'

The game had not quite broken yet.

'What does he know about life inside a house?'

'Mm.'

Nearly.

'The boy sees these fat-gutted Pharisees, with their hands folded piously in their sleeves, and he believes everything they say.'

'You mean, like the brother who comes into *The Hawk*?'

Albert turned to gaze blankly at him.

'The Tub. Yes. If the Tub told him they served roast swan every night in there, he would believe him. What does he know?'

'What does he know about life in a guardroom or a shearing barn?'

Albert turned to him and raised his eyebrows.

'Mmh?'

Bertrand pursued his point.

'What does he know about anything except life at an inn? For all that it is a good one,' he added hastily.

'He is too young.'

'He is not a baby, Albert. He must find out for himself. You went off to be an archer, I would wager.'

Albert waved dismissively.

'That was different. Times were hard.'

'And your father had a lot of mouths to feed.'

'Exactly. And what do I have?'

'Vico.'

'Vico is Livia's son, not mine.'

'You have *The Hawk*.'

Albert growled.

'And they think they are going to get it. Well, they can think again. Monks have their uses, you know.'

'For all that they stink?'

'For all that they stink.'

Bertrand felt himself getting into deep waters, and turned back to solid land.

'You have Lenore.'

Albert looked at him again, and the pain in his eyes suddenly made Bertrand feel sorry for him.

They both looked away and buried their heads in their mugs.

At last, Albert heaved a huge sigh.

'If Hedi were here…'

'Hedi?'

'Hedwiga. My first wife.'

'Ah.'

'Hedi was – everything. She always knew what to do. Lenore was not always as you see her now. Only after my Hedi – '

He stopped, trying to hold back the tears. Bertrand waited.

Albert sighed and blinked.

'Why should I be telling you this?'

'For the same reason you confess your sins to a travelling priest. You will never see him again.'

Albert composed himself as best he could.

'When my Hedi – went – Lenore could not understand. Her mother was everything to her. She was everything to me too. But I was older. I had my company. I had responsibilities.'

'A company of archers.'

Albert turned to him in some surprise.

'Yes – yes.'

'In Calabria.'

Albert stared again.

'Yes. But Sicily too.'

Bertrand shrugged.

It was time now to keep him on the move. He was responding well.

'I neglected her. Simon did not know what to do, poor lad. So she turned for comfort to…'

'Elsewhere.'

'Yes.'

There was a pause. Bertrand was afraid that he might run back to cover. But he suddenly spoke again.

91

'Lenore used to talk to her, you know. To Hedi.'

'Why not? We pray to dead saints.'

'That is what my Hedi was – a saint.'

This was most unpromising. Bertrand had to steer him away from maudlin dalliance.

'Does Simon miss his mother?'

'Of course he does. That is why he has these fancies – first a merchant, then a priest, then a monk.'

Bertrand's mind leapt back thirty years in an instant. He saw himself almost as God would have seen him. The shock was dazzling and painful at the same time.

'He is searching, Albert. He means no disrespect or ingratitude.'

Albert thumped his mug on to the bench beside them.

'But if he goes…'

'Does he not want the inn?'

'That is what he says. Idiot. Graceless idiot. If he goes…What will become of this place? I shall not live for ever, you know.'

Bertrand made an expansive gesture.

'You are big and strong.'

Albert was not listening.

'If he goes… My Hedi is gone. Lenore is – is not with us. If Simon goes, I have nothing.' He grimaced with pain. 'Nothing.'

Bertrand suddenly felt sorry for his own father. At last he understood the old man's distress. It was pain that his son did not want to be a soldier, and it was pain that his son wanted nevertheless to leave home. He would have neither pride to ease the separation, nor company to ease the shame.

* * * * * *

92

Proprietary and self-possessed, like all the cats since the dawn of time, Thomas sat in the corner of the window alcove. He gazed disinterestedly at Bertrand and his dinner.

Bertrand had heard Livia call him by name. He now did the same, offering a titbit of unwanted gristle. Thomas turned away and stared over Bertrand's shoulder as if he were not there.

Bertrand made a face at him, then turned to concentrate on his stew, squinting in the candlelight. It guttered in the draughts that shot through the shutters like the sharp sticks that cruel boys used to torment caged animals. The early darkness of late November was made gloomier by the clouds that had been gathering all day. A wind was getting up.

'Thought I should find you in the quietest corner.'

Bertrand looked up.

'Not surprised. Nobody would choose to sit here.'

Arnaud sat down.

'You came then,' said Bertrand.

'You asked me – remember?'

'Tore yourself away, did you?'

'Oh, shut up. Livia! A bowl, please.'

When Livia brought it, and the inevitable dark bread in her apron pocket, Arnaud grinned.

'And I do not have to pay. I am the guest of your favourite customer.'

Arnaud laughed at his own joke. Livia said nothing. She bent over and placed a mug of beer without having been asked.

Bertrand watched her withdraw towards the kitchen.

'What on earth did Albert see in her?'

Arnaud wiped his spoon on his sleeve.

'What is in front of us is the answer to that.'

'But she is such a change from Hedwiga.'

Arnaud looked up in surprise.

'Albert told me,' said Bertrand.

'I never knew Hedi.'

'You speak as if you did.'

'That is because she is so real to Albert.'

'It took me a long time to get it out of him.'

'Oh, he does not talk about her. But he thinks about her. All the time. You can tell.'

'No wonder Livia has a long face.'

'She would have a long face whatever Albert did. Come on, Bertrand. You have seen Italian widows. Italian wives, come to that. Remember all those ghastly creatures round scaffolds in Apulia? Hair drawn tight back. No sign of lips. Implacable.'

'So why marry a fellow like Albert, and come all the way here?'

'Same reason, really. They were both left with mouths to feed. He had Simon and Lenore; she had Vico. He needed a cook and housekeeper; she was looking for a roof and a provider. It made a sort of sense.'

'But she must know she comes second best to Hedi.'

'I expect so. And he comes second best to *her* first husband, whoever he was.' Arnaud grunted. 'Everyone comes second best to Livia – except her precious "Ludi".'

'She is a long way from her home.'

'I fancy that that does not trouble her. She is not the pining type. She is not lonely either.'

'Albert is.'

'I know. And Livia is no help. Poor Albert. Bad enough to be lonely. Worse still to be alone. And that is what Albert is. He has lost his beloved Hedi. Lenore is…you have seen

Lenore. And Simon is – well, you have seen Simon too.'

Arnaud scraped his bowl, sat poised with his last piece of bread in the air, and gazed absently at the cat.

'He is not a bad lad. Not really. Albert is not a bad man. Like all of us, he tries.'

'You take a lot of interest in Simon.'

Arnaud sniffed.

'You forget. My eldest boy would have been about his age – now.'

It was the first time Arnaud had referred to that awful time since – almost since it had happened. Bertrand had sat up with him night after night, while he wept. Then he had cleaned him up morning after morning, after he had tried to swill the grief out of himself with cheap Apulian wine.

Arnaud took a swig of his beer.

'He leaves food out for her, you know.'

'Who?'

'Simon. I said he was a good boy.'

'Does Albert know?'

'I expect so. But he says nothing, for fear of upsetting Livia.'

'Why does Livia hate her?'

'Livia hates anybody who will not work. Even the cat works. Though you would not believe it, to look at him. Catching rats in the barrel house. Livia even makes him sleep there. Everybody must do his bit. Or they go.'

'Why does Albert put up with it?'

'You have eyes. He can not cope with her, and he can not cope without her. That is what infuriates Simon. He knows his father can not stand up to her. He is ashamed of him.'

'He wallows in ideals,' observed Bertrand.

'All he can afford, poor lad.'

'So it is Livia who holds the place together.'

'Not entirely. Give Albert some credit. It is his inn after all. Livia is a second wife, and Vico is only a stepson. Let us say that it is she who stokes the fire, but it is he who provides the fuel. He works very hard, you know. He is a man of many talents.'

Working even harder now, if what Arnaud had said about recovering from the sackings was true. He would need all his many talents – especially his low cunning. What was he cooking up with the 'stinking monks'?

'He was an archer, I believe.'

Arnaud blinked over the rim of his mug.

'How did you know that?'

'As you said, I have eyes. A sergeant, I should wager.'

'True. A good one. He was picked out by the Hautevilles.'

'The Guiscard? If he was, he must have been good.'

Arnaud shook his head.

'No. By Roger – the youngest. In my book he had the longest head of them all. All twelve. The Guiscard had the power, but Roger had the depth.'

Bertrand nodded in appreciation.

'Then Albert must have been very good indeed.'

Arnaud sipped some more beer, and gazed into the distance again. Then he growled.

'God! To be with the Guiscard now, eh?'

'The Guiscard is dead. Has been for years. And you, my friend, are too old. Like Roger, picking grapes in his castle in Palermo. Like Albert.'

'And like you.'

'Yes. Like me too. The difference is, I know it. I accept it.'

'Do you like it?'

'No.'

'Then there is no difference between us. You try to make men listen to your old stories, and I try to make men obey old rules. Like your stories, they are wearing out.'

'Is the platform idea not working?'

'Yes – for the moment. It will be a five-days' wonder. What will happen when it is finished? Eh?'

Arnaud placed his empty mug on the table.

'Have you heard the latest news?'

'What?'

Arnaud leaned forward like a conspirator.

'I have heard,' he began impressively. 'I have heard that Raymond is coming here.'

'Raymond?'

'His Grace Count Raymond of Toulouse. Now, my brave tale-spinner, you tell me: why would he be doing that?'

Bertrand smiled.

'*You* are doubtless going to tell *me*.'

'He is coming to meet His Holiness.'

'Even I can work that out, Arnaud. But tell me why.'

'You know what a good son of the Church Raymond is. Our brave Urban is the holiest of men. At least, as the Bishop of Rome, he ought to be. We have the Pope here; we have a Church Council here; we shall soon have the holiest, most God-fearing count south of the Loire joining them. The city is bursting at the seams with riff-raff from the four corners of Christendom. And the native citizens, after four disasters in two years, are weak, frightened, and puzzled, waiting for a sign, a portent, a gesture, a glance from God – anything. I tell you, Bertrand…'

Arnaud shook his head. Then he clapped his hands to his knees.

'Thank you for the dinner.'

Bertrand put out a hand.

'Before you go – '

Arnaud paused.

'What?'

'I did what you asked me to do.'

Arnaud looked blank.

'What was that?'

'Warned Vico about that soldier.'

Light dawned on Arnaud's seamed face.

'Oh, good. It will reach Albert soon enough.'

'It will reach him sooner than you think; I told Livia too.'

Arnaud looked impressed.

'Brave of you. I bet she shook with terror.'

Bertrand pursed his lips.

'As a matter of fact, she reacted. Not much, but I would swear she reacted. My guess is that she already knows about him.'

'The Limper?'

'Yes.'

Arnaud shook his head in reluctant admiration.

'An amazing woman. She knows everything. You can never surprise her. She just wipes her hands in the dishcloth and looks at you.'

'Where does she get it all?'

'The cathedral – where else?'

Bertrand looked blank. Arnaud grinned.

'Did you not know? Bertrand, old friend, you must be slipping. Oh, yes – always praying, our lady Livia. Or so the neighbours think.'

'Ah.'

'Oh, yes. Sit in a pew, put your bag down beside you, stay there long enough with your head down, and you hear everything. People think you are talking to God; they do not realise you are listening to them. You are part of the furniture – like servants. But the things you catch. It is almost as good as being in a confessional. And what you miss in the nave you pick up in the square afterwards.'

'Well, that may be. But Vico knew too – I would swear to that as well.'

'Of course – Livia told him.'

Bertrand looked unconvinced.

'If you say so. But Vico knows something.'

'Makes a change. He is the most ignorant oaf for miles.'

'Are you not concerned?'

'What about?'

'This soldier?'

Arnaud screwed up his eyes.

'What are you suggesting?'

'I am not sure. But it seems odd: you tell me about – '

' – the Limper.'

' – the Limper. As if it is some new knowledge, which you pass on to me, almost as restricted information, which I am to handle discreetly. And when I tell Livia and Vico, they behave as if they already know.'

'So what?'

'And Vico shooed me away.'

Arnaud laughed.

'And where have they buried the body – in your chicken-house?'

Bertrand looked shamefaced.

'Maybe. But should you not – well, investigate? You are the Mayor, after all.'

Arnaud laughed again.

'Bertrand, I can not be the servant of your lively imagination. First you want me to investigate a dead soldier who has been strung up in the forest for a week, and who was almost certainly sent to Hell by the men he had betrayed. Now you want me to look into a murder that has not yet happened.'

'How do you know?'

'Bertrand, I told you about the Limper because I wanted to protect Albert and his family from him. Now you are suggesting that I should have protected *him* from *them*.'

'Well?'

'On what evidence? Because Livia stands still and says nothing – as usual? Because Vico stoops a bit lower – as usual?'

'He had his pitchfork in his hand,' said Bertrand lamely.

'He *always* has his pitchfork in his hand. Oh, come on, Bertrand – you will have to do better than that. I have a city trembling on the brink of I know not what.'

He clapped his hands to his knees again.

'I really must go.'

'Why?'

'To be ready.'

'For what?'

'If I knew that, my old friend, I should sleep a happier man tonight. Thank you once again for the dinner.'

He leaned over to stroke Thomas, who showed no sign of gratification. Arnaud swore at him under his breath.

'Then talk to your precious Livia. It is the only time she strings more than five words together. Unless she talks to the Tub.'

He patted Bertrand on the shoulder as he passed.

'Ask Thomas. See if he noticed anything. Oh – one last thing. Something else came out of the Bishop's palace this evening. The Pope plans to preach in French.'

'So what? He *is* French.'

'Oh, Bertrand, do not be so dense. When did you last hear a bishop preach in anything but Latin? And what did it matter what he said? We shall have an enormous crowd out there, ready for any madness, and they will be able to understand every single word he utters. I tell you, no good will come of it.'

'You controlled those drunken soldiers,' said Bertrand.

'Easy,' said Arnaud. 'A few men-at-arms mad with beer, who would be sober in the morning. And I had a traitor who was both greedy and convenient. Now I could have a whole city drunk – on words. And for how long?'

'Only words, my friend.'

'They are your tools. They were the tools of Jesus. Look what he started.'

* * * * * *

Six

HUGH OF TOURNAI threw the last of the lees from the bottom of his mug into the nearest gutter. He gazed round the near-empty cathedral square. Over half the braziers were dead. Many stallholders were already taking down their awnings.

'Pack up, Robert. We are wasting our time.'

'Do we move on?'

'No. We wait.'

'What for?'

'People to come to their senses. Look at it – a madhouse. A week of crowds like Jerusalem at the Crucifixion. Now – as empty as the grave. Enough to give anyone the shivers. Unnatural.'

'They are all waiting. Outside the city.'

'Let them wait. I have business to do.'

'You mean you are waiting for the Bishop to pay you.'

'Mind your tongue.'

'Well, you are.'

'All right – what if I am? I am also waiting for all those other bishops to forget their precious Pope and their precious Council for just a few hours. They will, they will.'

'Why are you so sure?'

'Because even bishops are human, like the rest of us. Put them all together like that, and they will look around. They will all want to live up to the others. And I shall be there to give them the chance to do it. Sooner or later. You see. And then…'

'You will make a lot of money.'

Hugh glared.

'And what is so wrong with that? We offer supply where there is a demand.'

'Yes – when the price is right.'

'It will be. Especially with Count Raymond. They say he lives like an emperor.'

'So what do we do now?'

'What *we* do is my business. What *you* do is what I tell you – pack everything up.'

'Why is it always me?' Robert grumbled. 'What are you going to do?'

'Look for somewhere for us to stay while we wait.'

Robert looked up in surprise.

'What is wrong with the wagon?'

Hugh gestured towards the ghostly square.

'Too dangerous.'

Robert stared.

'What! Here?'

'I told you – unnatural. I am off to find an inn with a safe stable yard. What the eye does not see it can not covet. Do as I say.'

Robert looked downcast.

'Can I not go and see? I promise to clear everything up first.'

'No.'

'There may be something wonderful out there – a miracle perhaps.'

'Yes, and a pig's ear. You have been listening to too many sermons, boy. Keep your head, or someone with a churchman's chasuble will charm it off your shoulders.'

Robert bent to his gloomy work.

'Nobody charms you, I suppose. No silver-tongued

soldier with a scar on his face.'

Hugh cuffed him.

'I want you here to keep an eye on all this. Especially now; anything may happen.'

'All right, all right – if you say so.'

Hugh pulled on his jerkin. Robert continued grumbling.

'We go everywhere, and we never see anything.'

'See that you double-wrap the red and the blue. No ends showing.'

'In case soldiers with scars come by.'

'Yes. And do not get charmed out of it all like me.'

They looked at each other and grinned. Hugh clipped him lightly on the ear as he passed.

*　*　*　*　*　*

'What are you doing with that?'

Vico paused only momentarily, and leered from his stoop.

'What does it look like?'

Simon was beside himself with rage.

'I left that for – for – '

Vico made a noise in his throat which was half chuckling, half hawking.

'We all know who you left it for.'

Simon gaped.

'You must have been spying for hours to notice that.'

Vico swept the food off the platter to the ground, where two stray dogs were already slavering.

'Bit late now.'

Simon felt almost stifled with his heart's angry beating.

'You – you offal!'

Vico wiped his greasy fingers.

'You should watch it better. I did.'

Simon tried to control his temper.

'I shall tell Father.'

Vico's eyes shone in their deep sockets.

'Do it.'

* * * * * *

Livia lifted the handle of the huge pot on to the hook over the flames with barely a grunt of effort.

She stood back and kneaded her hands in a cloth.

'They will all have to eat, Thomas. When it is all over, they will all have to eat.'

Thomas arched his back.

Vico came into the kitchen, still smiling to himself. He saw the cat, and hung back in the doorway.

'Make that animal go.'

Livia flapped the edge of her apron.

'Off, now, Thomas. You know how Ludi fears you.'

'It is not fear.'

'Whatever you call it. It comes to the same thing.'

Vico growled.

'If you are like that, I shall not stay. I shall go to hear him.'

Livia did not trouble to turn round.

'You too will come back – when you are hungry. There will be work to do later; do not forget.'

Vico's face cleared.

'I have done a good morning's work already.'

He turned to go, and bumped into someone coming in. He stood back with a scowl.

'There was nobody at the front, so I came through,' said Hugh of Tournai.

Vico glanced at his mother. Livia put down her cloth.

'A place for me and my boy,' said Hugh. 'And for my

wagon. My money is good. See? Two days in advance if you wish.'

Vico's brow bent under the weight of suspicion and ill humour.

'What is wrong with the square? Or outside if it comes to that?'

Hugh pointed in the direction of the west gate.

'Have you been outside there today? Have you any idea what is happening?'

'The square is empty,' said Vico, who obviously knew.

Hugh was losing patience.

'You are an inn. You offer places. I am asking for places, and I have good money. Do I get them or not?'

He opened a palm and displayed silver coins. Vico's eyes gleamed in spite of himself.

'Why?' said Livia.

Hugh tossed his head in impatience.

'Because I have already been robbed, and I have no wish to be robbed again, by that mob out there. Now, for the third time, do I get my places?'

Livia nodded. Vico stepped forward, but Livia stopped him with the smallest gesture of a finger. He backed again, hunched and frowning.

As he was counting the money into Livia's hand, Hugh had an afterthought.

'You have not had any soldiers staying here recently, have you? I have to be careful, you see.'

A whole covey of glances flitted between Vico and Livia. Livia shook her head.

'Good,' said Hugh. 'I shall go and get my wagon. My boy is watching it in the square at the moment.'

When he had gone, another pair of glances flew.

* * * * * *

Albert went to the door of the barrel-house for the third time to listen. He had seen Vico go indoors. Simon had stumped off somewhere, apparently in yet another rage. Livia, he knew, would be in the kitchen. The inn was empty. The yard was empty. Now was the best time.

He went to the deepest corner, and, putting out all his great strength, moved away a near-full barrel. He kicked aside the cat's box. Behind it, he used his knife to prise out a loose stone in the outer wall. He placed his lighted candle carefully so that he could see inside the hole. Licking his lips, he slid out a wooden box. Sitting astride a pile of old beams, he placed it before his splayed knees.

Using thumbnails as strong as chisels, he prised back the ornate clasps. The box alone, made by a master craftsman in Poitou, had cost him three weeks' sergeant's pay. He lifted the lid. It was even lined. He undid a leather pouch, tipped out some coins into his palm, and began counting...

Did he have enough? Would the prior drive an even harder bargain? Should he keep some back for Simon? Perhaps that old minstrel was right; he should let the boy go. What was there for him in a place like this? Perhaps he *was* cut out to be a scholar. Perhaps that was God's Will... And what about Lenore? She was getting worse, not better, for all his prayers at wells and shrines. What was the best way? A house for her too? ...Would he be able to deceive Livia? ...Could he hide this box from Vico's squint eyes for much longer? After all, there were only so many places in a crowded inn, and nobody could be alone for much more than a call of nature, if that.

He paused with a handful of silver coins in each palm, and rested them on his thighs.

Who would there be left? ...

He heaved a colossal sigh. It was hard. Was this what God wanted? Why was it that what He wanted so rarely tied in with what you wanted yourself? Could he be sure that it was indeed what God wanted? It hurt, and what hurt was usually the right thing – or so the churchmen said. But how could he be sure?

He sighed again.

Hedi would have known what to do. Hedi had always known what to do…

* * * * * *

Robert paused with a bale still in his arms. A thin figure had appeared at the corner of the deserted square. It was the girl. Still half-naked, so far as he could see. Though she excited no male longing in him, he wanted to throw the cloth to the ground, rush across the square, and put his coat round her shoulders. Even as the thought came to him, he knew it would be hopeless; he would not get ten paces before she would bolt. There was something about the way she held her head, about the sharpness of her movements. Ever alert, like a bird hopping round crumbs in a yard.

Then she stopped, knelt down, and clasped her hands in an unmistakable attitude of prayer.

Robert, having restrained his desire, now frowned in puzzlement. Why did she not go into the cathedral? There it was, a stone's throw away. There was no shrine in the square, no cross, no statue, no old well where the crones told stories of ancient spells and miracles. The girl's tense, bowed shoulders told of rapt concentration. What was she reacting to? What was she waiting for? Even at that distance, he could almost feel the urgency of the wasted body. Once, and once only, she looked behind her, and her glance flung fire across forty paces. An instant later she had resumed her original attitude, but Robert's memory stayed burned for years afterwards. The eyes. He had never seen such eyes.

Then it was the turn of his ears to be bewitched. At first it was a faint, confused murmuring. Robert stood up from wrapping the last of the bales – the red and the blue. He cocked his head to concentrate more. It was barely more than a rustle from distant trees.

It grew, though, like a gathering storm – not loud, but unstoppable. He glanced up in the direction of the Bishop's palace.

The soldiers were the first to come round the corner, their heavy iron-shod boots ringing on the stones – the first clear voice to speak out of the rumbling. Only a handful of them, but dressed formally, with regularity in their stride.

Behind them came a rustle of monks, their black habits swirling in the swing of their step, crosses and tassels on girdle-ends swaying on ample chests and stomachs. Chaplains, priests, and deacons carried a small forest of crosses on long poles. Others swung censers, their smoke hanging like God's Breath in the still air.

Riding through the holy smoke, a detachment of horsemen sniffed, and waved away the last wisps with gloved hands. Their equipment was not local. Exotic trappings hung from their bridles; colours spoke of long summer sun. When a richly-dressed nobleman swung into view, Robert knew, or thought he knew. It had to be Count Raymond of Toulouse; nobody near Clermont wore clothes like that, or had the money for them. Robert and Hugh, with their woollens and their linens, had travelled south as well as north. He had 'covered ground', as he had boasted to the fat minstrel. He had heard about Count Raymond, and what he had heard tallied with what he was now seeing.

The talk in the square had been full of a great nobleman coming to Clermont, and Raymond's name had been on the edge of every beer-greased tongue. Very holy, they said – for a nobleman. A great pilgrim.

Robert pursed his lips. So that was what a virtuous count looked like.

Pages and private chaplains jogged uncomfortably behind the great man, and another squadron of cavalry kept them on the move.

Then came a gap. Robert kept looking intently. A suspicion, born of much procession-watching, made him suspect that the gap was deliberate.

Round the corner came the Bishop's retinue – another purposeful parade of black habits preceding the tall silver crozier. The gold thread of the swaying mitre – the bishop was not a very good horseman either – shone in the sun. A proud stable-boy, scrubbed and combed, led the bridle. Half the Bishop's household followed.

Robert continued to stare. Behind the last of the valets and constables came a cluster of nodding mitres. Robert was mystified for a moment. Then he remembered – the Council! He had heard about the great gathering of bishops from all over Christendom, but he had never thought to see one – out in the open, in full view. Bishops were creatures that humble folk saw rarely, and then only one at a time. He could have sworn that he caught sight of a scarlet cap or two as well; he had heard of cardinals, but he had never seen one. Hugh was right – he would never do business on a day like this. They must have been preparing for this procession for hours, days.

Servants and chaplains jostled each other in bad horsemanship or over-eagerness to cut the finest figures. But Robert noticed that, though bad looks were thrown about in large numbers, there was no swearing. It was then that he realised – there was hardly any noise at all. Nobody spoke. No sergeant barked orders; no constables shouted warnings; no soldiers showed off.

It was all rustle and jingle, scuff and clatter, rattle of scabbard and slap of leather. Robert swallowed.

He glanced towards the girl, who had not moved, either her position or her stance. Crazed she may have been, but not stupid; she had taken up a place close enough to see everything, but far enough away to be in no danger from the horses. Certainly a much better view than Robert was getting, but he dared not move closer for fear of scaring her off.

Then came another gap, a longer one. This time Robert was quite sure it was deliberate.

He was used to bright colours in his trade, but nothing in it prepared him for the burst and blaze, the dazzle and shine, the onslaught on the eyes, that followed. Exotic materials the like of which Hugh of Tournai would never have been able to stock, or protect. Gold and silver thread as profuse and gleaming as sardines tumbled from a barrel. Poles and pikestaffs and standards shimmering with devices and badges and emblems and pennons. Reliquaries encased with jewels which clung like barnacles to a long-neglected hull. Harness such as he had never seen on anything so ordinary as a horse. Garments which he would never wear in a thousand years – stoles and chasubles and capes and cloaks. Held by such pins and belts and buckles and clasps. And the rings!

Within this magical forest, this spell-ridden, teeming,

trotting and jiggling grove of riches, right in the middle, nodding alone, was a crown, a tiara, which must have come down from Heaven itself.

Still clutching his bale, Robert dropped to his knees. As he did so, he knew, beyond any shadow of doubt, that this – this – was the crowning event of his life so far. This was what he would bore his grandchildren with till they would prefer to go out into the dark rather than listen yet one more time to the story of the day when he saw a pope.

He did not see the remainder of the crowd that followed – the last chaplains and clerks and novices, the pleaders and suppliants and petitioners and clients, the piemen and water-carriers, the pickpockets and cutpurses, the orphans and urchins and cripples and beggars – and everybody else.

By the time it had all passed, Robert had come back to his full senses and scrambled to his feet, glancing round quickly to see if Hugh had noticed what he had been doing. The girl was gone. The square was practically empty.

In an arcade on the far edge away from the cathedral, two men sighed, each for different reasons.

Arnaud wiped his forehead.

'So far, so good.'

Bertrand did the same.

'I think I begin to get some idea of what it was like to follow Jesus in the crowd when he went out of Jerusalem on to the hillside.'

Arnaud grunted.

'They had no idea what they were going to get either.'

*   *   *   *   *   *

'Where are you going?'

Simon paused in the doorway.

'To hear him, of course.'

'Must you?'

Simon gazed in wonderment.

'Surely you are coming too?'

Albert made a vague gesture.

'A lot to do. Livia says there will be a lot to do when they get hungry afterwards.'

Simon sneered.

'Let Vico do it. He has time enough on his hands.'

Albert let his eyes drop.

'What he did was – not good, I agree.'

'Not good! Father, *he stole her food*. Threw it to the dogs. If we are not careful, she will starve.'

'She will not stay still. God knows where she goes.'

'It is you who should know, Father, not God. I can not do it alone. Vico waits and watches, like a cat at a hole. He could not watch both of us.'

'I know, I know. I will speak to him.'

Simon sneered again.

'Just as you speak to Madame Livia.'

He had never found a satisfactory way of referring to his stepmother.

Albert flushed.

'That is my affair. My affair. Madame Livia works hard.' (Neither had Albert.) 'You do not have the worries and the responsibilities.'

'I am worried about Lenore. You should be too.'

'I am. I am.'

'Then in the name of God do something!'

Albert stood up.

'All very well for you. You and your precious scruples.'

Simon sighed. It was all going the usual way.

113

'It is impossible to reason with you.'

Albert swore.

'That is the scholar's excuse. Pretending we are beneath your great mind.'

Simon pulled on a tattered coat.

'I am going. There is no point in listening to this.'

Albert tried to rein in his temper.

'Can you not wait a moment – just a moment?'

'Why?'

'It is just that – well, there is a matter I wished to discuss with you.' He spoke as if the words hurt.

Simon tilted his head in disgust.

'Well, let us wait until Madame Livia says you have the time.'

Albert waved a huge arm.

'Damn you to Hell! To think – I was just about to – '

'About to what?'

'Never mind.'

* * * * * *

Robert squeezed into the back of an uncovered wagon, which threatened to overbalance with the press of bodies crammed on to it. Nobody so much as looked at him. All eyes were on the platform.

He had missed the High Mass. Not that he cared much about that. High masses were for noblemen and saints. What worried him far more was what would happen to him when Hugh found out where he had been. Well, he would cross that bridge when he came to it. The bales were safe; he had seen to that. He could not for the life of him make out what Hugh was making such a fuss about.

He had seen a pope; now he had to hear one. If he could not make out a single word, it would not matter. It would be the only chance in his whole life, and if it cost him a beating it would be worth it.

He stiffened as he caught sight of the girl again. Lonely and exposed as before. He was just about to jump down from the wagon and go across to her, when he saw a young man approach her. To his surprise she did not recoil from him. She slipped a hand into his, as gratefully as if she had found a sheepskin coat against the November air.

Robert shrugged. Ah, well…

*   *   *   *   *   *

Arnaud whispered in Bertrand's ear.

'There he goes – look. Just like a cat.'

Bertrand followed the direction of Arnaud's nod.

Vico had climbed up the scaffolding, till he was above the platform. Zealous cathedral staff had draped bright hangings to provide an exotic backdrop to the Mass. Vico had raised himself to the topmost bars, and there propped himself with the ease of a cat on the top of a door.

'I saw him rescue a child like that once,' said. Arnaud. 'From the top of a tower. An hour later he had his hand up her skirt.'

'Swine,' said Bertrand, who was not really listening. He was sure he had just seen Albert in the crowd. He smiled in spite of himself. So retired sergeants of archers from Alsace were no more proof against the occasion than ageing minstrels or mayors.

They gazed in wonder at the size of the gathering. They trembled at the fierceness of its concentration on the figure at the front of the platform. As His Holiness made his way towards the makeshift lectern, it was as if the whole assembly had created a joint will of its own, intent on forcing a miracle out of the lonely figure in the towering crown. You could beat a hammer against the silence. With the wordless intuition of old friends, Arnaud and Bertrand looked at each other and asked the great question with their eyes…

Pope Urban raised his head and lifted his hands high. His voice rang clear like an abbey bell on a windless winter morning, over a flock as still as a snow-dumb countryside.

'My children in Christ… '

* * * * * *

Seven

'JE-RU-SA-LEM! JE-RU-SA-LEM!'

For the twentieth time a group of young people went by, their lungs bursting in frenzied, discordant unison. Lone voices were raised in frantic entreaty, offering to sell furniture, tools, carts, clothes, anything. Snatches of hymns and chants and prayers, out of tune, out of time, poured through cracks in shutters, their only common feature their urgency and their passion. Wheels ground and bounced over complaining cobbles. Boots and clogs beat a tattoo as of an invading army. Rattling, clanging. Cows groaned. Dogs barked.

Running through everything, like a pulse – soaring over everything, like an avenging angel – giving the whole rush of energy a single voice – was the constant refrain, bawled and bellowed through gapped and blackened teeth from eager throats raucous with repetition: *'Deus le volt! Deus le volt!'*

Inside *The Hawk* Bertrand de Montclos leaned forward, kicked a wayward log back into the flames, sat back, sighed, and shook his head.

'God wills it.'

He did not need to peer through the shutters. He knew what he would see if he did – the popping eyes, the dancing Adam's apples in whiskered, scrawny necks, the skin stretched across bulbous cheeks, the tongues lapping against lower lips.

Curious how it was hard to drive a single man mad,

but easy to craze a crowd. He understood very well; bewitching an audience was his trade. In Pope Urban he recognised a fellow-expert in the mystery.

But he had never seen a madness of such awesome fire. He would have wagered that it was new to His Holiness too. He would have wagered again that His Holiness had never expected anything like this.

For three days the city had not slept. It showed no sign of exhaustion. It was as if Urban's words had struck a magic spark amid a gigantic forest which had been dried in years of burning sun, and now the flame, with demonic energy, was consuming everything in its path. There seemed nothing to do but wait until it had burned itself out. How long, how long?

Bertrand shook his head again.

Till they had reached the Holy Land? How many years would that take? Till they had found the forgiveness of their sins? How many years would *that* take? Or would the madness and the hope be snuffed out in the frosts and snows of the mountains, in the parched summer months of Italy, in the rat-infested holds of Venetian merchantmen, in the bloodstained fetters of Dalmatian pirates, in the ambushes of the Magyars and the Bulgars?

Bertrand wiped the last of his bread round the edge of the bowl. Livia was serving her stew in bigger portions; the flood of customers had shrunk to a trickle. Everybody had too much else on his mind. Or her mind. One of the many amazing things about this madness was that it was infecting the women as well. One and all, it seemed, they were obsessed with raising money, making provision for long absences, preparing for a long journey – no time to linger, lounge, or gossip.

It was causing havoc with *The Hawk's* trade. Albert must

be worried out of his wits – as if he did not have enough to worry about already. Had he been able to float that loan that Arnaud was hinting at? It did not seem likely; William the Tub had been conspicuous by his absence of late. Perhaps he could see precious little in the way of firm security or sound chance of repayment. Perhaps Livia had found a convenient Jew to haggle with. In present circumstances – with half the city off its head – it might not be as difficult as it seemed. Child's play to a woman of Livia's resource.

She would know that there were suddenly dozens of tight-faced, slit-eyed individuals everywhere, who were prepared to advance money, buy goods at knock-down prices, look after houses and plots while their owners were away, give guarantees, swear promises, negotiate agreements. Had not His Holiness himself assured the children of his flock that a crusader's property was sacrosanct in his absence?

Bertrand pushed away his bowl. Well, Livia may or may not have given *The Hawk* a breathing space for the future, but there was certainly plenty of space for breathing in it right now in the present; Bertrand practically had the place to himself.

Except for the residents of course. Nor did they have time for him. Albert did not sit beside him to complain. Vico had given up abusing him; it seemed his barrel-rolling and his log-carrying tied his lurid tongue. He went about more hunched than ever, as if he were clutching a secret to himself. Simon suffered in silence. Lenore flitted past outside now and again, like a bat in the shadows of an empty vault. Livia brought his stew or his cold bacon, his beer or his bad wine, and fished his piece of dark bread out of her apron pocket.

'So you were wrong,' said Bertrand, looking up at her. 'They did not all come back to eat.'

Livia wiped her bony hands in the cloth she always carried.

'Madness.'

Her only comment. But expressionless. Bertrand had no means of knowing whether it was said out of annoyance, bafflement, or contempt.

Company was in very short supply. It was as if they had forgotten his existence. The daily routine of the inn became the only aspect of normality in a world turned upside-down, and they clung to it as would a shipwrecked voyager to a tossing spar. Since there were few customers to react with, they reacted with each other, apparently oblivious of his presence.

Bertrand sipped and watched from the shadows as Albert had an altercation with a pedlar, rather the worse for wear, who had come to scrounge a keg for his journey.

The cheeks and neck reddened.

'Get out. You stink.'

The man blinked and swayed.

'I give you good money.'

Albert spat.

'Call that a fair price? What do you take me for – an idiot? I am not mad like the rest of you.'

The pedlar swore.

Albert waved a huge arm.

'Get out – and no pissing on the doorstep, or I shall break your neck.'

Livia watched, but said nothing. Albert growled.

'Well, what was I supposed to do? Let him have it?'

'We do sell beer.'

'Not at those prices. You keep to your kitchen, and leave the rest to me.'

Worry was destroying Albert's common sense. He was losing control again, so he blustered, and there was no reasoning with him.

Livia tried just once. She pushed back a wisp of hair.

'Where will the next customer come from?'

Albert glared.

'Is the madness my fault? Is the Pope my fault?'

'Nothing is ever your fault, Albert.'

Albert beckoned her to a table.

'Tell me, tell me. You think I never take responsibility. You think I can not decide, is that it? That I never make up my mind. That is what you always mean. Admit it.'

Livia stood still and stared.

Albert stood up straight, and pointed to his own ample chest.

'Well, I have decided. I am going to do something about Simon. Maybe about Lenore too. Then you will have nothing to nag about. Put that in your stew and stir it.'

Livia bent to wipe the table, her hand moving methodically over the ring-stained wood.

'I hear you, Albert.'

'You wait – you just wait.'

* * * * * *

When Bertrand returned from the privy, it was Vico that Albert was abusing. Which was unusual. He complained about Vico behind his back, but this was the first time Bertrand had seen him raise his voice to his face, as it were.

'Who do you think this house belongs to? You? Your mother? Ha!'

Vico hunched down further as if in self-defence. Albert loomed over him.

'And keep your filthy tongue to yourself. I know my son and I know my daughter.'

'Tell that to Mother.'

Albert almost aimed a blow at him; the effort of restraint nearly choked him. Vico turned to go. Albert pursued him with swearwords.

'Your precious mother will never give you what you want, and nor will I. She has not the means. And I do not have the inclination.'

Again the long word – inclination. It heightened the sadness of Albert's predicament. He was intelligent, but had little instinct for the skill in human management which might help him, if not to get out of it, at least to survive in it.

The neck flushed again as Albert leaned forward the better to shout.

'Do you hear? Never. You will get nothing. Because I – I say so. *You* tell *that* to "Mother" .'

An hour later Albert was losing his temper with Simon. Simon was giving as good as he got.

It was as if the whole family could not leave each other alone.

Bertrand sighed for the tenth time. It was indeed some kind of a miracle, against which nobody was proof. Everybody around him may not have been rushing to go off on a crusade, but everybody was certainly, it seemed, going mad.

*　*　*　*　*　*

It had started with the first man to wave his hands. What had possessed him? Who could tell?

Up to then, the crowd had been quiet. Not a rustle, not a murmur. Enough to parch the throat.

'My children in Christ...'

From the moment he began, His Holiness had cast a spell. At first the spell of a storyteller. Bertrand understood that. Admired it.

And such stories. The miseries suffered by the pilgrims to the Holy Land – the insults, the robbings, the imprisonments, the offences to the women. No lurid detail was spared. Festering untreated wounds, dank cells, leering jowls through the grills, torn skirts, pleas for mercy scorned.

Then the defeats and disgrace endured by the Greek Emperor – the raidings, the burnings, the lootings, the desecration of holy places by devil-possessed infidels. The billowing cloud of hellish eastern black magic that now loomed over the precious city of Constantinople itself, where the broad, rich streets and the miraculous church of the Holy Wisdom were now under threat – the famous gold paving and the cool marble floors about to be trodden by the rushing, scuffing, stinking, naked feet of a million Turks.

Still no noise from the crowd. Bertrand felt uneasy. The stories were about to make way for another kind of spell – of sheer magic.

'What should we do, my children?'

There was a tenseness you could hear, a tautness you could feel on the hairs of the arms and neck. Bertrand looked round. They were waiting for the last syllables of the spell which would set the magic in motion.

'Crusade.'

There it was.

Holy war. Succour to the suffering pilgrims. Aid to

the beleaguered legions of the Emperor. Liberation of Jerusalem itself. Become a soldier of Christ, a deliverer of the golden city and of the Holy City, an agent of revenge and justice against the Devil-begotten infidels who should go back to the Hell whence they had come. If ever God's Will was clear, it was here and now. Could anybody doubt it?

Up went somebody's hands.

'Deus le volt!'

God wills it!

A score of voices answered him.

Urban sensed the moment, and instinctively played to it. Bertrand found himself agreeing; it was what he would have done.

God would lead, God would protect, God would guide.

Up went another pair of hands.

'Deus le volt!'

A score more of voices opened.

God would advise, God would support, God would conquer.

'Deus le volt!'

A hundred voices this time. Urban seized the reins of opportunity. Bertrand felt a stirring of unease. The horse was showing signs of getting out of control.

Soldiers should wear the cross, take the cross, give themselves to the cross, place themselves under the divine protection of the cross. The journey would be long and hard, but what better service of God could there be?

'Deus le volt!'

A thousand now, and more than once.

A man's property would be sacred while he was away; God would see to it. No risk, no hardship, no danger was too much in such a mission. It was the sacred duty of all Christendom to rescue the Holy City from the filthy, bloodstained hands of the infidel.

'*Deus le volt!*'

The crowd now had only one voice.

'*Deus le volt!*'

It was now not only a response, but a challenge. What was His Holiness going to say next? They were hungry for another burning sentence to respond to.

Urban was now taken up himself with the passion of the moment, carried away by his own oratory. Convinced that he was the agent of the Divine Will, the mouthpiece of God Himself, he threw the reins on the neck of the argument. He was no longer a storyteller, or even a magician; he was a prophet.

As the servant of the servants of God, he could assure his children in Christ that their greatest hope in all the world would be realised. What did they all long for more than anything? The forgiveness of their sins. That forgiveness he, as the channel of God's Grace, could promise them. War would no longer be a crime, killing no longer an affront to Divine Mercy – provided it was killing of infidels. Every split Moslem skull was a step nearer to Paradise.

'*Deus le volt! Deus le volt! Deus le volt!*'

Bertrand felt a thumping in his chest.

The crowd burst like a swollen river against a crumbling flood bank.

Bertrand fought his way to where his friend Arnaud was standing beside his horse. Bodies jostled him all the way; it was like a mob fleeing a fire.

Arnaud spat.

'God preserve us – and I do not mean Urban's God.'

* * * * * *

Bertrand stooped amid the forest of rushing feet and tenderly lifted a bruised white elbow.

Burning eyes looked up in to his. Bertrand bent lower and spoke slowly and clearly.

'If you stay here, you will die.'

As he struggled, a young man stopped dead in his headlong flight, and stared. Bertrand gestured urgently.

'Grab her other elbow.'

Lenore made no protest as Robert took her arm. He touched her as if she were a holy relic, staring and gaping. Bertrand shouted above the noise.

'Hold her, boy! Lift her.'

Robert jumped back to some of his senses.

'Where do you live?'

Bertrand interrupted.

'Never mind the questions. I know. Come.'

They steered her through the great gate and towards *The Hawk*.

Robert looked up.

'How do you know this is the place?'

'Because I am staying here. Just do as I say. Get her inside.'

Robert tried to ask her questions.

'Where is the young man you were with?'

Bertrand looked up between his puffings.

'What young man?'

'She was with a fellow. I saw them. Just before he began.'

'That was her brother. Was that Simon, Lenore?'

Robert stared.

'You know her name?'

'I said I was staying here. Lenore, was that Simon? Where is he? What has happened to him?'

Lenore sat peaceably on the bench where they had placed her. She put her hands in her lap.

'It is the Will of God. I knew there would be a miracle. I prayed for it.' She looked up at them. 'I prayed for it, you know. The Blessed Saint Margaret told me it would come.'

'No doubt, no doubt,' said Bertrand.

Robert frowned.

'Who is this Simon?'

'Her brother.'

'And he left her – in the middle of that crowd?'

Bertrand rebuked him with a look.

'The madness. You were running too. Where is Hugh?'

Robert tried to pull his thoughts together.

'He – er – he went off to find a place for us to stay, a place to put the wagon. He was afraid of what might happen in the square.'

Bertrand nodded grimly.

'Very sensible of him.'

He looked round.

'I suppose he could be here. It is the nearest to the gate.'

Robert looked about vacantly, as if he expected Hugh to pop out of an alcove.

'He needs to know where you are,' said Bertrand.

Robert found more sense returning, and with it some fear.

'He will kill me when he finds me; I left the wagon to go and hear him.'

Bertrand smiled drily.

'I doubt that somehow. Under the circumstances. Now go and see if he has brought your wagon back here.'

Robert looked round again. Bertrand made a gesture of annoyance.

'Not here, stupid. Out in the yard. Go out of here and follow the street round to the back. Down the alley. Right round to the stable arch, where the horses go.'

Robert looked helpless.

'But supposing I meet someone.'

'You will not. Everyone was out there, listening to him. The place is empty. But it will not be empty for long. Now go.'

Robert bolted. Bertrand made a quick sign of the cross over his chest. It was not the first time he had lied to Robert. He turned back to Lenore.

'Where is Livia, I wonder?'

He made as if to go and look for her, but felt a grip like iron on his arm, and turned in amazement.

Lenore's eyes were burning holes again.

'Do not call her. She is not here.'

Bertrand stared.

'You mean Livia was there as well?'

'I saw her. I knew she would go.'

Bertrand opened his mouth to ask her how she knew, but found the eyes boring into his, and changed his mind. Whatever this poor child knew, she knew by inspiration, not by thought. Unless, of course, she simply knew what Arnaud knew – that Livia used the cathedral as her clearing house for news.

Lenore's next remark confirmed it.

'She will stop in the cathedral and pray. As it is a special day, she will pray for a long time.'

More than likely; there was a lot of news to pick up.

'Then she will return.'

Bertrand detached his arm from her white hand, and

stood up. What was to be done now? He had rescued the girl from being crushed by a mob. He had done his best to reunite the boy with his master. Simon, admittedly, could be anywhere, but Simon was young and able-bodied, and could take care of himself physically, even if his mind was a mess. How had he become separated from his sister? Surely not by design; Simon was very attached to her. He despised his father for his weakness in the face of Livia's treatment of her. Probably simply the crowd, the rush, the madness. The madness! How many things would in the coming days and weeks be blamed on the madness?

Albert was bound to return sooner or later, and he was big and strong enough to keep his feet in any crowd. Heaven help the citizen who got in his way.

Livia would also come back, for sure – when she had got what she wanted at the cathedral. Vico? Well, Vico could also look after himself. Devil take Vico – as he probably would one of these days – and good riddance.

If only Arnaud would walk through the door.

Robert did instead. He was still gaping.

'How did you know?'

He pointed weakly behind him.

'Out there. In the yard. Just as you said.'

'I am a magician in my spare time,' said Bertrand. 'Now, the next thing you must do is find Hugh.'

Robert nodded vigorously.

'I know. To tell him.'

Bertrand tossed his head in impatience.

'He knows, you bonehead. He put it there.'

Robert now tossed his.

'No, no. Not that. To tell him that I must be going.'

'Going?'

'On crusade. I am taking the cross.'

'Yes, yes, yes, I see. Like everyone else.'

Lenore gazed ecstatically up at Robert, and clasped her hands.

'Oh, Robert, the saints and the angels will bless you.'

Robert looked down at her, as if he could not believe his own ears. This precious creature not only knew his name; she was actually approving of him, admiring him. Pleased to be near him. After her previous starings and silent flittings, the change almost unmanned him. He swayed on his feet with the intoxication of it.

Lenore seized Bertrand's arm again.

'We must prepare.'

'Prepare what?' said Bertrand.

'For our departure. Before Livia comes back.'

She flashed one of her scalding glances at Robert.

Robert swallowed.

'What − now?'

'Of course. It is the Will of God. I have always known it would come. It is just that I did not know how. Now I know. Now hurry. We do not have long.'

Robert and Bertrand looked at each other. Lenore stood up and clapped her hands.

'This is no time for fear. I say we must go. God will provide.'

Robert stammered.

'But I have to see Hugh first − to tell him, you see.'

Back there before His Holiness and his lectern, he had made a huge unconscious romantic decision. Now he was being called upon to make a conscious practical one. It was much more difficult.

Lenore took hold of both his arms and focussed her eyes on his. He recoiled from the heat.

'You want to go? To go with me? With Saint Margaret?

Yes? Say you do.'

Robert nodded. Lenore shook him.

'Say it!

'Yes. Yes!'

Bertrand wagged his head. Lenore turned to him and smiled. Actually smiled. The shadows in her cheeks disappeared. Her skin glowed.

'Poor old man. You must have longer to make up your mind. I shall make us some soup.'

From mysterious corners she produced some unsavoury-looking grasses, nettles, and herbs. Bertrand sniffed. It was a long way from Livia's miracles, and a long way from Livia's vegetable bag – which she pointedly ignored.

'Are you sure?'

Lenore placed a pot before herself and began chopping with one of Livia's knives.

'I have learned a lot in the forest. And before that, my mother taught me well.'

For the life of him, Bertrand did not know what to do. He was worried about Simon. Was the boy smitten by the same madness? Why had he deserted his sister? Was he preparing some beast of burden in the back of another inn yard somewhere? Was Lenore keeping his secret? Had she indeed remembered him? In the fevered state of her mind, it was impossible to tell to what extent she was capable of clear thinking, and how much she wandered. And it was well known that those who were distant in the mind were capable of seeing things that were too far off for ordinary mortals to notice.

Was she afraid of Livia coming back, or was it simply that she wanted to begin the great journey as soon as possible? One thing was for sure – Bertrand himself was afraid of what might happen if Livia returned and found all this going on. Or perhaps she too would be in some kind of disturbed state. Though – from what he knew of her – that seemed unlikely. If Arnaud was right, she would return armed with all the latest news, and that much more formidable.

Robert was completely bowled over by this domineering wraith, and apparently quite content to surrender the initiative to her.

Lenore began to stir the mixture.

'It is God's Will. And I know that the Blessed St. Margaret is telling me too. We shall all go together. This is God's way of protecting us on the journey. Simon will come too. And Father. We shall all go to Paradise together.'

Father! Bertrand had forgotten about Albert for a moment. Had he too succumbed to the madness, as Lenore seemed to think?

As if by magic, Albert appeared in a doorway.

'What are you doing with her?'

Eyes were screwed up in suspicion. The beefy arms hung slightly forward as if tensing themselves for trouble. The cheeks were beginning to flush.

'We found her,' said Bertrand. 'In the path of the crowd. If we had not pulled her away, she would have been killed.'

'It is true, sir,' said Robert.

Albert turned his glare on to Robert.

'And who are you?'

Robert blushed and stammered. He was still recovering from the admiration of his paragon; he could not adjust in an instant to this suspicion and hostility. Albert waved an arm.

'Well, you can get out.'

Lenore spoke from the hearth.

'No, Father. All is well. We are all going together.'

Albert frowned.

'Going? Where?'

'To Paradise, Father.'

Albert looked round the kitchen.

'Where is Livia?'

He addressed the question to Bertrand. In the tension of the moment, he forgot the 'Madame'.

Bertrand tried to explain. Albert listened, his face darkening with each apologetic sentence.

'And you put her up to all this, eh? Interfering busybody.'

'No, Father. It is not the will of Bertrand.'

Bertrand stared. How had she learned *his* name?

'It is the Will of God,' said Lenore. 'Do you not see? See how He has caused Madame Livia to go to the cathedral, so that she can not stop you going.'

Albert bridled.

'Livia can not stop me doing anything. Anything.'

Bertrand did not yet know whether Albert had been swayed by the madness or not, but it was clear that, whatever his state of mind – doubt or decision, depression or elation – he still felt the need for bluster. Lenore had no doubts.

'She can not stop any of us going, Father. In a little while, I shall have some soup ready for us to eat, and we can be on our way. God will provide for us thereafter. Just as he provided for the Blessed St. Margaret and all his other blessed saints.'

Albert swore, more in bafflement than in anything else. Things were moving too fast for him. He took it out on Robert.

'Leave us, leave us. And keep away from the flat of my hand.'

Robert opened his mouth for perhaps for an instant, then thought better of it, and skipped through the door. Albert waved another hand.

'And you too.'

Bertrand left with rather more dignity. As he cast about in his mind for the next best inn to go to, he thought that at least he had not been forced to drink Lenore's soup. Poor Albert. Lenore would talk him into it, if she was given the time, just as Livia always talked him into everything. But then, perhaps, he really wanted to go. Like all the others. Or, like Robert, he *thought* he wanted to go.

*   *   *   *   *   *

When Bertrand went back to collect his donkey, Albert took him back, despite what he had said. He then followed Bertrand to the chicken house and watched him. He had almost reached the gate before Albert could bring himself to speak.

'Stay, damn you.'

Poor Albert. He needed an ally. But why he needed an ally, he did not know. Not clearly.

He beckoned Bertrand into the barrel house, and filled a couple of mugs.

'Suppose I were to put her into a house – what would it cost? Would it be right?'

Bertrand thought of the tight-lipped abbesses of his acquaintance. They may have been paragons of virtue in their care of their sisters and novices, but they drove a hard bargain with the outside world.

He had no idea what it would cost Albert – in money.

But he had watched Albert for many days now. Thanks to Albert, he was beginning to understand, after all these years, his own father too. He knew exactly what it was going to cost Albert – in pain of the heart.

* * * * * *

The uneasy truce lasted only another day.

Livia had returned at last, more silent and purposeful than ever. But not before Bertrand had seen Vico stealing from her.

It was just as it had been for several days; they had forgotten his existence. Vico came through the door, and crept towards the corner where his mother kept her few private things – a sanctuary that not even Albert dared to invade, Bertrand had observed. Not only did he not notice Bertrand in the shadows; he did not even look in his direction. His furtive glances were directed to the main door and the back entrance.

He lifted the lid of the great oaken chest, and began rummaging. Clothes and mysterious parcels were turned out. At last he grunted with satisfaction, and tugged something out of a grubby linen bag.

Bertrand must have moved slightly, because Vico whirled round, his slit eyes glowing like coals, his huge cheekbones white with the force of his sudden shock at discovery.

* * * * * *

'Get out – now. And take your mangy donkey with you. Think yourself lucky I do not have it impounded to make up for it.'

Bertrand stared, his beer untouched.

'Make up for what?'

Albert was containing his temper, but as usual only just.

'First you fill my son's head with stupid ideas; then you put my daughter up to her madness. And still I keep you here. But now you have gone too far.'

Bertrand turned to Arnaud to seek a meaning. Arnaud shrugged. Albert flung an arm in Arnaud's direction.

'You may know the Bishop's Mayor and all, but a thief is a thief.'

Bertrand tried to argue.

'Albert, what are you speaking of? What have I done?'

As he said it, Bertrand knew that, whatever it was, or was not, Albert was more than furious; he was hurt too. He had favoured a travelling minstrel with his confidence, and that minstrel, he was apparently convinced, had somehow betrayed him.

'Please, Albert, tell me. Just tell me, and I shall go.'

Albert turned a flushed face towards Arnaud.

'The cheek of the man. I shall tell you, Arnaud. You will not punish him, because you lot stick together. But I tell you your friend is a thief. A thief from under the roof that shelters him.'

Arnaud looked at Bertrand, who spread his hands in bafflement.

'How do you know, Albert?' said Arnaud.

A noise behind them caused them all to turn. Vico had sidled in, his face creased into a mask of devilish pleasure.

Bertrand suddenly understood.

'You surely can not accept the word of – of that?'

Vico scowled.

Albert swore.

'What do you take me for – a fool? But I take the word of my wife. Why should she lie to me?'

Livia was now visible behind Vico. Nobody had seen her come in either.

Arnaud tapped Bertrand on the arm.

'Do you want me to make an official enquiry?'

Bertrand looked from Albert to Vico, to Livia, and back to Arnaud.

'No. It is not worth it.'

A family, it appeared, was still a family. Who knew what were the depths and currents of the waters that ran under this Clermont inn?

Bertrand sighed and stood up.

'Come, old friend. Show me another inn.'

'Good riddance,' said Albert, determined to have the last word.

Bertrand made a face at him behind his back, and furtively pocketed Livia's piece of bread beside his soup bowl.

He met Livia's eyes as he turned to go, and was quite sure she had seen him take it. She was wiping her hands on a piece of cloth. She said nothing.

* * * * * *

'Well, at least there is no Albert,' said Arnaud.

Bertrand half-nodded.

'No Livia either. And no stew.'

Arnaud laughed.

'No anybody very much. You will have the pick of the place. I have served myself with beer several times in the last few days.'

Arnaud answered the question Bertrand's eyebrows raised.

'I shall pay Nicholas when he returns.'

'If he returns.'

'He will. Not everyone will stay mad. He will grow some sense again. But it is no good leaving money here now.'

Bertrand nodded. People may have gone mad, but they still knew unguarded money when they saw it.

Arnaud swore.

'God's Face! Everybody is rushing. Nobody is sitting. Worse, nobody is thinking. I tell you, Bertrand... '

'You have been saying that since I arrived.'

'It is true. It is exactly as I have been saying. The madness is everywhere. Only this morning they found that the Bishop's palace has been robbed and looted in the night. You know those red curtains he bought? Gone. Cost a small fortune.'

'So he says. He is mean, remember?'

Arnaud was not impressed.

'You have met Hugh of Tournai. Can you see him letting his best stock go at a bargain price – to a churchman? For once I think my Lord Bishop is telling the truth. Half his trunks have been turned over too. I have seen them.'

'Who?'

Arnaud shrugged.

'Does it matter? We shall never find out. I have lost half my constables already. The Council bishops are leaving in droves – worried to death. Soldiers are pouring in from God knows where. Now Raymond is worried.' He laughed without humour. 'His Grace the Count of Toulouse is worried – says he can not feed them. Ha! *Now* he says it.'

'Why did he do it?' said Bertrand.

'Urban? God knows. He is regretting it now, I can tell you that.'

Bertrand pressed him.

'Arnaud, you have been in and around the Pope's household ever since he arrived. You must have some idea.'

Arnaud sipped his beer. He was just opening his mouth to explain when the door burst open. A man came in and slammed it behind him. It banged back open again.

Arnaud swore at him. The man turned and fixed the catch with a bad grace.

'Oh, all right, all right. Keep your whiskers on.'

He banged on a table for attention, looked round, and turned to Arnaud for an explanation. Bertrand recognised him, but said nothing. The man ignored him and continued to talk to Arnaud.

'I want a meal, and I am prepared to pay for it.' He gestured over his shoulder. 'More than those animals out there.'

Arnaud got up and drew him a drink. The man looked keenly at him.

'Who are you?'

'The Mayor. I always draw the drinks in taverns made empty when the city goes mad.'

The man took it without thanks and sat down beside them. When he had finished he sighed hugely. He turned back to Arnaud.

'Then you may be the one I should talk to.'

'Try me.'

' I have a complaint.'

Arnaud nodded. 'You are of Hugh of Tournai – yes?

Hugh tossed his head.

'Yes. Late of the Flanders cloth trade. As from this afternoon, victim, pauper, refugee, and crusader.' He pulled open his jerkin and pointed to a flash of red on the chest of his shirt.

'You do not seem very happy about it,' observed Arnaud.

Hugh snorted.

'Would you be?'

He flung an arm towards the door.

'Out there – out there – I have just lost everything. And where were you, I should like to know?'

Arnaud refused to take offence.

'I can not be everywhere. You have seen.'

Hugh nodded vigorously.

'Yes, I have seen. And, like everyone else, I did not think it could happen to me. But it did. And it will happen to you too. You see. I even took precautions. I thought I was safe. I thought I had been clever.'

'Tell me,' said Arnaud, who could already guess.

Hugh got up and drew himself a drink.

'Mind you, I should have seen it coming. With that devil-begotten hunchback.'

'Vico?' said Bertrand.

Hugh looked at him.

'If that is what they call him.'

'Vico?' said Arnaud. 'What has he to do with it?'

'Hugh has put his wagon in the yard of *The Hawk*,' explained Bertrand. 'For safety.'

'And I paid in advance.'

'What happened?'

'When we went out to check up on things, we found this evil little troll going through everything.'

'We?'

'I have a boy – Robert.'

'Ah – so you found him,' said Bertrand. 'Good.'

'Yes,' said Hugh, frowning at him. 'With his head full of some mad girl. Not your doing, I hope. 'Matter of fact, come to think of it, that may have been how it started.'

'Go on.'

'Well, Robert said he came upon this creature – '

' – Vico – '

' – Vico – said he was interfering with his mad girl. Robert went for him. More fight in him than I had thought – good for him. Anyway, I pulled them apart, and that was that. I complained to the owner, but he threw me out. Bad-tempered bastard. I asked for time to find somewhere else, and said I would be back for the wagon.'

Hugh took another swig of his beer. Even in adversity, he enjoyed telling a good story.

'Well, not long afterwards, as I say, we came back to the yard, and there he was – knee deep in my stock. We both went for him this time, and gave him a good hiding with his own pitchfork. He went off swearing blue murder, and that was that again.'

'Did he actually take anything?'

'No – we caught him in time. But he had one of the bales open. One of the best too.'

'Not the red, by any chance?' said Bertrand.

Hugh turned to him in some surprise.

'Yes, as a matter of fact, it was.'

'Why do you ask?' said Arnaud.

'Tell you in a minute. Go on, Hugh.'

Hugh took a deep breath.

'But what happened *then*! They came from nowhere, and they came from everywhere. One minute the yard was empty, the next it was a mob. They took everything, everything.'

'The cloth.'

'Everything. But – yes; it seemed to be the red they were after. They just tore up everything else looking for it. I always get Robert to double-bind it, you see. It was no use; they found it in the end. After all, that oaf Vico had found it.

141

'The wagon was smashed. Wheels in pieces. I saw Vico at work with an axe on them. They ransacked the mare's stall. She took fright and bolted. Lucky for her − they would have killed her. I shall never find her; someone will have taken her by now. My tools, our spare clothes, my reserves − all gone.'

'Your money?'

Hugh looked sidelong.

'What do you take me for? I may be unlucky, but I am not stupid.'

'What will you do now?' said Arnaud.

'More to the point, what will you do? You are the Mayor.'

Arnaud spread his hands.

'You have seen this place. You have seen the city. You have seen *The Hawk*. Half my constables have joined the mob. What can I do?'

Hugh nodded.

'That settles it then.'

'What do you mean?'

'We are off.'

'Where?'

'Jerusalem, of course. Where else?'

Bertrand and Arnaud stared.

'Both of you?'

'Why not? There is nothing here. I have no trade, no stock, no gear. And − it appears − no justice. Out there, when that mob descended, I would have committed murder to save my stuff, and was prepared to risk Hellfire for it. In the Holy Land I can do the same thing and be sure of going to Heaven. What choice do I have?'

'So you will go − just like that?'

Hugh smiled for the first time.

'No – not "just like that". All those crusaders – on their weary way to Jerusalem – remember I live on the road – I know about distances – those crusaders will need clothes, material. They will need the likes of me. I shall do business, take it from me.'

'Will you take Robert?'

'Of course. He thinks he is going to save the Holy City, but he will finish up selling good cloth in the end, just like me.'

He stood up, drank the last of the beer, and put the mug on the table.

'What about the girl?' said Bertrand.

'He will get over her. He only wants to save her. We all get over girls like that. I expect you did – once.'

He paused at the open threshold.

'Who knows? It could have been a sort of sign. *Deus le volt* – eh?'

He even shut the door carefully.

Arnaud turned back to Bertrand.

'Vico again, eh?'

Bertrand shook his head.

'Amazing.'

'What is?'

'Livia's grip on that household. She tells Albert that it was I who tried to rob her, not her own son. And he stands by her. Believes her. He was not blustering, Arnaud; he was genuinely hurt because he thought I had betrayed his trust. Livia had convinced him.'

'Now she has done it again.'

'Exactly. Vico gets his hands on Lenore. Robert goes for him. She tells Albert that it is simply a young lout throwing his weight about. And again Albert believes her.'

'Maybe it is because he has a chance of doing something that she approves of.'

'Maybe. Anyway, we have a clear motive for Vico raiding Hugh's wagon.'

'The cloth. I suppose he was going to sell it.'

'A bit subtle for Vico, I should say.'

Arnaud stared.

'Surely not for himself?'

'He did not ransack his mother's chest for large stocks to sell.'

'God. That creature on crusade. Makes you want to cross yourself at the thought.'

'Or Livia put him up to it. She would have had an eye to the sales potential. They are short of money, remember? She forgave her lovely Ludi for stealing from her, and put him up to stealing a lot more from somebody else.'

Arnaud looked more hopeful.

'More like it.'

'I will tell you something else,' said Bertrand. 'I would wager that the looting is Livia's work too.'

'How so?'

'It did not just happen, my friend.'

'There are gangs like that all over the place at the moment. I should know; I am the Mayor.'

'Arnaud, nobody in any gang said, "I know, lads, let's go and have a look in the stable yard of *The Hawk*, just in case there is some red cloth tied up in a draper's wagon there." '

'So Livia got them?'

'Can you see Vico thinking that one up? Or organising it? Vico would have simply set fire to the wagon when nobody was looking, leaned on his pitchfork, and admired the view.'

'You mean – ' Arnaud swallowed ' – Livia called up that crowd?'

'She did something. Why else would a mob suddenly burst into Albert's stable yard, at the very moment when Hugh's wagon was there? And Hugh would be outnumbered too; no chance of her precious Ludi getting another beating. Half an hour of pious prayer in the cathedral precincts, and she would have her mob. Child's play – to Livia.'

Arnaud blew out his cheeks.

'Some woman, eh?'

'Yes. At least when she calls up a mob, she knows exactly what to do with it. What is His Holiness going to do with the monster *he* has created?'

'God knows.'

'Well?'

Arnaud looked blank.

'Well, what?'

'Why did he do it?'

'Who?'

'The Pope. Why did he do it? You were going to tell me when Hugh came in.'

Arnaud gazed into the dregs of his beer.

'Politics – what else?'

Bertrand nodded.

'I guessed as much. Tell me.'

'You can work it out for yourself. The Emperor has stolen a march or two, and the Antipope is still causing trouble. Urban wants to regain the initiative. By proclaiming a holy war, he will kill several birds with one stone. It will take eyes away from the Emperor, and cut the claws of the Antipope.'

Bertrand made a noise of disgust with his lips.

'God preserve us – two popes.'

'Not the first time, and probably not the last. But you see, surely. By putting himself at the head of this holy war, Urban is doing something that the Antipope – what is his name? – Clement – Urban is doing something that is beyond Clement. If Clement were to proclaim a holy war as well, he would become a laughing-stock. And there is something else too.'

Bertrand raised his eyebrows. Arnaud made him wait until he had refilled the mugs.

'These Church councils. They will sit and they will debate, but not much will get done. And the reformers will get hot under the cassock about the delay. If Urban sends thousands off to the Holy Land on a war against the infidel, there is nothing more righteous than that. The reformers will have to stay silent; they dare not argue against it and say he is misdirecting his energy.

'It will also get rid of a lot of trouble round here,' he added.

'What do you mean?'

'You have seen. The soldiers. Armies and their looting parties; robber barons and their toughs; gangs of mercenaries, selling their swords to the highest bidder. With the famine and the pestilence and the flood and the drought, they have been hungrier than usual, and have terrorised more than usual. Vico turned a bunch of them away from the *Hawk*, remember? Now – at a stroke – Urban has turned them all away. And not only from Clermont; my guess is that a thousand mayors like me will thank their stars when the madness reaches them.'

'So you approve,' said Bertrand.

'No.'

'But you said – '

'I know what I said. But now I say this too. Urban will put a lot of soldiers on the march away from here, but he will put thousands more on the march towards us. They will come swarming in from every corner of Christendom – to make sure that the stories are true.'

'What stories?'

'That you really can go off on a killing spree, and be sure of going straight to Heaven – so long as you are killing the right people. They will want to see Raymond and Urban with their own eyes. And I have no doubt those noble princes will oblige.'

'You are surely exaggerating.'

'Think so? You have not heard the rumours I have heard.'

'What rumours?'

'I have heard already a strong word that Robert of Normandy is interested. I know Robert, and I know Norman knights, and I tell you I do not look forward to their arrival. And God knows who else will join the throng. There is a man called Godfrey, I believe – Godfrey of Bouillon – Flanders. If they are coming from as far as Flanders, who else can we expect?'

'Godfrey of Bouillon – I have heard of him,' said Bertrand. 'Well thought of, I believe.'

'And who will there be to keep the city going?' said Arnaud. 'These men will find a ghost city, and they will tear it to pieces. Especially if they find that the stories are not true.'

'Do you think Urban foresaw all this?' said Bertrand.

'No, I do not. I think he never looked further than gaining a lead over the Emperor and silencing the reformers. He was using the situation in the East as a tool in his campaign. Now he is appalled by what he has done.

I have watched him – up there in the Bishop's palace – when the reports have been coming in, and he has gone white. White, I tell you. But he is enough of a player in the game of politics to stay in the saddle. The ride is terrifying him, but he is staying in the saddle.'

Arnaud swung an arm round the empty interior of the inn.

'And now look at this. What has he done to all these poor devils?'

He spat.

'God's Will. *Deus le volt!* What has he done? Bewitched them. More like Devilry than the Will of God. How many of them are soldiers? What do they know of war? What do they know of their – what was it? – their "Eastern brethren"? People in the next *town* are foreigners. How many of them would know a Turk if they saw one? Not one of them has any idea where the Holy Land is.'

'It will not stop them going.'

Arnaud leaned across the table in his earnestness.

'Bertrand, you and I know what it is like. How many of them will get over the Alps, never mind to Palestine.'

It was Bertrand's turn to lean forward.

'These are not greedy soldiers; they are poor souls who worry where the next meal is coming from, and the next disaster. He has offered them freedom, Arnaud. Freedom from the drought and the pestilence and the floods. Freedom from fear and worry.'

'Freedom? Freedom to be robbed in the Apennines? To starve in Calabria? To drown in the Adriatic? To be enslaved in some Turkish market?'

'No, old friend. Freedom to save the home of Jesus Christ. Freedom to stand on the most sacred spot on the face of the earth. Freedom to go to Heaven. To die doing God's work, and to receive full remission of their sins, which lie heavy on a man's soul. It is the chance of a lifetime. To escape – to Heaven. Only fools like you and me would refuse such an offer.'

* * * * * *

Bertrand came in from feeding Tristan. He drew himself a mug of beer and flopped on to a bench.

He sipped moodily.

Why was he so tired? He had done nothing for days. Nothing but listen and watch. He had gleaned whatever it was that the city of Clermont had to tell him. He was ready to tell a story or two, but there was nobody to listen to him. Only Arnaud would talk, and Arnaud was in no mood for stories.

And yet, along with his tiredness, there was unease. Why did he stay? Everything he saw here saddened him. He could be of no further use to Arnaud.

True – there might, or there might not, be a mystery surrounding that second soldier. The one who had sworn revenge on Vico for driving him and his mates away, and for helping to get them arrested. Had he turned up again at *The Hawk*? Had Livia and Vico done something to him or with him? But he would get no help from Arnaud, beleaguered as he was by events. No interest either; why should his old friend give any attention to a death which may not even have happened, when the city was falling to pieces about his ears?

And yet – if he went – where was he to go next? If Clermont was anything to judge by, the whole of Burgundy, Provence, and the Auvergne would be in ferment. Perhaps the whole of Christendom. Stories were flooding in from all sides. There were tales of a mad preacher who was stirring trouble in a score of places; he was said to be goading armies of peasants to unimaginable orgies of havoc. Arnaud had mentioned soldiers coming down from as far afield as Normandy and Flanders. Bertrand's own wagging ears had caught references to Frisia, Brabant, Brittany, Lorraine, Swabia, Anjou, Champagne, Vermandois, and a host of others. God bless us – they were even coming from England. To get away from Rufus, or to get away from their weather?

It was known that the Pope planned to preach elsewhere, and who knew what further madness that would release? It was as Arnaud had said: His Holiness was terrified of the ride, but he was staying in the saddle.

Outside, in the street, against the constant drumming of the rain, hundreds of feet still beat the tattoo of desperate urgency that he had been hearing for days now. Voices were still raised.

The door banged open and shut again. Arnaud took off his cloak and shook it. He went, almost from force of habit now, to the first barrel and drew off a mug of beer.

He came and sat beside Bertrand, and drank thankfully.

'Thank God you are still here.'

'Not for much longer, my friend. I have it in mind to go tomorrow. I am waiting only for the rain to stop.'

'Well, you can forget your plans for tomorrow. I need you here now.'

'What has happened?'

'It never rains but it pours – to coin a phrase. Albert is dead.'

Bertrand was genuinely upset. 'Poor Albert.' How many times had he said that to himself. How many times had Albert's circumstances, and his reactions to them, made him think of his own father. Suddenly he felt real loss.

He crossed himself.

'God have mercy.'

'Amen to that. But I need you.'

Bertrand was puzzled.

'Why? I am not a priest.'

'I do not need a priest; I need a second brain. Albert was killed.'

*   *   *   *   *   *

Eight

'**I AM A** minstrel, Arnaud, not a seer.'

'You understand human nature, and you have the time.'

'I told you – I was just on the point of leaving.'

'Well, you can put it off for a few days, surely? You have done nothing but sit on your arse for a week or more.'

Bertrand did not take offence.

'I was…gathering material. You know that. You have seen me work before. Besides, I thought you told me to mind my own business.'

Arnaud nodded.

'Well, now I am telling you to get involved. Bertrand, do not play the innocent with me. You can not pretend that nothing has happened in the last week. The whole city is mad. In five minutes you can have a crowd; in ten you can have a hanging party.'

Bertrand nodded in agreement, albeit reluctantly.

'All because of some loudmouth at a street-corner.'

'It is worse than that. There is some crazy hermit preacher loose in the countryside, and who knows what he can set going? If he brings even more people into the city… Bertrand, I have a murder on my hands.'

'You had another one a few days ago. I told you all about it.'

'That was different.'

'Why?'

'It was outside the city, for one thing. It was before

152

the madness, for another. And anyway, he got what he deserved.'

'Hanging?'

'Bertrand, you and I have been in sieges with the Guiscard. How many traitors did he persuade to betray their brothers? How many of them lived to enjoy their blood money? Traitors are fools as well as vermin. For once I agree with Vico.'

'Vico?'

'Vico probably put them on to him. After all, he knew who the traitor was. He brought him to my house, remember?'

Bertrand shook his head. Vico had probably made money out of it too. Or Livia had. God and the angels – what a household!

'All of which is beside the point,' said Arnaud. 'I repeat, I have a murder on my hands, and nobody to back me up. The Pope is bewitched by the effects of his own sermon, and can think of nothing but the next one up country. The Bishop is terrified of the mob, especially after they tore down his curtains, and has locked himself in his own palace.'

He laughed without mirth.

'And he is supposed to be guarding crusaders' property while they are away.'

'What about your constables?'

'Ha! Half of them either have gone or are going. At any rate they are no use to me. You are the only sane man I can turn to.'

Bertrand looked unconvinced.

'Laying it on, my friend.'

Arnaud looked awkward.

'There is one other thing.'

'Well?'

Arnaud flushed slightly, as if the confession was a sign of weakness.

'I liked Albert. God gave him a rough share of life. For all his sins, I liked him.'

One old soldier to another. Bertrand smiled, and patted his friend on the wrist.

'So did I, Arnaud. But not for the same reason as you.'

Albert had brought Bertrand's father back to life again. It had somehow given Bertrand a second chance to understand him.

Suddenly Bertrand did not feel quite so tired. Nevertheless, he tried not to show it. He scratched a cheek.

'Tell me about it.'

'Albert is dead. On the floor. In *The Hawk*.'

'How?'

'No idea.'

'Who did it? Do we know?'

'Could be anyone.'

'That soldier – the one who came back.'

'The Limper. Yes – it could be. Not a scrap of evidence so far.'

'You are sure he is dead?'

Arnaud sniffed.

'Bertrand, you and I campaigned for fifteen years in Italy with the Hautevilles. We both know a dead body when we see one.'

'Who found him?'

'Vico.'

Bertrand tipped his head in disgust. Vico again!

'How long had be been dead?'

'Vico says he was not there a few hours before, because

he was loading logs before the fire, and nobody was there then.'

'Does Vico say anything else?'

'Yes. He says Simon did it.'

'Does he, by God? Did he see him?'

'No. But he says they were quarrelling shortly before.'

'How does he know that?'

'He saw them at it.'

'Did they see him?'

'No. You know Vico.'

Vico – the great listener at knotholes in the walls. How he got his stoop.

Arnaud shrugged.

Bertrand began to understand a little more. Arnaud was telling the truth about liking Albert, and feeling sorry for him. He was no doubt telling the truth too about the city, and the madness. But he was not telling the whole truth. Arnaud was concerned for Simon's safety. He had good reason to be, with Vico bawling Simon's name everywhere. Arnaud liked the boy, took an interest in him. Simon was about the age Arnaud's boys would have been, if they had lived. Just as Bertrand saw part of his father in Albert, so Arnaud saw part of his sons in Simon.

Bertrand smiled to himself, and at himself. Here they were – two old campaigners, who had survived by their wits, their luck, and their ability to avoid the coils of sentiment, and they were both allowing themselves to become tugged in by the sticky strands of memories and heavy hearts. Ah, well – so be it. To business.

Bertrand pursed his lips.

'Does Vico's lively memory stretch yet further?'

'Only that Simon was raising his fist – and his voice.'

'Do you believe him?'

'Vico practises most of the deadly sins with equal ease, and that includes lying. So he could be lying now. On the other hand, Albert is most certainly dead; I have seen him. And it must be somebody's fault. And we know that Simon and his father had arguments. We have seen those too.'

'So you do believe him?'

Arnaud shook his head doubtfully.

'For the life of me…Bertrand, we both know that truthful men tell lies sometimes. So liars must tell the truth sometimes. Stands to reason.'

'Is this one of the times?'

Arnaud spread his hands.

'How do I know? I have nothing to go on.'

'You have human nature.'

'That is your mystery, not mine. Why do you think I am asking you to help?'

'What do you think Vico's motive is?'

'What for – lying, or telling the truth?'

'Either. We agree he does not like Simon. Yes?'

'Yes.'

'So if Simon did kill his father, it would be in Vico's interests to say so – loudly.'

'To get his hands on the inn.'

'Precisely. Or so he hopes. My guess is it would have been over Albert's dead body. Well, now – alas! – it is. And convicted murderers can not inherit. With both Albert and Simon out of the way, the only creature standing in his way is a crazed waif who is slowly dying of neglect.'

'And if he is lying?'

'If I were Vico, I should say exactly the same thing – Simon killed his father – for exactly the same reasons.'

Arnaud started as a sudden thought struck him.

'Do you suppose Vico did it himself?'

'If he did, I should not have expected him to stay close. Thrust and parry in questioning is not in his line. What I mean is – '

' – he has not the brains. I agree.'

'The question still remains, would he even have the brains to cook up a story like this?'

'It is a very simple lie,' said Arnaud.

'A weak one too,' said Bertrand. 'I agree that Vico may have thought up the original lie, but he would not have thought up the details.'

'About the quarrels and the raised fists?'

'Yes. There we see another brain at work.'

'Livia.'

'Yes. And I would wager that if that first soldier – our friend with the scar – was tricked into a trap for his comrades to seize him, it was Livia who thought up the details of that too. It would have been beyond Vico. For the same reason Vico could not have killed Scarface himself; he would never have the imagination to string him up with that expensive red cloth; he would have been consumed with greed and stolen it.'

Arnaud's eyes were beginning to glaze.

'So what do we do now?'

'Easy. Get Simon to deny it. That will do for a start.'

'We can not find Simon. He has disappeared – gone – vanished.'

Bertrand clicked his tongue.

'Awkward.'

'Yes. Simon is a good boy. We both want him to be innocent.'

'If I know Simon, he almost certainly *is* innocent.'

'But *proving* him innocent, my friend. There lies the problem.'

Bertrand raised his eyebrows.

'We prove him innocent by proving someone else guilty. Who else could have done it?'

Arnaud shrugged again.

'Almost anybody. You have seen them.'

Bertrand had seen them – tipsy pedlars, drunken carters, boorish Gascons, deserters looking for trouble. To say nothing of half a city of madmen. Any one of them could have aimed a blow in temper – or even in self-defence – not intending to kill.

Arnaud was only voicing what his eyes had seen.

'Albert was not the most popular of men – with the world or with some of his family. You have seen him.'

Yes, I have seen him, thought Bertrand. He was not always raising his fist. He was not always swearing. Bertrand had seen the pain cross his face when yet another flurry of words with his son ended in high tempers and loud exits. He had talked to him in his barrel-house about his first wife – his dear Hedi – seen him close to tears. He had listened when Albert had discussed putting Lenore into a house.

Bertrand had been in *The Hawk* barely more than a week, and he had seen all that. Surely his own family, after years, saw some at least of it. No – Albert was not a bad man.

He looked at Arnaud.

'Are you suggesting one of his own family did it?'

'Vico is.'

'We shall come back to Vico. I take it you do not suspect Vico.'

'After what you have just said – no. Not yet anyway.'

'And we do not think Simon is capable. That leaves – '

'Lenore? Bah! Impossible. To attack a man twice her size? She is not that mad. And she loved him. In the old days, when Hedi was alive – '

'Yes, yes, I know. Albert told me.'

'What possible reason could she have?'

'That leaves only one.'

They sat in silence, both thinking of the woman who never gave warning of her approach, whose strong hands were always busy – kneading dough, chopping vegetables, humping great pots of stew, lugging her lumpy bag of vegetables through the dank morning streets, banging out bowls of slops in the alley. Who never hobnobbed with the customers (except one), who never joked, who never answered back when Albert lost his temper. Just twisted the cloth in her hands.

If their suspicions were right, she was capable of setting one mob to sack a wagon, another to string up a traitor. Bertrand felt a slight chill.

'What does she say?'

'Nothing. She does not even deny or support Vico's story. She says she saw nothing and heard nothing. And my guess is – as a matter of interest – she feels nothing. Not a flicker of grief – even of regret. When I was asking her the questions, I half expected her to pull a piece of bread out of her apron pocket and put it on the table in front of me.'

Bertrand thought.

'Is there anybody else?'

Arnaud's eyes popped.

'Surely not the Tub?'

'Livia often talked to him, and she talked to nobody else.'

159

'You mean, she put him up to it?'

'Well?'

'Oh, come, Bertrand. If you wanted a man done away with, would you ask a monk? There are hundreds of men better qualified for that sort of dirty work.'

Bertrand smiled.

'Ah – so you are learning something about human nature. Well done.'

Arnaud ignored the jibe.

'We have to face it that it could be one of hundreds. Even with the falling trade. They came for Livia's cooking, not for Albert's good temper. If it is a customer, Christ and Mary, Bertrand – we shall never find him in a thousand years.'

'You said the inn has been almost empty for the past few days, ever since – '

' – ever since Urban, I know. Still…'

'Well, that narrows the choice.'

'To no purpose. Few have been in there, I agree. But – of those – a third have already gone. A third are on the point of departure. A third are roaring round the city, deaf to all reason. I can not arrest anxious travellers and staring zealots by the score, with only a handful of constables, purely on suspicion. How could I question them all? Where would I keep them all? How would I feed them all, with half the city tradesmen gone?'

'What about our second soldier?'

'The Limper? Yes – that is a possibility, as we said at the start. But how to find him. And if we do, how to prove it – especially as Vico says it was somebody else. And Vico and he shared a plot to hang Scarface.'

Bertrand tried again.

'Was Albert robbed? Has anybody been throwing his

160

money around?'

Arnaud gaped.

'Bertrand, *everybody* has been throwing his money around – spending a lifetime's savings in order to kit himself out for the great journey. Selling everything to raise more money, only in order to spend it on – ' Arnaud slowed his speech and piled irony on top of each word ' – the – Great Quest – to the – Holy Land.'

He snorted.

'Paying a king's ransom to get shifty foxes to look after their property.'

'I thought the clergy were going to do that.'

'What I said – shifty foxes.'

Bertrand lifted his shoulders in a huge shrug.

'You are not making it very easy, are you?'

'If it were easy, I should not be asking you. Will you at least come and see?'

'If you can not find any evidence, how do you expect me to?'

'Second pair of eyes. Second pair of ears. And – '

Arnaud stopped himself.

'Well?'

Arnaud hesitated.

'If you must know, people take little notice of you. You have become part of the woodwork. You are no threat. They think I am.'

Bertrand smiled drily.

'What you mean is – they think I am a fat old minstrel, half buffoon and half sponger, and they might let down their defences in front of me.'

Arnaud grinned.

'Something like that. Shall we go?'

*　*　*　*　*　*

Outside the rain had stopped. Bertrand looked up at the sky.

'Brightening up.'

Arnaud growled.

'Getting colder. Frost tonight, my guess.'

Bertrand looked sidelong at his friend.

'You do look on the bright side, I must say.'

'Saves a lot of disappointment – in the long run.'

Round the corner came an extraordinary sight. There must have been twenty or thirty of them – and every one a grandmother. Indeed, one or two of them held small children by wriggling forearms.

Flashes of red showed below capes or on jutting shoulders. Clumsy bars of colour barely tacked on. If Bertrand had not known about the sermon, he would barely have recognised them as crosses. Rickety hand-carts were being bounced over the cobbles, the traces eating into the bunched flesh above knotty wrists.

Such crones would normally have stood aside from force of habit. Now they came on like a slender stream swollen with the flood of a sudden spring thaw, revelling in their unwonted vigour. Arnaud stopped and tried to reason with them.

It was a waste of time.

'We have taken our vow. To delay now would put us in danger of Hellfire.'

'But His Holiness did not mean you to start *now*.'

'Now or later, it may not matter to you. It matters to us. Some of us may be dead by the spring. How do we get to Heaven *then* – eh, young man?'

The grins of triumph shone through gleaming gums – triumph at an argument well won, triumph at the vindication of purpose, triumph at putting authority in its place.

Arnaud swore and went on his way.

'Save your temper, Arnaud,' said Bertrand. 'They are enjoying the luxury of being right as they see it.'

'Will they enjoy the luxury of lingering at death's door in the next few weeks, when it gets really cold?'

'Yes – if that door opens to Paradise. When you are as close to death as they are, my friend, you may think differently.'

'And what about the rest of them? This hermit, you know, is stirring up the countryside now. They are already leaving the towns. Before long, he will have them leaving the fields. The fields! You know what that means. God, Bertrand – even Urban said they should stay for next year's harvest.'

Bertrand shook his head.

'He said it too late, and he said it too quietly. They will never listen now. The spirit is loose.'

'You mean the Devil is.'

Bertrand put on an innocent expression.

'I thought the saying was *"Deus le volt"*, not *"Diabolus le volt"* .'

'Oh, *very* clever!'

'Ah! Here we are.'

They went in under the creaking sign of *The Hawk*.

* * * * * *

The burning stare met them. Livid eyes in a parched face. Bertrand was getting used to it. It seemed that every time they met he startled her.

After a moment's rigid silence, she returned to what she was doing.

Arnaud touched his elbow, and they went through to

the stable yard. Vico scowled over his sweeping, but said nothing.

'Where is your mother?' said Arnaud.

'In the great church.'

Livia and her prayers again.

'Will she be long?'

Vico shrugged.

It was Bertrand's turn to touch Arnaud's elbow. He jerked his head and led his friend to the barrel house, where he drew two mugs of beer. They sat together on a bench near the door, drank, and gazed out at the hardening sky.

'Albert liked it in here,' said Bertrand. 'His work. His beer. He felt at home. No unwanted company. No awkward decisions to take.'

'No Livia.'

Bertrand smiled sadly.

'Yes. Curious how even the most hostile families respect some niceties. This was Albert's private place, and not even Livia intruded. Vico did not come in here unless Albert told him in the course of a day's work.

'By the same token, Albert would not have dreamed of rummaging through Livia's big chest. That was why he was so shocked when Vico did.'

'Vico is an animal.'

'True. But Albert still credited him with some regard for family etiquette. Because *he* could not have done it, he did not believe that Vico could have done it. That was why he was so scandalised, and why he was so ready to believe Livia when she told him I had done it. You see? Albert was at heart a decent man.'

They sipped in silence for a while. Poor Albert! Bertrand thought it, and he knew Arnaud was thinking it too.

He gestured towards the main building.

'Do you think she has finished by this time?'

'I should say so.'

'Surprised?'

'Yes,' said Arnaud frankly. 'For a start, how did she know her father was dead? And for another, how is it that Livia is willing to allow her to lay out the body?'

Bertrand smiled.

'It is perhaps a good thing you asked me along.'

Arnaud frowned.

'Oh?'

'Do you not see, Arnaud? If you loved your sister, and she was your only sister, who would you tell first when you found that your father was dead?'

'How do you know he knows?'

'Because he is not here. He is not here for one of two reasons. Either he really did kill his father, in which case he would have bolted. Or he did not kill him, but found out, and went to tell his sister, as I said. If he did not know before, then he would be here, in which case he would know by now.'

Arnaud frowned.

'You are saying that Simon went and told her?'

'It makes sense.'

'How did he know where to find her? In those woods.'

'How else does she get fed – if only now and then? You said yourself that he tries to smuggle food out. Look at her, Arnaud – she is on her way to starvation. She must have been out there for months, on and off. He must know some of her secret places by this time. I would guess Albert knew too, but was too busy to go, or too frightened of a scene with Livia.'

'Suppose Simon really had killed his father. You know

165

'– a row – a chance blow.'

'If it was an accident, it would still make sense. He would still have to tell somebody. Even ask for advice. We have seen that Lenore still retains powers of decision. She sees things. He would have been desperate, ready to listen to anybody.'

Arnaud nodded.

'I suppose so. What if he did it on purpose?'

Bertrand acknowledged the point.

'That, I grant you, presents difficulties. But at least it would explain his absence. Fear of arrest. Either way.'

'What do you mean – either way?'

'Either he killed his father – by accident or by design – or he did not. Whatever happened, he dare not come back. Everyone knows he used to quarrel with Albert. Who would believe him now – especially with Vico shouting murder from the rooftops?'

'So – the sooner we find Simon the sooner we shall find out what happened.'

Arnaud clapped his hands to his knees and made to stand up. Bertrand stopped him.

'How do you know where to go?'

'Bertrand, if Simon knew where to find his sister, *she* knows where to find *him*. Even I can work that out.'

'I thought you wanted me to handle this?'

Arnaud hesitated.

'What will you do? Follow her?'

'Maybe. Maybe not. The trick is not to frighten her. You would scare her to death, with your big stick and your hobnail boots. She is canny enough to lead you a dance through miles of forest if she thinks you are trying to catch Simon.'

'Why will she not try to trick you?'

166

'Because she thinks I am a buffoon. Everybody does. You said so – remember?'

'All right, all right, clever clerk. You make a point. Now what?'

'I have a question for you. Why would Livia go to the cathedral at a time like this?'

'The usual reason, I should say.'

'Listening.'

'Yes.'

'Nothing else?'

Arnaud frowned.

'You do not mean praying, surely?'

Bertrand shook his head.

'No, old friend, I do not. If your son was crying murder, and blaming somebody, what would you be doing at the cathedral – praying to God for guidance, or – '

Arnaud clapped a palm on his thigh.

' – spreading the word. Of course.'

'That is why Lenore knows she has time to lay out her father. She knows that Livia goes to the cathedral, and she knows, generally speaking, why. Mad she may be, but not stupid.'

Arnaud nodded.

'I agree. She certainly must know Livia very well, for all that she is almost certainly afraid of her. And Livia knows *her* very well, for all that she resents her.'

Bertrand looked intently at him.

'Tell me, tell me – what do I not know?'

Arnaud smiled.

'You know all the theories, but you do not know all the facts.'

'Well?'

'The pestilence.'

'What about the pestilence?'

'Lenore caught it.'

Bertrand raised his eyebrows.

'And?'

'Livia nursed her through it.'

'What!'

'Oh, yes. The only case in the house – by some miracle. The place was boarded up. Livia had no choice. They were not allowed to leave. She could not turn Lenore out – I could not permit it. So, if the house was to survive – and its inmates, and its trade – Livia had to nurse her through it. So she did – just like that. Wiped her hands on her cloth and got on with it. No wonder she did some praying. And no wonder she has done some since. Real praying, I mean.'

'To make sure it does not return.'

'Something like that.'

'You would have thought it might make her like Lenore.'

'Yes, you would. Instead, she hated her. Hated her, I think, for bringing the whole house so near to ruin. She thinks Lenore provoked it by her wanderings and her consorting with the Devil knows what in the forest. Who can say that she is wrong?'

'So – when it was over – she turned her out.'

'In effect – yes.'

'I thought it was because Lenore does no work.'

'That is what she *says*. But my guess is that Livia has never forgiven her for their brush with Death. And – it is only a private idea of mine – Livia has never forgiven her for the fright of it. Livia enjoys being in control. She has always coped. Have you noticed, for instance, that she seems the only one in the house who is not affected in some way by the madness?'

'So far as we know.'

'Well – yes. The closest she came to losing control was during that time. You know how we all mess our leggings at the thought of the pestilence. Well, Livia was scared too – for a whole week she was scared out of her wits. I know; I was the one who had the place boarded up. But there was a greater call on her mind – the house. Survival. Property was all. And she survived. Now she can not forget that it was Lenore who made her so frightened.'

Bertrand shook his head.

'No wonder the poor creature looks so awful.'

'Enough to scar a healthy body and mind for good. She was half mad before it struck – losing her mother. Now she is three parts gone. Half dead with the physical strain while it raged, and a walking ghost with the near-starving since. How long can her heart stand up to it?'

'God, what a household.'

'Just wait till Livia gets back.'

'What will happen?'

'Livia will turn her out again. You see. Or Lenore will leave before she gets back. She has the instincts of a hunted fawn for the approach of danger.'

'Was it instinct that brought her here? Or Simon's news?'

'Hard to tell. She does have intuition. How did she know where to kneel in the square when Urban came past? Yet at the same time it was common sense, if you think about it. She may have heard about her father. Or she just knew. Who are we to say? She loves her father. She knows that Livia, whenever troubles come, always takes herself off to church to begin with. She thought she would have enough time to do what is necessary for Albert. And she is right.'

Arnaud stood up.

'Now put down your cup and come with me. By the time we get back inside, I should guess that Lenore has gone, and Livia has returned, and Albert has been given the necessary ministrations. And Livia will be furious. Would you care to bet against it?'

Bertrand followed him.

When they entered, Arnaud glanced round, turned to Bertrand and spoke with his eyebrows.

Livia took a deep breath when she saw them. If Bertrand had not just been listening to Arnaud, he would not have known what she had been thinking. Her control was remarkable. Perhaps the smallest whitening of the knuckles as she turned the cloth in her hands.

Arnaud stood beside the table where Albert had been laid out.

'I am sorry, Madame Livia, but we have to inspect the – um – '

Livia nodded.

Arnaud and Bertrand peered and prodded and lifted corners of clothing. They turned him over and looked again. While Bertrand carefully turned him back and replaced everything as Lenore had left it, Arnaud turned to Livia.

'You are aware, Madame, that your son Vico says there was an argument, followed by a struggle. That Albert's son Simon grappled with him, there may have been a blow, that Albert fell dead.'

Not a trace of animation showed. The kneading stopped.

'That is what I have heard.'

'Do you believe it?'

She shrugged. Arnaud repeated the question.

'Do you believe it?'

'Do you?'

'It is not my function, Madame, either to believe or disbelieve. Rather to prove or to disprove. And I have to tell you that, after our examination of your husband's body, the evidence for Vico's story is deficient. There is not a single mark there.'

*   *   *   *   *   *

Nine

THE HAND WENT into the apron pocket and came out with the familiar dark bread. Bertrand looked up, nodded his thanks, and began to spoon up his soup.

It was as if nothing at all had happened...

'Go back there,' said Arnaud. 'Tell her I shall pay for you.'

'She will never take the money,' said Bertrand.

'Oh yes she will. I know Livia. Besides, you will be part of a return to normality. It will give her an excuse to go shopping again, and drop by the cathedral.'

Bertrand smiled.

'The great bag.'

Arnaud nodded deeply.

'The great bag.'

Bertrand looked doubtful.

'She will never speak to me.'

'Has she spoken much up to now?'

'Why? To what purpose?'

'Just an idea.'

'What do you want me to do?'

'Wait. Watch.'

'What for?'

'A slip, a mistake, a hint – something. If there is any guilt, your mere presence may force it out. And remember, they underestimate you.'

'How can I refuse after such a compliment?' ...

Bertrand hunched himself over the table to protect his

soup from the wicked draughts. It was getting colder.

There had been no rustle or whisper from either of them for three days.

How was that staring phantom going to survive? How was Simon if it came to that? She at least was used to it. Who was looking after whom? Simon was hardly the robust, pragmatic survivor, and they had all seen how masterful Lenore could be − in *The Hawk* just after the sermon. Robert was hers, body and soul. If she had announced her intention of gaining an audience with the Pope, Robert would have gone with her.

Bertrand slurped another spoonful.

He could not in all conscience sit here for ever. He had as good as promised that he would make some effort to locate Simon by following Lenore. But then again, Arnaud had asked him to sit tight for a while. He could not do both.

Yet, despite Arnaud's hopes, he had seen absolutely nothing. Arnaud, worried out of his wits by the state of the city, had not found time to come and talk with him. Everything had slipped away. The event was dead; Albert was dead − and buried. Still no sign of emotion from Livia. Certainly no word, no comment, no glance, no tell-tale mannerism − nothing. She was exactly the same as when she nearly tipped the slops over him on that first evening. Customers, such as there were, ate and drank, paid, and left.

Vico came and went in his stooped, surly way. If anything he was busier than he was before; the stable boys had gone − whether to join the crusade or simply to stay at home until the madness was past, it was impossible to know. He laboured long hours to keep the stables clean, and relentlessly piled the muck on to the midden in the corner. Bertrand had to admit that he made a far better job of it than the boys had done. Vico, if nothing else, was a worker. A donkey, maybe, as Albert had said, but a willing donkey.

Bertrand took out his knife to deal with an apple – a rare treat for *The Hawk*. What on earth had he done to deserve this mark of Livia's favour? If it was indeed such. Perhaps she had saved it for Brother William, who had let her down. No sign of him for days. Further evidence of the suspension of normal life, both inside and outside the inn. Could it be that even some of the brothers had taken the Cross in addition to taking the cowl? Would they be allowed to?

They could plead necessity – both for them to go, and for the crusaders to have some form of spiritual comfort. There could not be many priests on the Great Quest to the Holy Land, if the complaints from Rome about the shortage of them generally were to be believed. Well, suitable ones anyway. That was one of the reasons why the Council had been summoned in the first place.

A resourceful brother could dress up his desire for liberty and adventure as a pious calling to provide solace and support to the Faithful in this most holy of enterprises, blessed – nay, instigated – by His Holiness himself.

Bertrand cut up the quarters. It was one of the advantages of having a faith that was rich in ritual, replete with elaborate traditions, groaning under the weight of prescriptive practice – you could find something in it somewhere to justify almost anything.

However – no Tub. No talk. No gossip. No clue. Nothing. Arnaud was away, thinking of a hundred other things, poor fellow. The trail, if indeed there had been any trail, had gone cold.

Bertrand ran his tongue round his front teeth.

Another odd thing – nobody talked about what would happen to the property. Who owned *The Hawk* now? Livia, as the widow? Simon, as the surviving son of Albert's body? What was the legal situation? Was it to be shared?

Bertrand found himself smiling. It was a very fanciful prospect – seeing that motley family working as harmonious business partners.

Livia of course was behaving as if her inheritance was natural and inevitable. It was in her interests to do so. Vico was certainly not going to challenge it. Simon was not there to challenge it. If he really had killed his father, he would be in no position to challenge it, whether he came back or not. Which in turn gave her a motive for putting the blame on her stepson; murderers could not inherit.

And the wretched Lenore was in no state to oppose anything, if indeed she was still alive in this cold.

The word 'will' had not been mentioned, either in *The Hawk*, or outside it. None of the family could read or write. If Albert had dictated a will, nobody had come forward with it. If any public body was holding it, it seemed that they too, like almost everything else, had been paralysed by the madness. Which meant that Livia would have things her own way. All she had to do was carry on as if nothing had happened.

Bertrand cleaned his knife and put it away. What was to stop him slipping away right now? He could see no way in which he could be of use. Why not leave and have done with it? Arnaud might grumble, but not for long. Simon would not know. Poor Lenore would probably not notice. Livia would not care. Vico would spit and heave his pitchfork…

And yet – and yet. He was fond of Simon. He wished

he could somehow put the boy on the right track, whatever the right track was. That was looking increasingly unlikely, with his continued absence adding daily to the scales of his apparent guilt. The priest had said, 'Woe to the murderer.' Bertrand had watched Livia's face intently, as she gazed at the altar across her powerful clasped hands. Her lips had shut into a flat line, her features into stone. Her silence had a hundred voices. If only in fairness, he would have wanted a single voice lifted in Simon's favour. But none came; the only one possible was hiding in a thicket in the woods, muffled inside a bony, bird-like body which might be crouched over the charred remains of another dead rat – if there was enough strength left against the cold.

He had begun to notice an ache in his heart over Lenore. Was it because of the injustice, or was it because of his sister? He had not spared her a thought for over thirty years. Suddenly the moon face and heavy-lidded eyes came before him with the clarity of a saint's vision. She was not like Lenore, of course; she was really short of her normal ration of wits. Lenore had all her wits; it was just that she exercised them in unusual directions.

She had known about the Pope's procession, and nobody had told her. She remembered where to find the ingredients for the soup. She was capable of ordering people about. Was it possible that, because of her voices from the saints, she was privy to secrets that were denied to those of God's creatures who prided themselves on their normality? Bertrand did not know. For the life of him, he did not know. But, if she did have access to any part of the Divine Mystery, it behoved the world to pay her some respect at least. Who knew what she might reveal? We could all do with a dose of God's Secrets. To write her off as an addled waif was unwise as well as unkind. Those burning eyes of hers scorched the soul, and no salve that he knew of would remove the marks.

He shook his head. This would never do. He was forgetting himself. Never become involved: that was the minstrel's rule. Remain an outsider. How else could he ply his trade of story-teller? His calling was to play on human feelings, not to be caught up in them. When the tender, hair-like strands of emotion began to reach out, that was the time to move on.

But he did not get up. Why? Why? He understood human motives, and he prided himself on being able to understand his own. So what was it?

He wiped his mouth, pushed away his bowl, and looked about him. The place was like the grave. Hardly surprising. Customers, since the funeral – those who were proof against the madness – had apparently made themselves content with fewer meals. Bertrand found himself missing the noise and bustle – the scuffing of feet, the grating of stools and benches on the ground, the swearing at spilt beer, the rumble of gossip and the bursts of laughter, all interspersed with Albert's voice raised above the din in livid, scowling annoyance.

Poor Albert. He was gone, and nobody was around to care. He had not been a bad man. A solid and reliable sergeant of archers. Certainly a loving husband and father. Probably quite a good innkeeper in the early days, when his precious Hedi was alive – to guide him, manage him, boost his confidence. He was maybe a sincere seeker of a second spouse, for the very best of reasons. Thereafter, he was out of his depth. Besieged by customers without the benefit of Hedi's patience and judgment; grieved by his daughter's fever of the mind; tormented by his son's lack of maturity and apparent disloyalty; disgusted by his stepson; and baffled by his new wife's lifeless manner – probably slightly afraid of her as well, as a man has a slight fear of anything he can not begin to understand. No wonder he got cross and waved his arms a lot. And yet he was prepared to contemplate his beloved son going away; he was prepared to put aside some of his precious savings to put his daughter into a house; he was prepared to face the awful prospect of being alone for their sake. No – he was not a bad man.

Bertrand sighed hugely. Was that why he was staying? Because a kind of natural justice told him that life, the world, *somebody* owed Albert something? No – he was not that much of a self-deceiver. He could not go on posing as an agent of Divine welfare.

He was not doing this for Albert, or God. Yet – thanks to Albert – and maybe God too, a little, because God took His time – he had come to see a side of his own father that he had never noticed before. The old man had not been able to bear the thought of his fat, lubberly, unsoldierly son going away. It had been as simple as that. Well, nearly.

True – he had bemoaned his son's lack of physical bravery and athletic prowess, his total deficiency in the military skills, his poor physique, his unmanly obsession with book learning. But he had loved him. He was concerned for him too. Out there in the world, it was dangerous. If his son had had half his proper share of muscles and wits, he would stand a chance of surviving, but to go off into the blue with none of the skills that a man needed in the world was madness. The old soldier would be left with the shame of an unmilitary son, and the prospect that, sooner or later, some willing traveller would bring him news of a tragic accident or sudden attack or chance mishap, and he would not even have a body to mourn over. That was why it had all hurt so much; Bertrand could see that now. It was so simple and clear. It now amazed him that he had not seen it years before.

He stood up and brushed the crumbs of Livia's dark bread off his chest. Now that he had worked out everything in his own mind, he found it easier to begin. Nothing like facing an unwelcome truth for clearing away a barrier to action. There were other barriers, just as there were other unwelcome truths that were slowly gathering at the back of his mind. Gathering in order to worry and challenge him on some future cold wakeful night. Time enough for those when the need was nigh.

He now knew that he was not embarking on this inquiry for Arnaud, or the city, or justice, or even for poor Albert. He was doing it for himself. It was a late opportunity for him to make some kind of amends to a sad, long-dead father.

* * * * * *

'An errand of mercy, Tristan. Maybe a hope for rescue. You will understand when we get there. At least it will make a change to sitting around all the time. I want no grumbling. The exercise will do you good.'

Bertrand tied the last of his bundles to his donkey's back, talking in the absent way that people do to babies and pets.

He was about to take the reins when he saw Vico slipping out of the stable yard into the street. Bertrand was hidden by Tristan's body and a huge pile of fresh droppings, so Vico did not notice him. The furtive stoop was much in evidence; he was almost creeping. One last glance over a rounded shoulder in the gateway, and he was gone.

179

Bertrand whispered in Tristan's ear.

'Now, where do you suppose he is going at this time of day, eh? Up to no good, if you ask me.'

He was now totally familiar with the routine at *The Hawk*; Vico never left the premises at this hour in the normal way of things.

'What do we do? Change plans? Or stick to our first idea?'

Bertrand answered his own questions by tying Tristan to a hook in a stable door. He put his fingers to his lips to Tristan, raised five fingers, and hurried after Vico.

Tristan would have counted up to more than five hundred before he returned. More like a thousand. He untied the reins, and leaned on the donkey's neck.

'Well, would you believe it, Tristan? What can he possibly have to tell my friend Arnaud? Oh, yes – knocking on the door. Saw him with these eyes. A confession, perhaps? Hardly. If it is, Arnaud will tell me soon enough. Meanwhile, I must find them – innocent or guilty – before it is too late. Look at that sky. Snow soon, or I am a cross-eyed Jew. Come, now. We have some talking to do.'

* * * * * *

Among the shanties and the lean-to's that festooned the city walls, the talk was of the weather. The madness had not gone away, but the weather was affecting it. Some were for staying until the worst of the frost had gone. Others disagreed.

'It will go soon enough. We usually have a mild spell before the end of December, and then we shall start. Only common sense.'

'Oh, no – get under way now. While the roads are firm under the frost. Get to the next city and under shelter before the new year. Stands to reason. Besides, the weather will turn in January. You see. It did last time.'

Bertrand shook his head. Men were allowing a lifetime of experience of the weather to wilt under the heat of desperate urgency and wishful thinking. Nobody really had the slightest idea. It was what they *wanted* to believe.

The very poorest and most miserable were staying put, because they had not the strength to do anything else. Hungry, cold, and listless, they were impervious even to madness.

Whatever the mood, few could spare more than a word or two for an inquisitive minstrel. They were preoccupied, one way or another, with the cold – to tolerate it, to use it, or to survive it.

'What, the ghost?'

'The one with the eyes?'

'Seen her, yes. Who could miss her?'

'She never spoke. Off her head, if you ask me.'

'No, I mind my own business.'

'Madwomen mean trouble – stay away from them is my advice.'

'How should I know? Better things to do.'

'Off in that direction, I think. No – not sure. Maybe past the monastery. Over there.'

'Oh, no – the forest. Like I said. Wandering. She would not know a road if she saw one.'

It took hours.

Then Bertrand had a piece of luck. He stumbled across young Robert, the cloth-merchant's boy. Almost literally; the boy was crouched against the wheel of a bare wagon, huddled against the wind. He was munching some bread and cheese.

'I thought you had gone days ago,' said Bertrand.

181

Robert looked a little sheepish.

'Hugh says we are not ready yet.'

Bertrand looked sceptical.

'So you are not going after all?'

'Oh yes we are. Both of us. In the spring. With Count Raymond. Hugh is up at the Bishop's palace now. See? We already have a new wagon.'

Bertrand suppressed a smile. Hugh of Tournai was infected by the madness like most others, but he had not completely lost his head. His merchant's instinct had reasserted itself, and he was now at the headquarters of authority, killing two birds with one stone — planning for the Great Adventure, and providing for their own well-being at the same time. Just as he had said he would. Negotiating a deal — the prerogative of the man of business since the dawn of time.

Bertrand ran his eye over the new wagon. Not really new, of course, and short of sound canvas cover, but in better condition than the previous one. Hugh had spent his money shrewdly. But then, with half the population of the city selling whatever they could to raise funds for the Great Journey, it would not have been difficult for a canny business-man like Hugh to locate a knock-down bargain.

'I wish I could help more,' said Robert. 'But honestly, it was only a glimpse, and she was too far away to hear me. If I had gone off to try and help, Hugh would have taken a whip to me. Besides, I should never have got near her.'

Further testimony to Lenore's skills.

'How did she seem to you?' said Bertrand.

'Terrible. She looked terrible. A bag of bones.'

'Where?'

'Over there. I heard the monastery bell, and I looked in that direction, and I saw her.'

'Which way was she going?'

'Towards the trees, it seemed. To her secret place, do you think?'

Bertrand felt a twinge of conscience. He had never told Robert of his earlier subterfuge. He would have to tell a priest one day. One day…

'Are you sure it was Lenore?'

'Oh, yes, I am sure. You do not forget a girl like her. The eyes have not changed.'

As Bertrand turned away, Robert leapt to his feet and seized his arm.

'When you find her, please come and tell me – tell me how she is.'

He looked over his shoulder.

'I dare not, you see. Hugh would kill me.'

*　*　*　*　*　*

Bertrand had followed trails in Italy with Arnaud – over baked earth, scrub, even outcrops of rock; picking up Lenore's track was not difficult, only tedious. And cold. And uncomfortable. He did not enjoy it.

He had the frost to thank for some assistance; the imprints of her bare feet had been hardened round the edges. He glanced up at the sky. If it had snowed since she had passed, he would never have found them.

As he approached the edge of the trees, he took care to step on fallen leaves, to avoid bare twigs. Every twenty paces or so, he stopped to listen. He stared at each bush, each thicket, each knot of bracken.

A bundle of dirty clothes under some brambles made him catch his breath. He had not expected to find her so quickly. Even so, he still approached quietly, half expecting the bundle to leap into life. A quick, burning stare, a flurry of dried leaves, and she would be gone.

But there was no movement. He bent to take a closer look, and received his second surprise. It was a full-grown man. He turned the body over.

He had been hanged. And mutilated – probably after death. The evidence tied round his neck. As if the disfigurements were not enough, he would have known from the clothes. A Jew.

So – the madness was now reaching out for more scapegoats. A payback for the drought and the famine and the flood and the pestilence. The infidels were too far away. The Devil was too powerful. Two or three old women had no doubt been despatched already, as they huddled over their pitiful fires of dried dung in tumbling hovels by reed-patches on the edge of a marsh. Arnaud had hinted at it as yet another of his headaches of office…

'A few may have done it, but half the city willed it. Who would give evidence against them? How can I interrogate and punish half a city?'

'A woman is dead. You might try.'

'With my constables? And my jail, built to hold a dozen overnight drunks? Not even Pontius Pilate tried to save Jesus, and he had the whole Roman army.'

Arnaud was right, of course. The whole Faith was built on the idea of a colossal scapegoat. Everyone understood scapegoats. Was it because humanity was following the precepts of the Church, or was the Church wisely building its grip on a simple truth – that men liked to blame anybody but themselves for their troubles?

With Albert, it was different; there was a definite cause there, somewhere. Albert was not jostled into death by a hundred blind and desperate hands…

Now this. A night raid on a moneylender's house; an

assault on his wife; the belabouring of his children, who escaped, crazed with fear and grief, into a street of slit eyes and teeth-baring oaths; the binding, the rope flung over a beam; the ransacking, no doubt in order to recoup the interest already paid. Then the body flung on to a cart under a pile of ordure or grain sacks. Or maybe a gag and a halter; a hustling of the victim through black alleys as if he were a frightened heifer to the slaughterhouse, with the certainty that nobody would pause to save a frightened Jew. Outside the city, far from women who sat up suddenly, wondering, in their beds, the screams and gurgles stifled by jeers and manic laughter. Finally, the dumping of the body off the trail in a forest thicket, where nobody in his right mind would go for weeks. By the time he was found, by children ranging far for kindling in late winter, the body would have rotted, and all signs of the manner of death would have gone. Convenient. And what a comfort to miserable, baffled minds which had thought they were doing God's work. The real guilt lay with those who had marked out one particular Jew rather than another, even if they did not put a hand on him.

Bertrand went on his way.

It took him another two hours. No smoke this time, as there had been on the day he had arrived at Clermont. But a larger clearing. Ashes though. No dead rat. But bones. Fresh ones, and, curiously, old ones too – of deer and oxen. Odd. He tied Tristan to a young beech. As before, he stood and looked about him. Total silence. But, as before, he could have sworn that he was not alone.

Then he noticed a sort of second, smaller clearing, leading off the first. He stooped to push away the brambles that hung across it. They were arranged almost artificially, as if someone had wanted to hide something.

185

As he leaned forward to get a better view, he understood. No wonder someone had wanted to hide it. There was a tell-tale mound, fresh, surmounted by a cross. Rather a better cross than the one he seen on his first day.

He knelt stiffly. Clumps of earth on top had begun to harden, but the whole mound was not yet solid. Then he remembered. He clambered to his feet again, and went to have a look at the bones. Of course – the antler. The end of one was dirty. He peered at the shoulder blade of an ox. Earth and scratches disfigured it. So that was what he had used. If it was indeed 'he'. Suppose it was – 'she'? Whoever it was, the death had come as a surprise. For some reason, no effort had been made to drag the body to habitation, or to go and tell anyone about the death. Nor had the discoverer of the body thought fit to go somewhere and obtain a proper tool.

Suppose the discoverer had not dragged the body because he – or she – was not strong enough? That would indicate…Then again, the cross was not like the first one he had found on his first day – lopsided and pathetic. So …

He had to know, sacrilege or no sacrilege.

He returned to the mound, knelt once more, and began scratching with the stained antler. Within minutes he had uncovered a torn hem, a pale, mudstained ankle, and a tiny bruised foot.

He found himself saying a prayer.

It was not easy; his sympathy for a dead soul fought a battle with anger at a supposedly merciful God who weighted the scales of life so unfairly against such an inoffensive creature – a creature who had none of the armour possessed by ordinary folk to act as a shield, however puny, against the thrusts and blows of a capricious Fate.

He bowed his head and did his best to concentrate on Lenore and not on theology. Perhaps Fate was not all that capricious after all. Her madness, according to Albert, had been only too normal in its cause – a loving daughter who had lost a saintly mother. Her treatment since had rather been the fault of Livia than the cruelty of God. Unless you blamed God entirely for the pestilence. A lot of folk did. Or was that simply making a scapegoat out of God Himself, according to human habit?

Her father and her brother had done their best to protect and sustain her; was it God's fault that their efforts had been found wanting? After all, God had given everyone Free Will – well, that was what the learned brothers had told him – though he had to admit that, as an unlettered young man grasping for learning, he had found the joint concepts of Divine Will and Free Will very hard to understand, much less reconcile. Put another way, had Lenore died entirely because of a malicious deity, or was her death the result simply of cruelty and neglect? Indeed, was it slightly her own fault? After all, if her mind had been that much stronger, it would not have cracked when they laid her mother to rest.

And yet – and yet – she had found a kind of peace that was all her own. She had lived in a different world, where perhaps the hardships and discomforts of daily life did not count for so much. She certainly had an insight that was denied to ordinary people. She had a passion and a certainty that others did not. She nearly carried everyone away just after the sermon. Robert was clay in her hands; Bertrand would go so far as to say that she had made him fall slightly in love with her.

And, in other ways, she was nobody's fool either. She had known where to find the wherewithal for some soup for her father, and had made it, and organised everyone else while she did it. She had been fully aware of Livia's usual movements, and had known exactly how much time she had to lay out her father's body. For a girl to do that at all, never mind calculate the time while she was doing it, it showed a strength of mind and familial devotion that was – well, unusual, to say the least.

Finally, she had the comfort of the Blessed Saint Margaret, which might put a smile on the faces of those around her, but that was all. She was the one who had the comfort, not they. Perhaps God was not so unkind or neglectful after all.

Bertrand finished his prayer and crossed himself. For a moment he continued to kneel. He leaned forward, scooped back the earth he had disturbed, and patted it into place almost fondly.

A body hit him from behind and sent him sprawling.

'Leave her!'

*　*　*　*　*　*

Ten

'**WHAT DO I** do, Bertrand? What do I do?'

Dried and drying tears blotched his face. His cheeks were hollow. He looked as if he had been dragged through a gorse grove by his feet. After his struggle with Bertrand, he seemed to have no strength left in his limbs. He had exhausted his entire resources.

Betrand pushed towards him one of the satchels that he had unloaded from Tristan.

'Eat! And drink! Go on, go on. You are not going to die, and you are not going to be hanged. Do as I say.'

Simon began, reluctantly at first, but with greater appetite as he progressed. Bertrand glanced up at the sky. There was more cold weather on the way, and, if he was any judge, snow too. Something would have to be done, and quickly…

The struggle had not lasted long – for which Bertrand was profoundly grateful. Simon had stopped as soon as he heard his name shouted. He turned his prey over so that he could see his face, and gasped in surprise.

'Bertrand! What are you doing here?'

Bertrand spat earth and leaves out of his mouth.

'I might have asked you the same question a minute ago. But now – '

He gestured towards the grave.

'When was it?'

'Yesterday morning. She just lay down and said she wanted to sleep. I could not do anything. I had no more food left. I could not leave her. I could not – '

Then had come the first tears…

Bertrand had to wait.

When the words began again, they were disjointed and without sequence.

'He used to take it from her, you know.'

'Who?'

'Vico. He used to steal the food I left out for her. The turd! The animal!'

'I caught him stealing from Livia too.'

'Not the first time.'

Simon did not even consider the remark important enough to warrant looking at him as he said it. Bertrand blinked.

'You mean, he made a habit of stealing from his own mother?'

'He stole from anybody – anything he wanted. I told you – an animal.'

'Does she know?'

'Oh, yes. But she will never admit it. Her precious Ludi can do no wrong.'

Bertrand nodded. Some of the pieces were beginning to edge towards a pattern.

Simon took a huge bite at a piece of dried pork, and stuffed a chunk of bread into his mouth as well.

'Whatever you say to her, whatever you prove – prove, mind you, against Vico – she just looks at you. You could kill her.'

He was talking with his mouth full, but at least he was becoming more animated. Some resistance was returning.

'I should not let anybody hear you make a remark like that,' warned Bertrand.

'Well, you could.'

Bertrand held up a soothing hand.

'Nevertheless... I am at the moment trying to establish that you are innocent of killing your father, and I do not want you going round declaring your wish to kill your stepmother.'

Simon flared, and immediately melted into tears again.

'I did not kill him.'

'Did you find him?'

'No. Vico did.'

'So Vico told you?'

'No. Lenore told me.'

Bertrand stared.

'How did she know?'

Simon shrugged his skimpy shoulders.

'How does she know anything?'

How indeed?

'So she just appeared?' said Bertrand.

'That is what she usually does. She was looking for me, actually.'

'To tell you.'

'To warn me.'

'To warn you?'

'To be ready.'

'Ready?'

'Ready for the lies.'

Bertrand held up a hand. This was going too fast for him.

'*She* came to tell *you*?'

'Yes.'

Bertrand allowed himself a wry smile. So much for his clever theorising with Arnaud. Simon sniffed.

'She feels responsible for me. Thinks I need looking after.'

Looking at him at that moment, Bertrand was not surprised. Simon wiped his nose.

'She thinks I am in danger.' He spoke of her as if she were still alive.

'From Vico?'

'From what Vico is saying.'

'She knows that too?' Bertrand found himself doing the same.

'Yes.'

It was pointless to try and get to the bottom of Lenore's clairvoyance, so Bertrand turned to the real trouble.

'Vico is saying you killed your father.'

'Yes, I know. He would.'

'Why?'

'You have seen Vico.'

Simon took a drink from a leather flask, and passed it back to its owner. Bertrand had a swig too.

'Vico says you quarrelled with your father.'

'Not true.'

'Are you sure?'

Simon hesitated.

'Not then.'

'But before.'

'Yes.'

'How long before?'

Simon began to lose his newly-won composure.

'How can I remember? We quarrelled lots of times.'

Bertrand decided on a sharp shock.

'Did you love your father?'

Simon's lip trembled again.

'He was a fool. He had all the authority, and he would not use it.'

'You mean he would not stand up to Livia.'

Simon lowered his head to hide his fresh tears.

'If you know, why do you ask?'

'On the day your father died, you say you did not quarrel. Is that right – on your oath?'

Simon lifted his wet eyes to Bertrand.

'On my eternal soul, I did not.'

'But you talked – yes?'

'Yes.'

'About your leaving home. About your wanting your share of the money. About your going on crusade.'

'No.'

'And he refused, and you lost your temper.'

'No!'

'And you lost control and perhaps pushed him and he fell.'

'No. No. No!'

The tears were now pouring down Simon's cheeks.

'It was not about me that we talked; it was about him.'

Bertrand was so taken aback that he lost the momentum of his questioning.

'Why?'

Simon wiped a hand across his face.

'I was not the one who wanted to go on crusade.'

Bertrand gaped.

'Albert?'

'He had been a soldier once. He said he would provide for me at the inn and leave it to me, and that he would give some money for Lenore to go into a house. I said the inn was run down and he would not be able to afford it. He said that he and Livia had made an agreement – '

' – a loan?'

'Yes. With a Jew.'

For two pins Bertrand could have told him which one,

but Simon was becoming distraught again.

'Bertrand, I do not want the inn. I do not want to be an innkeeper. I want to – '

'Yes, yes, yes.'

Days before, Bertrand had heard enough about all the wonderful things Simon wanted to do.

'Did you tell him this?'

'No. He had heard me say it many times before. I did not want to make him angry. Besides, I did not think he would ever pluck up enough courage to tell her what he was planning to do.'

Simon put down the remainder of the food in order to shake his fists.

'I tell you, Bertrand, we did not quarrel. In fact, it was the one time for months when a meeting between us did *not* end in a quarrel. It was in the barrel house.'

'The barrel house?'

'Yes. He is always in his best moods there. Funny. Perhaps because he is near his precious beer. He loved his beer, you know – the best of it, that is. Very proud of it.'

Simon began to snivel again. Bertrand called his mind back.

'What happened?'

'He called me in specially. He had tried to talk to me before, on the day of the sermon, and I was too stupid to listen. And now – '

Simon succumbed to fresh waves of weeping. Bertrand pursued him one inch further.

'So, when you left him, he was well.'

Simon rocked to and fro in his grief and anguish.

'Yes. Yes. I did not know till Lenore told me.'

A thought struck Bertrand.

'Did Vico accuse you straight away?'

'No.'

Simon stopped sobbing as the implication struck him.

'Then... by the saints! So it was... The devil! The fiend! He deserves to – '

Simon's moods were swinging wildly – a clear sign that his nerves were stretched on the rack.

'But he accused me later. He came to gloat. Over Lenore as well. Said we would both hang.' He shuddered. 'Those gums of his. I should like to smash them into his face.'

Bertrand tried to head him off before he let loose another storm of oaths and threats. First Livia, then Vico. At this rate he would be accounting for the whole family. He laid a hand on Simon's arm.

'Just because you are not guilty, it does not mean that he is. We have no proof.'

Simon whirled on him.

'He told me about finding Father dead. Father was alive when I left him. Vico hated him. Vico is a liar. Look how he gloated over Lenore and me. Is that not enough?'

'No, Simon, it is not. And you know it is not. What interests me is why Vico did not accuse you to your face straight away.'

'Because he was guilty – I said.'

'No. If he were guilty, why did he not accuse you at once, to hide his guilt? Why wait, and do it later?'

Simon fidgeted in his impatience.

'Let us go back and face him with it.'

'No. You would never get near him. Some wild crowd or other would tear you to pieces before Arnaud could save you. With Vico bawling his lies in the corner. You are forgetting the madness. And you are forgetting that you have a motive.'

Simon began to look tearful again.

'I told you – it was Father, not me, who – '

'I know. But who would believe it? After every customer in *The Hawk* has seen you and Albert quarrelling. When every customer knows what you keep saying you want to do. After the Pope's sermon. And you are forgetting something else.'

'What?'

Bertrand gestured towards Lenore's grave.

'How are you going to explain this? Two meetings with members of your family, and they are both found dead.'

Simon could not take any more. His face collapsed in agonised grimaces and more tears.

'I must be cursed. First my mother. Then my father. Now my sister. What terrible sin have I committed, Bertrand? Why am I punished like this? What do I do? What do I do?'

Bertrand packed the remains of the food into his satchel, and fitted the stopper back into the flask.

'You listen to me, and you do what I say.'

While Bertrand tied the satchel on to Tristan's back, Simon continued to rock to and fro, thoroughly immersed in his misery.

'My mother was a saint. A saint. And I was not a good son. I was lazy. I was selfish. That is how I repaid her. My father was not a bad man. He had provided for me. He loved me. I understand that now, Bertrand. And how did I repay him? By throwing his generosity in his face. And my sister. I did not listen to her. She knew things, you know, Bertrand. She was wise. She thought I was so innocent. Yes. *She* thought *I* was innocent.'

'That hardly surprises me,' said Bertrand. 'Now – get up, and pull yourself together. Never mind what an awful human creature you are. Whatever you are, you are not a murderer, and you must help me to do something about proving it.'

Simon did his best to respond. Bertrand got him to leave both clearings as natural as possible, so as not to raise the suspicions of any observer, casual or otherwise. Simon resisted, but Bertrand forced him to remove the cross. They took great care to seal the inner clearing with more bracken and bramble.

Bertrand took Tristan's reins.

'Now. I want you to go to that house near here. I came past it when I was looking for Lenore's trail. What is it called?'

'St. Fulbert's. It has only about twenty brothers.'

'Good. All the more room for you. Go to St. Fulbert's. Ask for shelter. Here. Here is some money. Tell the Guest Master I shall bring some more in a few days.'

Simon was struck by a thought.

'Suppose they already know?'

'Why should they?'

'Monks find out everything. God knows how.'

'Yes, I expect He does.'

'Suppose the Tub knows.'

'He has not been near *The Hawk* for days.'

Simon insisted.

'But suppose he does. Suppose he has told the abbot.'

Bertrand sighed.

'Well then, you ask for sanctuary. They will have to give it. Stay there. Stop worrying. And wait for me.'

'What will you do?'

'I shall have a word with my friend Arnaud. He may have some news.'

After Vico has knocked on his door, he should have.

Simon paused on the edge of the forest before they parted.

'Why are you doing all this? You hardly know me.'

'Did I say I was doing it for you?'

'But you owe nothing to my father.'

No. But I owe something to my own.

* * * * * *

'Witchcraft?'

'That is what Vico says.'

'Do you believe him?'

'Of course not. But what I think counts for nothing. It is what the *city* will believe that worries me.'

'Arnaud, Lenore has been dead at least two days. She can not cast spells from the grave.'

'She was alive – well, half alive – when Albert died. That is enough for a crazy mob.'

'You had only to look at her.'

'Yes, *you* did. Bertrand, you are a sensible, mature man. You are not a member of a frightened, bewildered crowd – a crowd that has been driven to frenzy by a pope's preaching. Kill the infidels, the Devil-worshippers, the sons of Satan.'

'And the Jews.'

'Yes. That poor devil you found will not be the last. Remember – four disasters in two years. They have to blame somebody. I have buried two lonely old women already. And now the Pope has given them a tailor-made scapegoat, and moreover given them a reason – a respectable one. Go and kill the wicked Moslems.'

'He did not mention Jews.'

'Makes no difference. They were the ones who crucified Him. They will do for a start. Right now, they will fall upon anybody who remotely fits the bill for a sinner.'

'Like Simon.'

'Like Simon. God help him if they find him.'

Arnaud clapped his hands for a girl to bring them something to eat.

'You see, Bertrand, if it were a private house, it might not have been so bad. But this is an inn we are talking about. Everyone knows it. Everyone knows that the daughter of the owner was off her head, a half-starved ghost who looted her stepbrother's rat-traps, who spent days at a time in the woods, lighting lonely fires and offering mysterious sacrifices. What you saw when you arrived was nothing new. Everyone knows that Simon regularly swore at his father. Imagine what a vivid imagination and a loud voice will do with evidence like that. We can have spells and death curses in no time. And Simon as the executioner. Especially with Vico spouting filth wherever he goes.'

'Can you not lock him up?'

'Why? He is the witness, not the suspect. And I can not lock up his mouth; he can shout through bars. Besides, half my constables are gone. I met two more of them an hour ago, draped in red sashes, and drunk with excitement, if not beer as well.'

Bertrand sat back, temporarily baffled. Arnaud pursued him.

'And if word gets out that I was party to your sheltering the chief suspect, I should not care to put money on keeping my own job.'

Bertrand sat up again.

'All right, all right. But does it not strike you as odd that Vico does things so – well, so late? According to Simon, he did not accuse him of the murder straight away. He

199

waited. Only accused him later on.'

Arnaud nodded.

'Yes, I know. And why does he wait till now to mention witchcraft?'

'Exactly. There is no word about it until you point out that there is no mark on the body. So the story about a struggle and a blow will not stand up. The next day, he comes to you – right through the city – with this story about the Devil and his spells. Arnaud, it stinks.'

'Of course it does. But how can we *prove* it stinks? Even if we get Vico to admit that he quarrelled with Albert – '

'He did. I saw them the other day. Albert was furious.'

Arnaud shook his head.

'Albert was always furious. Everybody saw that. But we have no evidence of a quarrel between Vico and Albert.'

'You have mine.'

Arnaud looked embarrassed.

'Yes. Well… '

Bertrand tilted his head in mild disgust.

'Yes. I see. I am only a minstrel.'

'You are an outsider, Bertrand. Outsiders do not count – you know that. Besides, you can not prove it. No, my friend, we have no evidence – not relevant evidence. Even if Vico did quarrel with him, and even if he admits it – '

' – which he will not.'

' – which he will not – that is still no proof that he struck Albert, or even that the blow led to death. No mark on the body, remember? If it was evidence in favour of Simon, it is evidence in favour of Vico.'

The girl brought some food. Arnaud gestured towards it.

'Tuck in. I have already eaten. I daresay you have an appetite on you, after all those hours out there.'

After a while, Bertrand lifted his head and licked loose crumbs from round his lips.

'It all comes back to Livia.'

'Livia?'

'Look at it, Arnaud. We both know that Vico could not frame a coherent piece of sensible evidence if you paid him a ransom to do it.'

'They are not very big lies, Bertrand. A quarrel, a blow, a fall. And now witchery. It is not exactly advanced theology. *The Hawk's* cat could have thought of that.'

'It is not the words; it is the timing. Do you not see? Do not accuse him of the murder straight away; do it when he and Lenore have gone off. Their absence would point to his guilt.'

'Mmmm.'

'And then, when the first story will not stand up – '

' – no marks on the body.'

' – no marks on the body. Then, come back with a better one. When they find the first story can be disproved, come back with one that can not.'

Arnaud frowned.

' "They"?'

'I said – it comes back to Livia. Vico would never have worked that out.'

Arnaud looked half-convinced.

'Maybe.'

'Maybe! Arnaud, use your sense. Look at what has happened since I arrived. First – that dead soldier, strung up with his own loot, so far as we can make out. Who brought him to see you? Who was the only one who knew which of them had done the betraying? Do you think Vico would have thought out such a devious way of doing away with him? Telling his comrades and arranging an ambush

201

and an abduction? Vico would have simply hacked at him with his axe, or got out his pitchfork.'

'Well, yes – '

'Then what about Hugh and his wagon? Could Vico have conjured up a mob just like that? No – he would have simply put a match to it. But Livia, after ten minutes down at the cathedral, whispering behind her bony hands, could have arranged that as easy as cut your finger.'

Arnaud opened his mouth, but Bertrand swept on.

'And, if it comes to that, what about our dead Jew? Have you checked yet to find out whether he had lent money to Albert and Livia? If he had, how easy for our pious Madame Livia to pay another of her quiet visits to the back pews and let out a few hints, and lo and behold! Yet another murderer of Our Lord has received his just punishment. It is too easy, Arnaud.'

Arnaud nodded.

'And now you are saying that it is Livia who has come up with the witchcraft story.'

'Yes. Vico does not think fast enough. Vico would not have the sense to *use* the madness. It is not that Livia thought up the spells and incantations idea – which is clever enough. It is that she had the wit to realise that the city was mad enough not only to believe anything, but to *act* on anything. It is brilliant.'

Arnaud shook his head.

'Proof, Bertrand. Where is your proof?'

'It runs through the whole business. It is the only thing which holds it together. Find me some other explanation that fits it better.'

Arnaud wagged his head again.

'No, my friend. You build a great house with your words, but it is built upon sand. It starts from a weak position. It suggests that the two of them planned it all in advance. Now, you tell me, Bertrand, how do you plan to kill a powerful man like Albert with no weapon? If you were Livia, how would you prepare Vico to have a row with him, coach him in what to say, time the blow so that nobody was there, and knock him down hard enough to kill him – and leave no mark on the body? He would have botched it. Or Albert would have half killed *him*. Livia may be clever, but she is not that clever.'

Bertrand smiled.

'One up to you, you stubborn old fox. But I think it is time we talked to somebody.'

'Livia? Never. She has hardly said a word since this started. Mouth slammed shut like a Spanish city gate against the Moors. You will never get anything out of her.'

'I meant Vico.'

'You will get nothing out of him either. Nothing truthful, anyway.'

'Not if he thinks he is being trapped, no. But, if he thinks he is trapping somebody else…'

Arnaud narrowed his eyes.

'What are you up to?'

Bertrand put his finger beside his nose.

'Trade secret. You asked me to help. Well, let me do it – my way.'

Arnaud shrugged.

'Please yourself. Do you want me to keep Livia away from him while you are at it?'

'No. That would alarm them both. They think I am harmless, remember? If they see us working together, I shall get nothing out of either of them. Leave it to me. I shall use Livia's trick – timing. Vital.'

Arnaud rose and began collecting the empty bowls.

'Wait till you see Livia. All in black now, she is. New too, if I am not mistaken.'

Bertrand smiled.

'What did I tell you? She did that with the money she got back from the Jew's house.'

Arnaud ignored the remark.

'She has even put on a black apron. Black braid in her hair. Just like those awful harpies we used to see in Apulia. I tell you, Bertrand, she is enjoying it.'

'We do not know if she killed him.'

Arnaud piled the bowls in the hands of the serving-girl.

'Either way, I swear she is still enjoying it. Does it occur to you that Livia appears to be the only one in the whole business who is not touched by the madness?'

'So you said. And yet she might have heard Urban – if Lenore is to be believed. She could have had the time.'

'Perhaps. So she too could still catch it. We thought Albert was impervious, and he proved not to be.' Arnaud laughed without mirth. 'Who will be touched by it next? Livia? Me? You?'

'Very funny.'

Bertrand found his neck flushing, and he did not know why. He stood up to try and mask his embarrassment, and tried to change the subject.

'I found young Robert.'

Arnaud looked surprised.

'I did not know you were looking for him.'

'I told him about Lenore.'

The surprise left Arnaud's face.

'Ah. What did he say?'

'Nothing. He wept. His face was like a sheet. I thought he was going to be sick.'

Arnaud grunted.

'What – again?'

Bertrand stopped on his way towards the door.

'Have you forgotten what it is like to be that young?'

Arnaud helped him on with his coat.

'I have not forgotten what it is like to mourn, if that is what you mean.'

Bertrand smiled softly.

'No – I am sorry. I was forgetting for a moment.'

Arnaud smiled too.

'So was I. So we are both getting old, my friend.'

They shook hands. Bertrand turned away, then turned back.

'By the way, have you considered trying to find out if anybody besides Albert drank Lenore's soup?'

*   *   *   *   *   *

Eleven

'**WOULD YOU LIKE** some more, Brother William?'

William the Tub smiled broadly and shook his chins in agreement.

'You make the finest soup south of the Loire, Madame. How could I refuse?'

He beamed as the tureen was tilted. Dark bread was lifted from the great pocket.

Bertrand nudged Arnaud in the shadows of an alcove.

'So he is back.'

Bertrand nodded.

'First time in days. All is back to normal at St. Fulbert's.'

'How do you know?'

'I have just been talking to him. Helped him to tie up his mule.'

'Why?'

'You wanted me to get something out of Vico.'

'So?'

'So – I keep Livia in the dark as much as possible. We do not want her to find out where Simon is, do we?'

Arnaud lifted his head in understanding.

'Ah. So you tell the Tub to keep his mouth shut.'

Bertrand gestured towards the happy brother, midway through his third bowl.

'Except when he is eating.'

'How did you manage it?'

'If you had spent time in a house, Arnaud, you would know.'

'I have. In Apulia. When I was wounded.'

'Then you have forgotten. Monks lead regular, predictable lives. So they love an intrigue. Breaks the monotony. Brother William was a very willing partner in our little scheme, I can tell you.'

Arnaud looked mildly surprised.

'But he loves coming here. I thought – '

'Just because he loves Livia's soup, it does not mean that he loves Livia. Or Vico. It means that he loves his stomach. A glutton is not necessarily a buffoon. Brother William is quite aware of what we are engaged in.'

'You told him?'

'As much as he needs to know. He already knows about Simon. He has probably met him there. I saw no point in trying to fashion an elaborate lie. Besides, he likes Simon; thinks he is a good lad – underneath.'

'So he will help us?'

'He will not allow Livia to pump him, if that is what you mean. I think he resents Livia's confidence that she can.'

'She has been trying hard enough for months.'

'That was for a loan.'

'She may still have need of it. Even if your Jew is her Jew, if you see what I mean.'

'Possible.'

They watched while Livia returned with another pot of beer. Bertrand chuckled quietly to himself.

'What is the joke?' said Arnaud.

Bertrand nodded in the direction of the two at the table.

'I suppose Livia could not have added to her inducements the prospect of a rather more – um – intimate favour, could she?'

Arnaud looked at the fat, sweaty jowls of the Tub, with spots of fat on his chins, and at the pale, drawn features of his rangy hostess, with her hair drawn back tight on the nape of her neck.

'Inconceivable.'

They looked at each other, and dissolved into stifled giggles like two serving girls.

'Do not worry, Arnaud. Livia may want to find out about Simon, and she may still want another loan, but William will not accommodate her.'

He waved a hand to dismiss the matter.

'What have you found out? Did Albert leave a will?'

'No.'

'How can you be certain?'

'I checked in the city chest, and in the diocesan court records. I do know my job, Bertrand.'

'You mean you got a clerk to do it.'

'Naturally. As you would have done. Luckily, there was still one at his post.'

They looked steadily at each other for a moment. Then they both laughed.

'A piece to you, my friend,' said Bertrand, 'if only a pawn. But you see, I am sure – Livia would have nothing to challenge. If Albert had given the inn to Simon by will, she would have had to fight. But if he has not…well, it would make it easier, at the very least.'

'You are robbing Livia of a motive – you do realise that?'

'Unfortunately, yes. Livia's only motive for killing Albert was the certain knowledge that he had left a will, and that he had left *The Hawk* to her. We know now that that was not the case.'

'She could have *thought* so, I suppose. Albert could have led her on.'

'Yes – he could. There is another possibility.'

'Well?'

'That she knew, or expected, that Albert would leave the inn to Simon, and her aim then was to prove him guilty, and so disinherit him.'

'No. We agreed before that she and Vico could not possibly have planned to kill Albert; he was too strong. And Vico would never have remembered his part.'

Bertrand stared across at William, and sighed.

'So we are stuck. Think for a moment, Arnaud. Where else could Albert have left a will? Where else could he have got one drawn up?'

Arnaud shrugged.

Bertrand clapped a hand on his thigh.

'Of course.'

He looked quickly over his shoulder to see whether William the Tub had heard. The brother was now midway through a block of cheese. Even so, Bertrand lowered his voice to try and mask his excitement.

'St. Fulbert's! The Tub comes in to collect rents from the property they lease out in the city. It is a regular – '

Arnaud punched him gently in the chest.

'Of course! St. Fulbert's.'

He was about to clap his hands when he stopped suddenly.

'Hold on a minute. Albert loathed monks. He fought tooth and nail against Simon going into a house.'

'True,' said Bertrand. 'Letting your son go into a house for life was one thing; using the legal services of a local prior was quite another. Albert was not a fool. He knew how tight and safe they were. And plenty of people to write out a will for him. Witnessed by – he could even have persuaded the abbot himself – how respectable could you get? For all I know, his much-vaunted hatred of the brothers could have been an elaborate plan to put Livia off the scent.'

'And Simon? Was that genuine too? Did he really want to go into a house?'

'Quite probably. Or he thinks he does. Albert understood him much better than Simon gave his father credit for. As my father probably did me. He felt sure that the boy was not cut out for the habit. Or at any rate not yet.'

Arnaud nodded.

'Yes. But do you think Livia found out – about the will?'

'Possible. She watched every move here. She knew everything that was going on. And we know about her lengthy "prayers" in the cathedral. So she knew most of what was going on in the city too.'

Arnaud dipped his head in agreement.

'Very well. But do you suppose she had also found out about Albert's plan to go on Crusade?'

'Equally possible. Albert was a braggart and a loudmouth. He might not have let the cat out of the bag, but he would drop large hints about having a cat inside it. It would have been his way of getting one over her. Livia was no fool either. This is one of the troubles of the situation. Everybody involved – Albert, Livia, Simon, Lenore – was intelligent in his or her own way. The only dunce is Vico. And Livia tells him what to do.'

'And he does it?'

'I think so. We can find no other explanation for what has happened.'

'So – you are saying that Livia got Vico to kill Albert, to stop him going on crusade?'

'No. Either way she would have lost him – either to the coffin or to the Crusade. No. That was not in her scheme

210

of things. She was willing enough to take a husband to provide for herself and Vico; she would not have changed those motives.'

'So Livia did not want Albert dead?'

'No. As I read her, she wants a roof for herself and Vico. If she can have it with Albert, so be it. If she can have it without Albert, so be it too. Probably so much the better. But I do not think she would have arranged it. Far too chancy. But now that he *is* dead, the will becomes vital. If it is in her favour, it will be easy. If it goes against her − or if there is no will at all − she must disinherit Simon.'

Arnaud leaned forward and jerked a thumb over his shoulder to where the appreciative Brother William was wiping the blade of his knife.

'Is it not possible that she is still trying to find out? Prime him with food, and out will tumble the required news.'

Bertrand shook his head.

'No danger. William will stand firm. If he will not tell her about Simon or about a loan, he will not give way about a will either. Besides, he probably does not know. Wills are not common property. Another thing that Albert knew about legal services was that they are confidential. He could rely on the Prior.'

Arnaud glanced at the gratified cleric, then turned back with a smile.

'In that case, old friend, you have just given yourself another errand.'

Bertrand nodded glumly, and stood up.

'I know − St. Fulbert's. But it will give me a chance to see how our young sufferer is faring.'

'God be with you.'

Bertrand tied the strings of his jerkin.

'Make sure you are still paying my bills when I am gone. And here is an errand for you.'

'Oh?'

'Go back to the day Albert died. Simon swears that they did not quarrel – remember?'

'Do you believe him?'

'Yes, I do. Because he admitted freely that they did quarrel at other times – often. But he is adamant that they did not quarrel on that day. They talked, as I told you. But they did not quarrel.'

'So?'

'So – suppose Albert still had a quarrel – with somebody else.'

Arnaud let his mouth fall open.

'With whom?'

'Whom do you think?'

Arnaud looked blank.

'Livia?'

Bertrand tossed his head in impatience.

'Oh, Arnaud! Livia never answered back. She suffered. Sufferers do not quarrel.'

Arnaud's face cleared.

'Vico then?'

'Exactly. Now ask yourself – why would Vico start a violent argument? Or even get drawn into one – because most conversations with Albert finished that way. They loathed each other. Why bother having a piddling little row?'

Arnaud screwed up his eyes in suspicion.

'Bertrand, you are playing games with me again. Like Lenore and the stew.'

Bertrand bent low and winked.

'I shall tell you the solution to both questions when I

get back. And God be with you too.'

* * * * * *

Bertrand took his time preparing Tristan for the journey.

'We have a queen among conspirators, Tristan. Everything falls her way, and she appears to have done nothing to bring it about. And when things begin to fall the other way, she disappears towards the cathedral, and – lo and behold – things start to go *her* way again. Genius, my friend. Genius.'

He tightened the saddle straps, grunting with the effort.

'We can prove nothing – nothing. We could tell her – face to face – what we think – what we know! – and it would avail us nothing. She would just stare at us, turn that cloth in her hands, and go and empty out some slops in the alley.'

Tristan shook his head. Bertrand patted his neck.

'And we are still no nearer deciding how Albert died. I suppose – '

He broke off as a sudden thought struck him.

Surely not – it was a mortal sin. Albert was as good a son of the Church as most. That is, he was as good as life allowed him to be. How could he hope to meet his beloved Hedi if he did that? True – he was deeply depressed, and men could do odd things when they were depressed, as he himself knew only too well. Travel and campaigning was not all victories and spoils and jolly songs round the old camp fire. Look at Arnaud when he lost his two boys. Bertrand had had to watch him day and night for weeks – in case.

'Mind you, Tristan, it would explain why there was no mark on the body.'

213

Bertrand fiddled absently with the reins.

'No, Tristan, it does not make sense. Men who plan that do not plan to do it in front of other people. They go somewhere quiet – on their own.'

He looked over his shoulder at the barrel house. That was where Albert would have gone. But they did not find him there – unless Vico moved him! And why would he do that? Unless Livia had told him.

He shook his head. The suppositions and possibilities were crowding in like ghostly trees in an enchanted forest.

Consider the practicalities. Where could Albert have obtained poison? That was the only way he could have done it. *No mark on the body.* Poison? Quite easily actually, when you come to think of it. Any resourceful peasant could have shown him half a dozen within a mile or two of the city. The trick would have been to hide it. Where was there any private place in the whole of *The Hawk?*

Bertrand led Tristan back to his hook in the wall, and secured the reins there.

There was nothing else for it; he would have to go and look. Though Heaven alone knew what he hoped or expected to find.

It was peaceful inside – just as he remembered it with Albert. Small wonder he had always liked it in here. No Livia; no Vico. Just his beloved beer. For a moment Bertrand was tempted to draw off a mug of Albert's best. Dammit – he would!

He sat and sipped on the bench he had shared with Albert – when Albert had first told him about Hedi. When he was close to tears.

That was certain! There was no imagination or speculation required for that. Albert loved his wife. He loved his daughter, and wanted to do his best for her. He loved his son, really, when all was said and done, and would have done his best for him too, if only he could work out what *was* the best. He loved his beer. He wanted to do his best for them all, and for the house – in spite of all those terrible disasters – flood, plague, drought, famine. And the terrifying sackings by the soldiers. And he wanted to go on the Crusade! To save the Holy Land, put his soldier's experience at the disposal of God, fight the Good Fight, go to Heaven at the end, and meet his beloved Hedi. No – Albert was not a bad man.

He was an intelligent man though. He was beleaguered, and he was often at his wits' end, but he was not stupid. Remember that, Bertrand, my boy.

He had a refuge – where Livia and Vico never went.

Bertrand put down his mug and looked about him. If Albert had hidden any poison, it was in here. But the walls were cold and damp – hardly the ideal place to store dried plants or roots. No picked fungus would last more than two or three days here, and Albert had been dead for getting on for a week.

Bertrand got up and began walking about. They could be in some kind of container, possibly. There was no cupboard, no alcove, no furniture – just Thomas' box against the wall. The walls were plain stonework, mostly bare, with just a few shreds of crumbling mortar – another sign of neglect. Another front on which Albert had had to retreat, poor fellow. Bertrand stooped and peered underneath the remaining barrels. Nothing. He knocked the bung out of empty barrels and squinted inside. He tried rattling them, and rolling them to and fro. Again nothing.

'What are you doing here?'

It was Vico, who had obviously come at the sound of

the hammer.

Bertrand picked up the mug and held it out for display.

'Helping myself. Sorry. I shall pay.'

'You will indeed.'

Vico almost snatched the coins from Bertrand's hand and stumped off to pick up his fork. Bertrand watched him piling the midden still higher. It absorbed him completely, just as he had been absorbed with burning the rats. It was like a child making mud pies. He seemed to have forgotten Bertrand's existence. He patted stray lumps of soiled straw into secure positions with great care. It was almost as if he were building something.

Bertrand came up behind him and kicked another lump towards him.

'Forgotten a bit.'

Vico whirled round, his eyes pinpoints of suspicion and menace. He brandished his fork.

'Get out – or you get this in your fat gut.'

Bertrand went.

* * * * * *

'Have you been to see her? Is she all right?'

Simon continued to speak of his sister as if she were still alive.

Bertrand raised a pacific hand.

'Be at ease. I knew you would ask that. I went to have a look on my way here. All is well.'

He did not tell the boy that the reason for his visit was to make sure that Vico had not been nosing around, to make sure that Vico did not even know of the grave's whereabouts. He had found nothing. Lenore was indeed at peace – at last.

And would remain so – he had taken especial care to

make sure that he was not followed.

Simon received the reassurances with a distracted air, which was understandable under the circumstances. Bertrand did feel sorry for him. He had after all had a great deal to bear. The sudden death of a father; the false accusation of his murder; and the fading away of a much-loved sister, of whose death he had been a helpless spectator. And now he was shut up in a strange building, still helpless while he waited for a near-stranger to bring welcome news. Bertrand anticipated his questions.

'No – we have found no conclusive evidence yet. But there are straws in the wind. Give us time. You are safe here. Livia will never guess.'

So long as Brother William's love of an intrigue was stronger than his appetite. Bertrand absently patted his own belt. A stomach was a powerful adversary of the conscience; he shuddered to think how many Fridays he had desecrated with a furtive cut of meat. And how few times he had confessed them.

However, there was nothing to be gained by worrying the boy about what might or might not happen. Bertrand put on an innocent air.

'So,' he said. 'How are you? Are they looking after you?'

Simon made a face.

'I suppose so. Nobody takes much notice of me.'

Bertrand raised his eyebrows.

'You are fed and housed and protected. The whole point is that you should *not* attract attention. The less they make of it the better.'

'They are not very holy.'

'What do you expect – a community of saints?'

'I expect somebody, somewhere, to behave like a

monk. Instead, I hear nothing but gossip and backbiting. You should hear the things I get told – in confidence, of course. They spend their time thinking how hard done by they are.'

His lip curled in disdain.

Bertrand had to make an effort not to come back with the obvious reply. The boy was running true to character. And he was also finding out exactly how monks – the monks Bertrand knew anyway – conducted themselves. They were ordinary men like any other, except that they had made the decision to live apart. Such a decision did not turn them into men of especial virtue overnight – or indeed ever. And living so close to each other made demands on their tolerance that were far in advance of those in a normal life.

For all his troubles, Simon was behaving like any other young man who had no idea where he ought to be going. The world went around him, just as the sun went around the earth. The world moreover – much less God – was not considerate enough to make it clear to him what he should be doing. Which was the world's fault. Probably God's too.

Still, if nothing else, the episode should provide him with valuable information as he made up his mind about whether he himself had the true calling for the habit.

Bertrand tried talking about more practical things like the inn, and how it was to be run. Simon was not interested.

'To the midden with *The Hawk*. The only thing I like about *The Hawk* is Thomas. He is a good ratter.' He smiled for the first time. 'And he is the only thing that makes Vico uncomfortable.'

That at least was positive. Bertrand decided to leave him there. He would keep until his next visit.

As he jogged along the path back towards Clermont and the Mayor's house, Bertrand chatted with his donkey.

'Not a bad afternoon's work, my old warrior. The grave is safe. Simon has plenty of self-pity to keep him company, and he is finding out that the habit may not be the answer to the problems of life. And I, Tristan? What have I been doing? I – I have been having a most interesting conversation with the Prior.'

* * * * * *

Arnaud stopped his pacing when Bertrand opened the door.

'Ah! Thank God! Vico has been to see me again.'

Bertrand sat down and helped himself to an apple from a wooden bowl.

'That explains why he was not following me. Well, what now?'

'It is uncanny – he is on to poison now.'

God's angels! It was indeed uncanny. Bertrand felt a slight thrill of fear. A few hours ago he had been considering the chances of Albert's having poisoned himself, and now Vico – sent by his mother – had come up with an accusation of poison, admittedly by somebody else. Because it most certainly was Livia's work; Vico would never have thought of that – not at this stage.

'What are you gaping at?' said Arnaud.

Bertrand told him.

'The woman must be a mind-reader.'

'Ha! I thought *you* were the mind-reader. Remember you told me that Lenore's soup might be tainted? Now we have Vico whispering poison.'

'I merely said that it might pay you to find out if anyone else drank Lenore's soup. If they had, it would give you a means of denying the very evidence that you say has just come forward. If they drank it and did not die, nobody can say Albert was poisoned with it − intentionally or otherwise. Did you?'

'Did I what?'

'Find out if anybody else drank it.'

'No. I could find nothing. And how did you know that Vico would talk poison ?'

Bertrand spat out a pip.

'Arnaud, where are your brains? It was going to be only a matter of time before Livia came up with it. Especially as the other means had failed.'

'Livia?'

'Well, it certainly is not Vico. By the angels, you are a Mayor. You do not need me to tell you. How many unexplained deaths set the gossips talking about poison? And nine out of ten are nothing but upset stomachs from rotten food. When was the last time you were rooted to the privy − less than a month ago. Eh? We all get it. Of course Livia would try it on.'

'You just said it shook you.'

'Even when you expect something unpleasant, it still shakes you when it happens. It is a reminder too of what we are up against. A most exceptional woman. I only mentioned the idea of poison in order to give you a chance to be prepared.'

'Well, I am not. Once again, I can not disprove it, and Livia knows I can not.'

Bertrand bit carefully round the core.

'No. But it is weak. How is it that she finds out so late? Did she dig up the body and poke about inside his stomach?'

'Very funny. As a matter of fact, Vico says she found

the remains in the dried pot.'

'Remarkable. And where is this deadly pot now – and its fatal contents?'

'Vico says she thought they were accursed, so she buried them. And said a prayer over it.'

Bertrand could see Livia banging the slop bowl against the wall of the alley.

'Yes, I am sure. Did she say where?'

'Says she can not remember.'

'How very convenient.'

Trodden by a hundred muddy feet – they would never find them now.

Arnaud sat down, still agitated.

'There is still going to be trouble. By the time Livia has finished down in the square, the city will smell those herbs from wall to wall.'

'Only a smell, Arnaud. We know that soup was harmless.'

Arnaud banged his table.

'Damn you! If you were Mayor, you would never say that. A smell is enough to set a crowd going here. This damned hermit I was telling you about is still preaching. Manors are being left half empty. They are coming here. I have never seen so many villeins in town at this time of the year. Hanging about at corners in muttering groups, smelling of pig dung and God knows what. I have even seen slaves, and God knows how *they* are going to stay alive.'

Bertrand nodded, and put up both his hands.

'Yes. I agree. I am sorry. The problem is still with us. We can put out the fire of weak evidence, but the smoke of rumour remains. And as long as the smoke of rumour remains, folk will say that there is no smoke without fire.'

They sat in silence for a while. Then Arnaud lifted his head.

'What about the other thing?'

Bertrand looked up.

'What other thing?'

'You said you would explain two riddles when you got back. The soup was one. What about the other?'

Bertrand smiled.

'Oh, you mean Vico and his row with Albert?'

'You said they did not.'

'I suggested that they would not in normal circumstances. But suppose something had happened that was out of the normal?'

'Like what?'

'Oh, come now, Arnaud. Like the thing that has been giving you sleepless nights for a couple of weeks.'

Arnaud frowned.

'Explain.'

Bertrand leaned forward.

'You and I heard him speak. We both *heard* the same thing, but we *looked* at different things. You were looking for trouble; I was looking at faces. Trouble is your trade; faces and feelings are mine.'

'I still do not see.'

'I watched a lot of people that day. One of them was Vico. Remember we saw him up on that scaffolding?'

'So?'

'I make it my business to watch faces, Arnaud. I see them change when I tell stories. I see men's souls come out of their eyes. All their loves, hopes, fears, desires, longings.

'Urban is a great speaker. He drew men's souls out too. I glanced up at Vico, and for a moment it was like looking in Lenore's eyes. They were on fire.'

Arnaud looked disbelieving.

'Are you telling me that Urban turned our Vico into a saint with one sermon? Bah!'

'No. I am saying that Vico is human like the rest of us.'

Arnaud spat.

'Oh, really?'

'No, no – listen to me. Look what Urban was offering. Heaven. Paradise. Forgiveness. *For ever.* Intoxicating to a virtuous man. But to a sinner like Vico – consuming like a fire.'

Arnaud stared for a while as he digested the thought.

'All right. So Vico wants to go on Crusade. What is that to do with – '

He broke off, staring.

'Exactly!' said Bertrand. 'It was not Simon who wanted to go; it was Vico. Vico did the obvious next thing; he went to Albert and asked him for his share, his interest in *The Hawk.* '

'Albert would never have given anything to him.'

'True. We know that. So did Vico, no doubt, in his more sober moments. But when a man is on fire, he does not see problems; he does not see the truth. He sees only his visions of the future. So he asks Albert. Now there *was* something to have a row about. Something quite new. No wonder feelings ran high.'

Arnaud pondered.

'It is still only a guess.'

'Have you got a better one? Remember I saw Vico stealing red cloth from his mother's chest.'

'And from Hugh the draper.'

'Well, there you are.'

'Is it any good asking Vico?'

'I doubt it – put like that. But, as I said, if we can get

him to think he is trapping someone else, he might trap himself.'

' "We?" '

Bertrand sighed.

'Very well. You will have to wait for the rest of my story then.'

Perhaps it would be as well if the Prior's news were kept waiting for just a little longer. Then it might be made to fit into a more complete pattern. Poor Arnaud had enough headaches.

As if he were reading his thoughts, Arnaud said, 'The first group is leaving soon. This cold snap is only delaying them. The first properly organised group, that is. The Pope is going one way; they are going another.'

Bertrand felt a vague stirring of envy, which surprised him.

'Urban is leaving?'

'He will spend a few nights at Cluniac houses on the way, and keep Christmas at Limoges. Or so his chaplains tell me. Then, more preaching in the new year. Tours, Poitiers, Saintes, Bordeaux, and Toulouse. Another rendezvous with Raymond.'

'So he is still running with his wild horse.'

'Oh yes. He is terrified, but he is still running. Anything to steal a march on the Emperor. I tell you, Bertrand, it is as much politics as it is anything.'

'But he is using the madness he has created, my friend, like any good intriguer. And Livia is doing the same. They could be fit companions.'

Arnaud laughed.

'If you put Livia up against Urban, who would you bet on?'

Bertrand laughed too.

'A nice problem. Now – I must be off to talk to Vico, before he comes up with something else.'

'He will be at *The Hawk* again, I expect.'

'Yes, and I know exactly where – feeding the midden.'

Arnaud saw him to the door.

'Good luck.'

'You too, my friend. Oh, by the way, any more sightings of that soldier – the second one – the one who was swearing vengeance on Vico?'

'The Limper? Yes, as a matter of fact. I nearly forgot. You can tell Vico we have found him. Or rather part of him.'

'Part of him?'

'Yes. His head, to be precise.'

'Where?'

'In a cloth, underneath Hugh of Tournai's wagon.'

* * * * * *

Twelve

'**I HAVE SOME** good news for you, Vico.'

Vico put down the whetstone and tested the edge of the axe with his thumb, but did not raise his head. Bertrand knew Vico had heard him.

'You know that soldier you helped to arrest? The one who swore vengeance?'

Vico still did not show any reaction. Instead, he bent and arranged a log endways on the block with exaggerated care. Bertrand continued regardless.

'You know he came back? I warned you about him some time ago. Well, you can tell your mother that you can both stop worrying. He is dead.'

Again, Vico did not show surprise. A leer of satisfaction crossed his face.

'Good.'

'The Mayor told me. The Mayor is my friend.'

'Yes,' said Vico. 'I have seen.'

He grunted as he brought the axe down. It was a neat split. Bertrand waited till he had put the two pieces on one side and placed another log endways. This game would have to be stalked with great care. He stood silent while two more logs were split. Vico looked at him sidelong once or twice.

'I daresay that must be a relief,' said Bertrand at last.

Again the sidelong, watchful glance.

'Yes.'

Bertrand tried a more direct approach.

'You will never guess where they found him.'

Vico's brows knotted, as if he were wrestling with some problem.

'No.'

'In the wagon of that draper who attacked you. So he must have been getting his own back on the soldier who stole his cloth. Did he ever tell you about that?'

No point in making the distinction between Scarface the Charming Thief and the Vengeful Limper. Vico was certainly not going to correct him, if indeed he remembered. If indeed he knew that the Charmer had stolen from Hugh in the first place.

Vico bent over his chopping. Bertrand tried again.

'So it will serve him right. Eh?'

Vico scowled in the effort of thinking of an answer.

'Yes.'

'Nasty piece of work. I think you did so well to see him off when you did. And not just him. The whole mob of them. Took courage, that did.'

'Yes.'

'I expect your mother was relieved when they went. You must be a great comfort to your mother. All the bad times we have been having.'

Vico swung the axe. Another perfect split.

'Especially now,' said Bertrand. 'These terrible events. Within the family. Takes bravery to give evidence like that. A lesser man would have shied away.'

Vico concentrated even more ferociously on his chopping.

'Yes, well…'

'No, I mean it. It shows a great sense of justice. No fear or favour. I like that.'

'Justice – yes.'

227

'No matter what is the cost. After all, you have to defend yourselves. Otherwise wicked tongues could cause no end of mischief. Nothing worse than a wicked tongue, I always say. I think you show great loyalty to your mother. And she is having the worst of it right now.'

Vico's frown was becoming nearly permanent.

'Yes…'

'They will find him, you know – in the end. My friend the Mayor tells me that. Then you and your mother can rest easy. My guess is that Simon will get what is coming to him. After all, what could be worse than an ungrateful son? That is why I admire you; you stick by your mother through thick and thin.'

Vico sniffed.

Bertrand picked up a piece of wood which had flown aside on impact.

'Oh, I watched things, Vico. I saw.'

'Yes.'

'Always quarrelling, were they?'

Vico got the axe stuck in the top of a log, and banged it on the block.

'Always. From way back.' Vico punctuated each phrase with a blow. 'Albert was a fool. A coward. Afraid of Mother. Simon hated him for that. Only half a man.'

'Often away was he – Simon?'

'Never did a decent day's work. I did all the heavy stuff.'

'And still do. Without a word of complaint. I admire you for that.'

Vico gave one final, savage blow. The log flew apart.

'Lazy little turd!'

'Where did he go?'

'God knows. Dreaming. In the woods mostly.'

'If he was dreaming, I expect he was easy to follow.'

'Yes. Fool.'

Bertrand held his breath, but Vico had not noticed. Bertrand dangled another piece of bait before he became suspicious.

'Comforting his sister?'

Vico leered.

'Call it that if you like. Christian folk would have another name for it.'

'Crazed, was she?'

'Not surprising, eh?'

He gave a dirty cackle as he laid down the axe.

Bertrand helped him to fill the box.

'Lazy and crazy – no right to *The Hawk*. Not like you and your mother. No justice, is there?'

'Mother will get it.'

Justice? Or *The Hawk*? Or both? Bertrand decided not to stalk the quarry too closely, and fell back a little.

'Albert, your father – '

'Stepfather.'

'Yes, yes, of course – stepfather. People seem to think he got what was coming to him as well.'

Vico scowled.

'Bastard!'

'Bit of a miser, I understand.'

'Mean as misery.'

'Did he keep your mother short?'

'He tried to.'

Vico allowed himself a twisted smile.

'Mean to you too?'

'Yes. Always.'

'It must have been a particular disappointment to you?'

Vico looked at him.

'How?'

Bertrand back-tracked.

'As I said – keeping your mother short. It must have struck you as most unfair. I expect he was generous to Simon.'

Vico shrugged.

'Not much… '

Bertrand blew an inward sigh of relief. The quarry had glanced over its shoulder, but had not bolted. Vico bent and lifted the full box with no trace of effort. The stalking resumed.

'Bully, was he?'

'Yes.'

'Eat too much?'

'Pig.'

'Drinker?'

'Like a fish.'

'Shouted a lot – red in the face?'

'Like a plum.'

'Easy to bait him?'

'Like a blind bear.'

'But your mother coped?'

'Mother managed – everything.'

The quarry seemed more relaxed. Bertrand ventured closer again.

'Still – when it happened – no warning – it must have come as a shock to your mother, poor soul. When you told her.'

'Yes.'

They reached the entrance of an out-house, where Vico dumped the box inside. He picked up the bar to fasten across the door.

Bertrand felt his heart beat a trifle faster.

'It must have been a shock to you – him dropping like that.'

Vico slammed the doors shut and dropped the bar easily into its brackets. He turned and stared blankly.

The quarry vanished into a thicket.

* * * * * *

Arnaud was quite right; the cold weather was keeping more people indoors. But there were still knots of bedraggled villeins at corners. The looks they cast over their bowed and bony shoulders were anything but Christian or charitable. Bertrand felt a twinge of alarm. He sensed that it would need only one voice raised to bring a score of them surging towards him.

Infidel! Turk! Saracen! Jew! Thief! Adulterer! Witch! Spells! Black magic! Murder! It would make no difference. They would not pause to *ask* questions, never mind listen to the answer. He was glad when he reached the Mayor's house. Even more relieved to see a couple of constables lounging near the door, thumping their arms across their bodies. Their red crosses were missing.

Bertrand risked a quip. He addressed the one he knew from his visits to *The Hawk*.

'Changed your minds then. The Pope took the spirit of the Crusade with him and left you behind?'

'We were drunk on the spirit, Bertrand. Now we are sober.'

'You can get drunk again.'

'But you can not *stay* drunk all the way to the Holy Land.'

'Others think you can.'

'That is their look out.'

He was a well-built young man, with a cheerful open

face. Bertrand liked him. But as he gave him a playful shove in the chest and went by to knock on the door, he felt a very slight twinge of disappointment – the sort of regret felt when someone one likes is about to miss a treat.

Arnaud opened the door himself. He looked as if he had been waiting for too long. He tilted his head towards the interior.

He kept silent till he had sat Bertrand down and the girl had brought him something to eat and drink.

'Well?'

'We have been looking in all the wrong places, my friend.'

'Where should we have been looking?'

'In the obvious one – under our own noses.'

Arnaud sat down opposite.

'You mean, you have found the killer.'

'No.'

Bertrand knew this was naughty, but he was enjoying himself. Arnaud was rising to the bait. He was getting impatient too.

'Bertrand… '

Bertrand smiled.

'All right, all right. I have spoken with Vico…'

'And?'

' …There is no mystery, Arnaud. Think about Albert for a moment – as we should have done at the outset. Thick neck, overweight, red in the face, weaker than his wife. An unsuccessful innkeeper, constant rows with the customers, the attacks of the soldiers, worry about trade falling, drinking too much. Then the excitement of a family argument. Work it out for yourself.'

'You mean apoplexy? So nobody killed him.'

'Life killed him, my friend. And you can not punish Life.'

'Can you prove this? Has Vico confessed?'

'No. He slipped out just before I could nail him down. But he did not deny it. And he knows I am on to him.'

Bertrand reached out for the pot of wine, and began pouring.

'He knows I am on to something else, too.'

'Oh?'

'I told him the Limper was dead.'

Arnaud leaned forward.

'And?'

'And nothing. He spent the next few minutes trying to do as little as he could. My guess is that he was baffled to know what to do. How to behave. His mother was not there to tell him.'

'So you think he did it?'

Bertrand shrugged.

'Do you know what Vico was doing while I was telling him? Sharpening his axe and splitting logs. How do you think the Limper's head was severed from his body?'

'Vico's axe is not the only axe in Clermont. Once again, we can prove nothing.'

'No. But it is interesting, Arnaud. Look at the number of times now that Vico has been to tell you of some new twist in the story. It seems he is never short of ideas.'

'You mean – after he has had time to talk to Livia.'

'Yes. Yet put him on his own, and he has no idea what to say next. The only time he was at all talkative was when he was running down Simon and Albert. Because that was what he really thought. I nearly had him. But, at the last minute, the shutters were slammed.'

Arnaud poured himself a drink.

'Pity.'

Bertrand held out his cup, and Arnaud obliged.

'Nevertheless, we have raised the pressure. Vico knows we suspect *something* – never mind what. And if he knows, Livia knows by now.'

Arnaud tilted his head.

'So we know, and they know we know.'

'And we know that they know we know.'

'True. And we know how Albert died – assuming you are right. But we can not prove it. We can not *prove* Vico wrong. So we are still no further forward. In fact, we are a step back.'

'What has happened?'

'There is another ingredient added to the mixture.'

'What?'

'The word is now going round that Lenore was most definitely a witch. Why? Because she was abnormally immature. She had no breasts to speak of.'

'Arnaud, she was half-starved.'

'That is not all. She had very little hair. And her bleedings had not started.'

Bertrand stared.

'But I have only just left Vico. He could not have got here in the time.'

'I picked this up in the square. This is Livia's direct work, not Vico's. It has the mark of her tongue. A woman's tongue.' Arnaud shook his head in reluctant admiration. 'I begin to believe what you say now. That woman is capable of anything.'

'She is coming more into the open. Not wasting time using Vico as the messenger. Getting impatient.'

'Or worried.'

'She will be more worried now she knows what I got

out of Vico.' He mused for a moment, then shook his head. 'Poor Albert.'

'Why do you say that?'

'Look at him, Arnaud. Beset on all sides. Every day of his life without his beloved Hedi was an agony of loss. Every day with his son was a strain and a regret. Every day with his daughter was a sorrow. Every day with Vico was a spit of disgust. Every day with Livia was a struggle, and a losing one. No wonder he was red in the face. That man spent his life swimming against the current, and being pushed back all the time. It was too much for him.'

'And it killed him.'

'Yes. I think it did. Of course I can not prove it. But you saw him. Albert would have gone under sooner or later, one way or another. Madness. Or seizure. I even wondered whether he might have killed himself.'

'Suicide!'

Arnaud said it in a shocked whisper, as if the mere thought was disturbing – which it was to any Christian soul. Bertrand shook his head.

'No – all the scales of common sense are weighted against it. That left violence – he would have snapped and attacked someone. But – I repeat – he was not a fool. He knew what was happening. He knew he was losing. And he tried to devise a means of escape. Give Simon the inn. Put Lenore into a house.'

'And what would he have done?'

'Not sure. Perhaps he was not sure either. Perhaps his plans were only half formed. But I am almost sure that they received a kick with Urban's speech. It could even have changed them. Suddenly he could see the way. Go on Crusade. Simon and Lenore would be provided for. Livia and Vico could go to the Devil. He was an old soldier; his skills would be useful. And he would go to Heaven. Maybe even take his beloved Hedi with him. There is no end to the hopes of a man whose yearning is painful enough.'

Arnaud growled.

'All that may be very well, but we have still to stop Livia exciting everybody with these rumours of witchcraft. You have been through the streets. You have seen.'

Bertrand had indeed seen, and he had been frightened. Arnaud leaned forward.

'Bertrand, we can not sit and simply wait for Livia to come up with something else. She will have us on the run all the time. How do we get evidence? How do we prove her wrong?'

'This is not about evidence and proof, my friend. It is about opportunity and timing. Livia and Vico did not plan to kill Albert. Nor did they kill him by accident. Nor did they particularly want him to die. But what Livia did was to realise that Albert's sudden death was a great chance. That was the clever part. It was what she has *done* with that opportunity − '

' − what she is still doing.'

'Yes. That is what we have to try and stop. If we simply try to scotch each rumour that she puts out, we shall be doing nothing but chase will o' the wisps, and we shall always be one step behind. And she knows that.'

Arnaud nodded.

'I agree. And there is something else too. She wants Simon found, so that she can turn the anger of a crowd on to him.'

'Just as she turned a mob on to Hugh's wagon.'

'Just as she probably put that head under it.'

'That is what you think?'

'I told you — I believe anything of that woman now. Why on earth would Hugh have killed him? He was not the one who had stolen his cloth. There is no axe in Hugh's wagon — I looked. And it was Hugh who brought me the head. He left Robert vomiting his heart out.'

Poor Robert — he was not very good with dead bodies. First a hanged soldier with half a face in a forest; then the dread shock of a girl's death; now a severed head under the very place where he might have slept — within inches of his own head.

Bertrand slapped his thigh.

'The bag!'

Arnaud grunted, and shook his head in wonderment.

'The great bag.'

They both fell silent, as they thought of Livia, on her frequent trips to the vegetable stalls, with her great leather bag over her sinewy arm.

Bertrand broke the mood.

'No good, Arnaud. Yet again, no proof.'

'We could look inside it for blood.'

Bertrand dismissed the idea.

'She goes to butchers' stalls too. Can you tell the difference between human and animal blood?'

Arnaud clung to his idea.

'Who else could it have been? Why would anybody else in the whole of Clermont put a severed head under Hugh's wagon? Why go to the trouble? They would have tossed it into the river. Come to think of it, why would anybody bother to cut his head off at all?'

'Unless it was already cut off.'

'You mean Vico?'

'Yes. Vico lost his temper and swung his axe.'

Arnaud stared.

'And cut off a head!'

'They say that the Saxons at Hastings could cut through a man's neck – chain mail and all – with their axes.'

'They were professionals.'

'So Vico just got a lucky strike. Then Livia has to decide what to do with the pieces. It reeks of her handiwork. If people see Vico skulking through the streets, hunched over a mysterious bundle, they will be suspicious. But nobody would take any notice of Livia with her bag of vegetables for *The Hawk*. She had tried to ruin Hugh once by violence. Now she could do it by stealth. Once again – genius.'

'All right, all right. But what about the rest of him?'

Bertrand sniffed.

'I am working on that.'

'Well, hurry up,' said Arnaud. 'Livia is still down at *The Hawk*, and she is pumping Brother William about the will. Sooner or later, she will discover, to her surprise, that St. Fulbert's is sheltering Simon.'

'So the Tub will crack, do you think?'

'If she can not get it from the Tub, she will get it sooner or later from the St. Fulbert villeins. I told you this hermit is disturbing them. They are leaving their manors in droves. The city is crawling with bemused peasants.'

'What does a peasant know about wills?'

Arnaud made a gesture of impatience.

'Bertrand, now it is you who is not using his sense. Livia will get something. Albert was a big man. If he went to St. Fulbert's to draw up a will, somebody, somewhere, will have seen him. And one of them, somewhere, will have seen Simon. Livia will find out, sooner or later. She will start the hue and cry. If Simon is killed or arrested, it will not matter then whether there is a will or not. We have to do something. Quickly.'

Bertrand gathered his thoughts.

'For a start, it is not worth chasing evidence; there is none. It is not worth trying to disprove Livia's new stories. She will simply invent more. It will go on as long as the madness lasts.'

'I know. If one story – only one – should excite a crowd, all the disproof in the world will count for nothing. Look at that lot out there. What do we do?'

'Do? We must go to the fount of the evidence, and get it turned off.'

'Livia?'

'Yes.'

'You will not frighten Livia.'

'No. But we might frighten Vico. And we might – we might just – be able to drive a wedge between him and his mother. If we split them, we might silence her.'

'How do we do that?'

Bertrand took another swig at his drink.

'Remember Italy and the Hautevilles? Robert especially. Remember they did not call him the Guiscard for nothing?'

Arnaud grinned.

'Cunning devil. You had to get up very early in the morning to catch out the Guiscard.'

'Exactly. Think of all those sieges. How did we get in at the end? Frontal assault? Too costly. Mining? Too long and tedious.'

'Treachery.' Arnaud chuckled. 'You can never beat it.'

'Right again. Pay someone to open the gates in the

night. Well, Livia will never surrender the citadel. So we get Vico to open the back gate when she is not looking.'

'How do we do that?'

'Pressure, old friend. Pressure.'

'Explain yourself.'

'I have been thinking on my way here.'

In between worrying about being set upon by a mob.

'It means a move on your part. If we are to force them out into the open – or at least Vico – we have to come out into the open ourselves. And we have to use all our available resources. If you do what I suggest, you can no longer use me as a shape in the shadows. Livia will have me out of *The Hawk* in a twitch of Thomas' whiskers.'

'What other resources do we have?'

'Hugh of Tournai for a start. He would welcome some revenge for his wagon. Especially if we tell him that Livia put the head under it. Robert is probably still under the spell of Lenore; he would jump at a chance to do something.'

Arnaud sniffed.

'A draper and his boy.'

Bertrand nodded towards the front door.

'I see you still have two strong young constables.'

Arnaud nodded.

'Yes. Two at least have come to their senses.'

'Good. I suggest you arrest Vico.'

'On what charge?'

'Murder.'

'What? But you said Albert died of natural causes.'

'Who said anything about the murder of Albert?'

'But nobody else has been murd – ' Arnaud stopped himself.

Bertrand burst out laughing.

'Arnaud, Clermont is awash with dead bodies. Our friend Scarface. Lenore. Those two old women. The Jew. And now Hugh's head – the Limper.'

'We have no evidence that Vico did any of those. Not real evidence.'

'Who cares? We make it up. Livia did. Think of the Guiscard, my friend. Cheat. They have been cheating all the time. If we want to win, so must we.'

'So what do we do?'

'Take them by surprise. Who is the one that Vico is least likely to have killed?'

Arnaud did not have to think.

'Lenore.'

'Good. Charge him with that one. That will shake him. It ought to shake Livia too. Surprise. Surprise! The Guiscard again, Arnaud. Catch them on the wrong foot, and they are already half way to falling.'

'What then?'

'This is the plan – or rather the suggestion. After all, you are the Mayor.'

'Go on, go on.'

Bertrand looked keenly at his friend's face for a moment, as if wondering whether he would accept what was coming. Arnaud fidgeted.

'Get on with it. Let me at least hear it.'

'Very well. Here it is. I want you to prepare two large cages, each one capable of holding a man. Fill one of them with the nastiest cats you can find. Hungry ones if possible. With so many people neglecting their homes in the last fortnight, that should not be difficult.'

Arnaud's eyes opened wider with each detail. Bertrand swept on, determined to get to the end before his friend could think of anything to say.

'Send your two constables to arrest Vico, and take him, and the cages, and the cats, and a lot of wood – dry wood which will burn fast – up into the forest behind St. Fulbert's. To the clearing where Lenore is buried. I shall tell you how to find it. You go too of course.'

As Arnaud was still gaping, Bertrand had the chance to continue.

'When you get there, this is what I want you to – what I suggest you do… '

* * * * * *

The next day, Bertrand walked his donkey to the stable yard of the second inn. He had no wish to be anywhere near *The Hawk* when Livia found out the part he had played in the arrest of her son. With hands like that, she was quite capable of throttling him.

In the cold air of a fresh winter morning, the plan he had cooked up did not seem quite so likely to succeed. He had been rather tickled with it when he had first put it together, especially when he had seen Arnaud's awed reaction. It made him feel clever. Now, after a poor night and a chill breakfast in Livia's kitchen, he began to notice all sorts of loopholes.

As usual, he voiced his thoughts to his companion.

'Ah, well, Tristan, just because I can see snags in the plan, it does not mean that Arnaud can. Whatever its weaknesses, it will come as a complete surprise to Vico, and surprise is half the battle – as the Guiscard would have said. There was a man for you, Tristan. Nothing ever took him off guard.'

It dawned on him that one of the Guiscard's trade secrets would stand them in very good stead now. Once you have a plan, carry it out, and carry it out with confidence and dash. 'If it was good idea yesterday, it is a good idea today.' That was what he used to say. The trick was not to fall prey to doubt. *Of course* it would work. *Make* it work.

But suppose it did not? What would the Guiscard have done? Bertrand knew the answer to that too. He would have laughed that great booming laugh of his, and sat down at once to think of another plan, probably better than the first.

So – yes – it was as well to stick to what they had decided. It was now in Arnaud's hands. When it came to action like this, Bertrand felt out of his depth. All he could do now was wait.

He patted Tristan's neck, and they turned up another street.

Ironic, though, that it was taking the two of them – a worldly-wise minstrel and an experienced soldier and magistrate – to out-think this stark, silent, lonely woman, who was proving to be the most splendid opportunist he had ever come across. Except possibly the Guiscard himself. Come to think of it, Livia would have made a worthy partner to the Guiscard. And the Pope. There was a trio. Between them, they would have defeated both emperors – the one in Germany and the one in Constantinople.

Whatever was to be the outcome, you had to admire the way she had faced events and had seized her chances. At the outset, she was nothing more than an innkeeper's drudge, a wordless servant whose place was to cook and serve and clean. Her husband was a boorish bully, and he had two children who, in the normal run of things, would inherit the property – which would, in all probability, leave her own son out in the cold.

It must have been an opportunity she seized when she married Albert in the first place. There she was, in a war-torn province of Italy, a widow with a young son, with probably no property and no funds. She had spotted this vigorous, successful sergeant of archers, who had recently lost his wife. True, he had two children of his own, but she could cope with that. And cope she did. It did not seem likely that she was ever in love with him. They each needed someone. It seemed a good arrangement at the time.

For Livia it remained a good arrangement, if a dreary one. Then had come the pestilence, which had threatened the business, the house, the future, their very lives. And the only way forward had been to nurse the feeble daughter through the worst affliction that God could bring upon a human being. She had been sickened, revolted, and terrified. But she had done it.

The authority that episode had given her must have been incalculable. And she had taken advantage of that too. By the time the pestilence had quitted the stricken city, she had become the hub of the household – no question. All Albert could do was bluster about it. The situation was so clear that it was alienating his own son from him. Simon could not bear to see his father, whom he loved and whom had thought could deal with everything, unable to cope.

What with the other disasters – the drought, the famine, and so on – and the sackings by the soldiers, it became clear that Albert was crumbling beneath the weight of worry and responsibility.

Then had come the final drama: Albert had dropped dead at Vico's feet, and Vico was looking at her asking her what should be done. In dealing with this she had risen to new heights.

Here was a chance to realise all her ambitions at the same time. Almost certainly she had not wanted Albert to die until she was sure of the inheritance. And she could not be sure of the inheritance until she had found out about the existence of a will. If such a will existed, it would almost certainly benefit Simon and Lenore. It would be hard to contest. But – if Simon could be accused, and convicted, of the murder, it would not only remove him from the house; it would remove him from the inheritance. Lenore would not have the wit to contest the outcome, and in any case, years of calculated neglect would sooner or later account for her. If that could be achieved, the very existence of a will – never mind what was in it – became an irrelevance.

But the best idea of all, in Bertrand's opinion, was to use the current madness. For all the hours she spent in the kitchen at *The Hawk*, Livia knew what was going on as clearly as the loudest market-cross gossip. All those trips to buy supplies for *The Hawk*; all those hours on her knees in the nave of the cathedral or round the porch. Madame Livia, with her great bag and her folded hands, was the perfect housekeeper, the perfect wife and lady of the house. Every trip she made to spread her poison made people think so much the better of her; it was brilliant.

She understood perfectly well how the crowd, any crowd, in the city could be worked up to a pitch of madness and hatred – of Jews, infidels, witches, murderers, the Devil, anything. There was no proof, but it was uncanny how Hugh had had his wagon destroyed; how the poor Jew had met his end; possibly how Scarface came to be hanging in the forest, with his leggings round his ankles, poor devil – all of them enemies of either Vico or herself, all of them despatched by packs of snarling beasts of human beings called into being at a flick of a whip – or rather a tongue – all of them faceless and formless.

Her only failure – so far – was not to turn another pack of human animals on Simon, but it was not for want of trying. She switched from one ruse to another with a speed and a richness of imagination that were – well, genius. Her command of timing was masterly. Again, the Guiscard would have been proud to call her partner.

Livia had not asked God to bring about Albert's death. But she had been very grateful for the opportunity that such an event had brought in its train. And – wonder of wonders – He had brought along the Pope as well, with a firebrand of a sermon – in French! Giving everyone something to blame. It was almost too convenient to be true. God surely was on her side. And God would equally surely help those who helped themselves.

Bertrand had struggled for years to pick the lock on the great problem of reconciling Divine Will with Free Will, and had argued long and hard with priests and monks and other holy men up and down Christendom for years. Livia seemed to have done it in no time at all.

They turned into the yard of Bertrand's new accommodation. It had been empty for days, but the landlord and his wife had come to their senses, and decided not to go on crusade after all. So Bertrand could look forward to a meal.

He saw to Tristan's needs, and went indoors. He helped out by lighting the fire. There was nothing for it now but to wait for the result of the plan he had outlined to Arnaud. He hoped his friend would have some news.

He certainly had some for Arnaud. He had spent some very interesting time in the stable yard of *The Hawk* before he left.

*   *   *   *   *   *

Thirteen

BERTRAND WAS NOT good at waiting. He was good at sitting, at watching, at gossiping, at loafing generally. He could muse and dream and doze with the best of them. But when something was impending – good or evil – then his mind, and above all his imagination, came out of hiding, and gave him no peace. Unlike his friend, he was not a good pacer. Arnaud could walk up and down for hours, grumbling and swearing; the heat and sweat somehow dissipated part of the worry. Bertrand merely found the exercise tiring, and it made his trouble of mind only worse.

Would Vico break under the strain? Would he just laugh at Arnaud's elaborate arrangements? Would he return to the city and come to wreak vengeance on the fat, busybody minstrel who had thought it all up? Would he invoke the even worse vengeance of his mother? At a pinch, Bertrand could contemplate the wrath of the hunched, scowling creature who was half-savage; he could face the huge cheekbones, the slit eyes, the wet lips drawn back in a leer of hatred from the grey gums and the gapped, blackened teeth; even the strength in the stooped shoulders. He knew he could almost certainly outwit him.

But the cold, silent widow with the tightly-drawn hair; the long, muscular neck and gaunt frame; the thick wrists; the miserly words spent only on her lofty, knowing cat; the restless hands that were forever twisting a strip of cloth

– that frankly frightened him. He doubted his ability to cope with that.

Suppose she found out where Simon was? With Brother William practically bursting out of his habit, how long could he – or his stomach – hold out? Would it be only a matter of time before she wheedled the truth out of him? And, once she had got it, what then? Was it going to be like Hugh's wagon all over again, except that it was not strips of red cloth that they would be after, but a human being?

There were only twenty or so brothers at St. Fulbert's, but there were twice the number of lay workers – field and domestic – who could easily be goaded to join a mob of instant zealots. There were enough of them loitering round corners in Clermont already. Had she pulled them into *The Hawk*, filled their fevered stomachs with stew and their fevered minds with hatred? Would those trembling, cloistered clerics be able to keep at bay the muttering crowd that Livia would be able to conjure up from alley and furrow, gutter and ditch, by some silent alchemy of her own? If they could not, he would have betrayed Simon's trust. His mouth went dry as he pictured the accusation in Simon's eyes when they thrust the noose over his head and flung the end of the rope over a bar of the scaffolding round the Pope's platform – where it had all begun.

Suppose she turned the crowd on to him as well? On Bertrand de Montclos – tale-teller, *jongleur*, lounger and loafer, watcher and listener? He was an outsider, a stranger, a disturber, an interferer. He had felt a thrill of fear merely passing those knots of surly villeins in the street outside Arnaud's house. Would Arnaud be able to do anything to save him – with only two constables left? And their loyalty would be suspect when it came to a crisis. Why should they risk their lives for a fat-gutted minstrel who, it seemed, never told stories? Well, none that they had heard.

What sort of a minstrel was he anyway? He had become one for all the wrong reasons...

In fact he had not become one at all – not at first. He had run away at first. Why? To prove a point against his father? Simply to escape the old man's disappointment? To prove a point to himself? He would never know. He crawled home, starving, after only a fortnight.

He did it again later. In a desperate attempt to win his father's approval, he had gone for a soldier. Joined one of the Hauteville brothers when he passed through from Normandy on his way to join the rest of the clan in the south. Which one of the brothers was it – Geoffrey? Serlo? Mauger? He could not remember at this distance of time. There were so many of them; it was a job to keep track. They bred like rabbits too; Apulia and Calabria were crawling with young Hautevilles.

He was a dismal failure – just as he had known in his bones before he started. No skill, no flair, no liking for it. No relish in the endless ambushes and skirmishes and burnings. Deaths and maimings revolted him. He disgraced himself more than once. The only profit he gained from the whole experience was a friend. Arnaud tried to console him.

'Nobody is a hero. I get scared too. In my first six months I messed my breeches twice and ran away five times.'

Bertrand began telling stories round the fire, out of impatience, not desire. Simply because everyone else made such a terrible job of it. They had not the slightest sense of drama or pace or timing; they could not get three simple facts in proper sequence; they had no idea of variation of the voice. It all seemed so obvious to him.

He discovered that he could make men listen, make them laugh, make them think. Make them see things. He found a new status. For the first time, he felt that he was not a liability to the party. He had a definite role to play.

So he played it. It was better than that of camp coward or camp pudding or camp wineskin, the butt of the jibes and the practical jokes. Almost overnight, he became curiously inviolate; he was special. He began to look for ways to enhance this peculiar position in which he found himself.

He watched his companions more closely, observed their quirks of behaviour and speech. He made mental notes of curious incidents that they came across in their travels and campaigns across southern Italy. He became acquainted with, and slowly learned thoroughly, the great stories and romances that warmed every chilled and lonely soldier round every camp fire in Christendom. He started to collect local anecdotes, and learned how to embellish them. He discovered that he had a knack for mimicry.

All the time he told himself that this was only a temporary measure; it was only a way of filling the time, and maybe looking for a way to make his fortune – until he was ready to enter a house and embark on the study of letters. He told this to everybody who asked him – even when they had not asked him. One day – one day – he would become a man of education, of reading and writing. A scholar.

Year followed year, and curiously he never seemed able to get round to it. There was always something – a new campaign, an illness (or, worse, an epidemic), a sudden reversal of fortunes, a change of leader (even the numerous Hautevilles were not invulnerable or inexhaustible), a mood of black despair, a friend who needed him (when the Saracens murdered Arnaud's children, for instance). Always something.

As time went by, he had moods of self-contempt, when he upbraided himself for dilatoriness. These would be followed by firm resolutions to make the break, which came to nothing – to be followed in turn by further moods of depression.

'But you are good, Bertrand. Why change? You are a born minstrel.'

Arnaud's reassurances only made it worse.

Other minstrels he met gave him compliments. This professional approval had a twofold effect: on the one hand he felt pride that he was learning a mystery, and sharing in the brotherhood of that mystery with other practitioners; on the other, he could not avoid the feeling that this very approval was binding him yet more firmly to the minstrel's calling, and making his ultimate escape that much more difficult.

He made the acquaintance of one of the greatest exponents of the minstrel's art – Taillefer – the lugubrious, consumptive, beer-soaked wreck who could fascinate, enrapture, bewitch, and transport audiences of thousands right across Christendom. Or so it was said. Taillefer was the first person to give him cause to doubt the value of books. The first person besides farmers and soldiers, that is – and his father; they merely equated scholars with unmanliness.

Taillefer gave him much better food for thought.

'Do not worry about books. You can read only one book at a time. You can write only one book at a time. You can *speak* to hundreds – thousands – and they in turn will talk to hundreds and thousands more about you. And the more often they speak, the bigger you and your stories become. Believe me, my young friend, the spoken word is the most potent instrument of human activity in this world. No wonder Our Lord chose it too. Did you ever hear of Christ writing?'

Well, it sounded persuasive, and Bertrand, flattered by Taillefer's interest, was very taken with it at first. He even toyed with the idea of changing his name, as Taillefer had done. (Bertrand never found out what his real name was.) But, as 'Taillefer' meant 'the cutter of iron', he wondered how it would sound to call himself 'Tailleper' – *'tailler-peur'* – 'the cutter of fear'. A very necessary process in an audience of soldiers before a battle. But the mood passed.

Taillefer offered him several compliments too.

'You talk well; you have a good memory; you watch people and you are beginning to understand them. Like me, you do not relish responsibilities; you are slightly "driven". But you like an audience. I know; I have watched you. You are not a saint, and you are not a hero. Nor can you face being tied to the village cross or to the city street. You have no craft or skill. You have not the acquisitive instinct of the merchant. You do not look cut out to be a soldier. What else is there? You are a minstrel.'

'You have missed one – what about the cloister?'

Taillefer shook his head.

'No, my young friend. If you had that calling, you would have been there long before now.'

It hurt, but Taillefer was right.

So he – Bertrand de Montclos – was a minstrel. He was not happy with it; it was simply better than what he had had before. And he was stuck with it…

The door was flung open, and Arnaud came in,

looking very grumpy. Bertrand felt his heart sink. Arnaud slammed the door, tore off his coat, and helped himself to a mug of beer, almost from force of habit. The landlord, who had repented of his earlier madness, came in, aglow with the efforts of restoring his business, and asked a question with his eyebrows.

Arnaud waved a hand.

'All right, all right, Nic, I have not been robbing you. The money is in the box. Now, get us something to eat – if your wife has come to her senses too.'

Nicholas opened his mouth to argue, saw that Arnaud had turned away, and changed his mind.

'Kat! Kat! …Katherine!'

Arnaud licked his lips, drank a huge draught, and smacked the half-empty pot on the table. He was still frowning formidably.

Bertrand fidgeted.

'Well?'

Arnaud looked blankly at him, then let his face dissolve into a smile.

'Sorry, Bertrand; you did it to me. But I shall not keep you dangling any longer.'

He beamed with pleasure and self-satisfaction.

'It worked. It worked. Like a charm.'

Bertrand tried to suppress a colossal sigh. Livia's hands slipped away from his throat.

'Yes?'

'He broke into pieces. Grovelled like an animal. Screamed like a rat in torment.'

'So we have him.'

'Yes.'

'And Livia too?'

Arnaud hesitated, and subsided somewhat.

'Well, not exactly.'

Bertrand sat back. He had thought it was too good to be true.

'Suppose you tell me what happened.'

Arnaud emptied his mug, and wiped his lips with the back of his hand.

'I did exactly as you said. I had the two cages made. We took them up into the trees where you said.'

'Did Vico make a struggle?'

'No. He was right off balance. I caught him in the stable yard, before he could make contact with his mother. My two lads had him out of the gate and into the street before he knew what was happening. And when I said he was accused of murdering not Albert, but Lenore, he was dumbfounded. Completely bowled over. No resistance.'

Bertrand began to enjoy it – the relief.

'You see? Surprise – you can never beat it. The Guiscard, remember?'

'Yes. And then I thought of something that would improve your plan.'

'Oh?'

Arnaud fidgeted in the excitement of his own cleverness.

'I remembered that boy who helped you to bring Lenore back to *The Hawk*. After the sermon?'

'Yes, yes. Robert. I told you to use all your resources.'

'Yes. Well. Robert of Tournai. Hugh's boy.'

'Hugh himself would have been better. It was his wagon that they destroyed.'

Arnaud looked smug.

'I got him too. You are not the only one with bright ideas, Bertrand.'

'I am sure. Just tell me.'

'I found them easily enough. You should see the mess out there beyond the walls, Bertrand – '

'Get on with it!'

'Yes. Sorry. Well, I had another good idea.'

'Oh, really?'

'Yes – "oh, really". Remember that Vico had molested Lenore? Well, I told Robert that Vico had killed her too, and that we had arrested him for it. He was ours at once. I think if he had had a knife in his hand, he would have gone for him then and there.'

'So far, so good. What then?'

Arnaud frowned.

'I do not think you fully appreciate the point. Robert really believed me. He did not have to act; he convinced Vico that he was in earnest. Well, he was.'

Bertrand smiled.

'Rest assured, Arnaud; I "fully appreciate the point".'

Arnaud growled.

'Well, all right. Anyway, young Robert was so furious, I had to pull him off. Vico did little to defend himself. It was as if all the fight had been shaken out of him. Hugh gave him a wallop or two for good measure. By the time we had dragged him as far as the west gate, he was in a dreadful state. And no Livia to turn to.'

Bertrand grinned smugly.

'Arnaud, you are beginning to turn into quite a philosopher.'

'A philosopher?'

'Imagination and compulsion – an unstoppable combination. Well done.'

Arnaud frowned. Bertrand smiled.

'Never mind. And the boxes?'

'When he saw those, he got worse. He was baffled, you see.'

'Yes, I do see,' said Bertrand. 'It was my idea.'

Arnaud was too excited to notice the irony.

'Yes, yes. Anyway – I had a couple of my stable lads to do the business with the wood. Vico was still mystified when we pushed him into one of the cages. That creature is so stupid!'

'When did he realise?'

'When we pushed the second cage up against his, and pretended to open it and let out the cats.'

'Was that it?'

'No. But it was when we lit the fire at the other end, and my lads began to push both cages towards it. It was not a sight I should care to witness again, Bertrand – the collapse of a human soul. I have never seen such fear. You could barely watch. One of the stable boys vomited on the spot. So did Robert.'

Poor Robert – it was his destiny to heave up his stomach every time something dramatic happened.

'Do not waste any sympathy on Vico. He was quite prepared to help destroy the life of another human creature. So he confessed.'

'To having a row with Albert, yes.'

'It was not Simon who wanted to go, but Vico himself.'

'Yes.'

'And he stole red cloth from his mother.'

'Yes.'

'And he was after the same thing when Hugh caught him in his wagon.'

'Yes. And Hugh made sure of that.'

'And he asked Albert for his share of the money to fund him.'

257

'Yes.'

'And Albert refused.'

'Yes.'

'And there were high words.'

'Yes.'

'And Albert dropped dead at his feet.'

'Yes.'

'And he went straight and told his mother.'

'Yes.'

Bertrand lifted his shoulders in a great shrug of satisfaction.

'Good.'

Arnaud shook his head.

'Not so good as all that.'

Bertrand frowned.

'Do you not believe him?'

'Oh, yes, I believe him. When a man is in such extremities, he tells the truth. But he was not telling the whole truth.'

'Livia.'

'Yes. We practically destroyed Vico out there in the woods. We had him so unbalanced that for a while he really thought he was between two kinds of Hell – the fire and the cats – and that one of them was going to consume him. Possibly both. Incidentally, how did you know?'

'About the cats?'

'I watched. I saw. You must have seen the same thing hundreds of times.'

'Yes, I suppose I have. But – '

'Exactly, my friend. You see, but you do not observe. I knew a man once who was like that with frogs. Put him anywhere near a frog, and he would go almost insane. Imagine the effect of letting loose a swarm of frogs all over him. It was the same with Vico and cats.'

Arnaud did not look convinced.

'I would have said that. But then something interesting happened. Try as I might, he would confess no further. Afraid he may be of cats; afraid he may be of Hellfire. But I tell you, Bertrand, there is something that terrifies him even more.'

'His mother.'

'Exactly. He would give away nothing more, no matter what I said. *He would not implicate her.* The spells, the witch-craft – the minute I brought Livia's name into it, he began to come back to his senses. He was still shouting and weeping, but it was different somehow.

'By that time the best of the fire was fading, and it would have taken time to gather more dead wood. The moment had passed. My constables offered to drag him out and rough him up – apparently he once pissed into their beer – but I knew that would be no use. Hugh and Robert offered to do even more. Still no use.

'I tried the cats again. I even let one loose into his cage with him. But he kicked out in panic and quite by chance broke its neck. It gave him back some confidence. He seemed to know, almost by instinct, that I had fired my shaft, and there was nothing more in the quiver. So – nothing more would he say.'

'Did you try him on the Limper?'

'Yes. I did that too. He confessed at once. No arguments. No wriggling.'

Bertrand tensed.

'Like the other confessions?'

Arnaud looked puzzled.

'No. That is the odd thing. He had partially recovered himself by that time, as I said. There were no tears and breast-beatings. He simply said "yes, I did it".'

Arnaud looked fixedly into his friend's eyes.

'And do you know what, Bertrand? I would swear he did not.'

'Of course not. He is protecting her.'

Arnaud stared.

'Holy Virgin! Do you mean Livia – that she – *with an axe?*'

'Look at those hands, Arnaud. She could have strangled him if she had wanted.'

'But Bertrand! *An axe!*'

'I do not say she attacked him with it – no. Vico probably did that, with his pitchfork. Just as he had nearly done the first time, when all those soldiers arrived together. We agree that he is perfectly capable of it. The soldiers obviously thought so, or they would not have gone away. Perhaps he killed him; perhaps he crippled him; I could not say.'

'But if he was already dead, why cut his head off?'

'Because he could not be hidden. It was Albert all over again. There they were, with a dead man – or a dying one – at their feet. What were they to do? In Albert's case, they wanted a body to prove something. But they could not blame this on Simon; he is cooped up at St. Fulbert's. They could not blame it on Lenore; she is dead. And there were the marks of Vico's fork all over him.'

'And Vico did not have the imagination.'

'Vico did not have the imagination. So – who?'

Arnaud sighed.

'Obvious, when you put it like that.'

'Livia decided that it was impossible to hide a body, or to move it without anybody noticing. They would have to compromise. The head was what identified him, and she could easily move a head.'

'The great bag.'

'Yes – the great bag. And she could put it – the head, that is – wherever she liked.'

'Underneath Hugh of Tournai's wagon.'

'Yes.'

Arnaud laughed without mirth.

'I wish I could have told that to Hugh; he would have beaten him up even more. Might have got something else out of him.'

He mused for a minute, then shuddered.

'To bend over a man, and calmly decapitate him. In the heat of battle, maybe, when you are staring mad or crazed with fear – but in cold blood. And he might not even have been dead.'

Arnaud crossed himself. Bertrand leaned forward.

'Arnaud, have you never seen a housewife like Livia slaughter a pig?'

'I have never seen a housewife like Livia – and that is that.'

Bertrand waited quietly for the next question.

'What did they do with the rest of him then?'

'Now think, Arnaud. You have just killed a man. You are in a stable yard. What is Vico usually doing with his pitchfork when he is not shoving it into soldiers' insides?'

'The midden!'

Bertrand sat back.

'There you are then.'

'How do you know?'

'I do not know for sure. But answer me this – has anybody else reported a headless body from wall to wall of Clermont? And can you imagine anybody moving a body through the streets and out into the fields or the forest without somebody noticing?'

'They moved Scarface, and they moved the Jew.'

'For all we know, both of them may well have been *alive* when they were taken out of the city. If I were going to kill either of them, I would have done it that way. Much easier. Besides, that was a small crowd each time. And nobody was going to be concerned about a whining deserter or a wailing Jew. But a woman and a man alone, struggling with a single body – with no head? Both of them known to one and all? Impossible.'

Arnaud nodded.

'Makes sense, I suppose.'

Bertrand smiled slyly.

'And I have been cheating; I do have evidence – well, a little.'

He paused. Arnaud sniffed.

'Come on then. Out with it.'

'After you had taken Vico, I had a good look round the stable yard.'

'Why?'

'Because I had noticed that Vico was very touchy about me being near the midden. His behaviour was not natural.'

'Could have been simply bad humour.'

'Could have been. I noticed, though, that he did not look anxious when he shooed me away from the barrel house – just mean as usual. But when we were near the midden – totally different. There was something else too. It was as if he could not leave the midden alone. He was forever patting the sides down, plugging gaps, making the shape perfect. Like a child with a mud pie. You do not do that with middens.'

'Vico was a bit soft in the head.'

'Want some more evidence? I had a look at his pitch-fork. There were stains on the tines.'

'With what he is usually picking up, hardly surprising.'

'I agree. So I had a look at the handle.'

'And?'

'Stains. I could not be absolutely sure, but I would say blood. Certainly recent.'

'What about the axe?'

'No stains. Livia would have had the sense to wash them off.'

Arnaud went through some hard thinking.

'So what do we do now? Release Vico on the charge of killing Lenore, and arrest him again for killing the Limper? Dig out the midden? Arrest Livia?'

'No. Let him go. Leave her alone. The midden can wait. There is a body there, Arnaud, as plain as if I saw it. And, frankly, in the state it must be in, I would rather not see it.'

'Livia will think they have got away with it.'

'No. Livia is much more clever than that. She now knows that we know a great deal. She will find out what we did to Vico, rest assured, from Vico himself if from nobody else. That will slow them down for a while. That gives us time.'

'Time?'

'Time to rescue Simon.'

'But you said he is safe at St. Fulbert's.'

'So he is – until or unless Livia can conjure up a mob. And we must not only save Simon's life, but save *The Hawk* for him.'

Arnaud spread his hands.

'We have no idea if there is a will. Nobody has found one yet. And whether there is or not, Simon says he does not want it.'

Bertrand shook his head in impatience.

'Oh, Arnaud, you know the boy does not know his own mind. And whether he wants to be an innkeeper or not, he is entitled to the property. He has the right to dispose of it. Do you want it to go by default to the other two – after what they have done?'

Arnaud looked keenly at him.

'Why should you care? You have explained Albert's death. What else do you owe him? What do you owe Simon? He is the one who should be indebted to you.'

Bertrand looked a little embarrassed.

'At the risk of sounding pious, I was unable to fulfil my father's wishes. I should like to be able to see to the fulfilment of another fond father's wishes.'

'How do we know what those wishes were?'

'I know.'

Arnaud pursed his lips.

'Bertrand, I have seen that look before. What have you been keeping back? If you have sent me all the way out there – '

'No, my friend. That, I assure you, was necessary. Now, armed with the success you have so shrewdly won, we can proceed further.'

'Why did you not tell me before?'

'Because this whole business, as I said, has been, on the whole, not a matter of evidence, but a matter of opportunity and timing.'

'Well?'

'Now – the time is right.'

'What for?'

'To tell you about a man I met.'
'What man?'
'The Prior of St. Fulbert's.'

* * * * * *

Fourteen

'**AH! I WONDERED** where you had got to.'

Arnaud shuffled up to allow Bertrand to get into the front of the crowd. Sparks and flames leapt into the crisp winter sky. They warmed themselves for a while without speaking, gazing at the circle of glowing faces.

'You see?' said Bertrand at length. 'Force of habit. They stay for the midwinter bonfire.'

Arnaud agreed.

'Yes, I am pleased to say some of them are coming to their senses. But a lot are still pretty crazed, and doing daft things.'

'Be grateful that some at least prefer the reassurance of *familiar* things. Let God take care of those who are beyond reason.'

'It is not that they are beyond reason; it is that they are beyond common sense. God might protect them if they are mad; it is unfair to expect Him to protect them if they are stupid.'

'You said they were all mad.'

'No. I said *some* were mad, and I said *some* were coming to their senses. But there are many others who should know better.'

'Even if their hopes are stronger than their experience?'

Arnaud stooped, picked up a faggot that had fallen from the pile, and tossed it back into the flames.

'Yes, if you like. I can sympathise, but I do not approve. To set off now, in the depths of winter, on a journey to

266

who knows where. Oh, yes – I know what you are going to say: they are looking for land as well as salvation.'

'You told me yourself that land was getting short round here.'

'It is. But who is to say that it is not short everywhere else? Do they honestly think that some obliging Turk somewhere will give them some? Or sell them some?'

'No. They will kill him and take it.'

'Exactly. And none of these bumpkins has any idea what that entails. We know what war is, Bertrand; they do not.'

A knot of men lifted an effigy on a long pole. Sparks soared and span round its grinning, bouncing mask of a face, lurid against the night sky. Arnaud inclined his head towards it.

'See what I mean? That – that is supposed to be a Turk or a Saracen. Or a Jew. Pitiful.'

'Harmless enough. There are no Turks or Saracens here.'

Arnaud grunted.

'Try telling that to the families of the dead Jews.'

He turned away, and beckoned to Bertrand to follow him.

'Come and have some supper.'

* * * * * *

Arnaud bestowed a fond but absent pat on the rump of the serving girl as she turned away from the table.

'Thank you, my lovely.'

He turned to Bertrand.

'Well? You saw him?'

'Yes.'

'You told him?'

'Yes. He was dumbfounded.'

'Did he believe you?'

'He did when the Prior showed him the will, and pointed out the relevant parts.'

'Simon can not read or write.'

'No. Neither could Albert. But Simon could recognise his father's mark. Anyway he believed the Prior. It was too outrageous to have been made up. And what possible reason could the Prior have for lying to him, when all Simon had to do was get it checked by the Bishop's clerks?'

'What did he say?'

'Not much. I told you – he was dumbfounded.'

'Did he mind?'

'No. He seemed – well, almost pleased. Do you know what I think, Arnaud?'

Arnaud pulled the stalk out of a pear.

'No. What?'

'I think he is so impressed with what his father has done. Just think, Arnaud. Albert, by the simple device of making over the inn to St. Fulbert's – '

' – on condition that it – '

'Yes, yes. By doing that, Albert has, at one stroke, provided for his son, prevented him from disposing of *The Hawk* on an immature whim, scotched the plans and plots of his shrew of a wife, and cut out his monster of a stepson. It is brilliant. And did I tell you that he had also persuaded the abbey to advance him some money for his expenses on Crusade? They would get it back by charging Simon a nominal rent for the duration of the lease. After it expires, he would pay nothing.'

'Ah – so Brother William will still have an excuse for coming to test the stew.'

They chuckled.

'Simon, as I say, is so impressed with this that he has regained respect for his father almost in one instant. You see? Albert was put upon, and he was beleaguered, but – I have said it before and I say it again – he was no fool.'

Arnaud frowned.

'Maybe so. But why, if the will existed, did the Prior say nothing about it before now?'

Bertrand answered without hesitation.

'Because the Prior is no fool either. He did not know whether Simon was guilty of murder. He did not even know whether Albert had *been* murdered or not. If he came out into the open straight away, he might have prejudiced the investigation. With Simon under suspicion, Livia would have put in her claim, and he might have been forced to declare in her favour, and he does not like Livia any more than you do. He knows about her from the Tub. Now – with Simon under his own roof and officially innocent, he can show his hand.'

'Albert's hand.'

'Yes, if you like. And I have no doubt it gave him a great deal of satisfaction. He has helped Albert to outwit the lot of them. He had even provided for Lenore as well – in the sister house of St. Fulbert's near Limoges. He had arranged it with one of the Pope's chaplains. They were going to finalise the details while Urban kept Christmas there.'

Arnaud sighed.

'Not necessary now – sadly.'

'No,' said Bertrand. 'But masses for her soul will be. That is where the money will go instead.'

'So in a sense he will still have provided for her.'

'Yes. I like to think Albert will be gratified at that.'

Arnaud made a face.

'The only thing he could not do was provide against his own sudden death. Poor fellow.'

Bertrand wiped his mouth.

'I think he did. I think he guessed that something like this might happen. Perhaps he had had some kind of warning attack. He tried to tell me things, you know, but he could never bring himself to say everything that was in his mind. There is something else too.'

'Oh?'

'Now that Albert is dead, he will not need the loan for his journey. So Simon can have that as well.'

'Or he can spend it on masses for his father.'

'At least he will have the choice.'

'Is Simon grateful for all this?'

'I doubt it. That young man is still rather busy being sorry for himself. So it was then that I sprang it on him.'

'What we agreed.'

'Yes. I called his bluff.'

'What then?'

'He took some time to understand the implications of it all. But he agreed in the end.'

Arnaud grunted.

'Just as well.'

Bertrand stared.

'You mean you have told them already?'

'You are not the only one who can spring surprises, my friend. You see, I have great faith in you.' Arnaud grinned. 'You should have seen the look on Livia's face.'

'How could you be so sure that Simon would agree?'

'Bah! He had no choice. The thought of revenge would have been irresistible. Am I right?'

Bertrand grinned too.

'Yes, you are. Tell me.'

'Well, I remembered what you said about driving a wedge. Luckily, Vico was still in a bad way from our previous little – er – subterfuge. I think he was ready to believe almost anything. When I told him that his mother had no intention of letting him go on Crusade, that she only promised to help him go if he peddled the lies about Simon and the spells and so on, he began to see that she had simply used him. As she had used Simon, as she had used Albert's death –

' – as she had used the madness, as she had used the mob against Hugh and the Jew – '

' – as she had used everything.'

'How did you prove it?'

'No need. Vico took one look at his mother's face. If she had denied it, I would have been in trouble. But she was so furious with me that she could not. You see, Bertrand? I am becoming something of a philosopher after all.'

'You are indeed, my friend. I take it you made clear the conditions?'

'Oh, yes. That was the part I enjoyed most. "Livia," I said, "Simon is not a vindictive boy, and he does not wish your ruin. Nor does he wish to continue with *The Hawk*. So he will make over the lease to you." '

Arnaud paused to shake his head in surprise at his own story.

'And do you know? She began to smile. Yes. What a woman! I thought, "I shall soon take the smile off your face." I said, "You will hold the inn from the abbey, and you will pay rent for as long as it takes to redeem the debt that you will owe on Simon's behalf. And for his expenses for entry into St. Fulbert's." '

Bertrand fidgeted.

'You are forgetting – '

'No, I am not. I said, "It is, moreover, conditional upon your good behaviour. There will be no more talk of murder, or of spells, or of witchcraft, or of poison, or indeed of anything which casts any aspersion whatever on Simon's character. One whisper out of place, or one default in payment of rent, and the abbey foreclose, and you and Vico are out. Is that understood?" '

'Is it?'

'Oh, yes, it is understood. I am not sure that Vico got the finer points, but Livia certainly did.'

'Did that take the smile off her face?'

'No.' Arnaud shook his head again. 'It is impossible to get at that woman.'

'Hardly surprising. She has got what she wanted. What she has plotted and schemed for ever since she met Albert.'

'But the lies, Bertrand. She would have sat there and watched Simon go to his death.'

'Just like those wives in Apulia, my friend. You and I have both seen them. Round the scaffold itself – angels of death.'

'Those harpies were just watching. Livia would have actually put him there.'

'Simon was not her own son. He was in her way.'

'Vico *is* her own son. And she lied *to* him, if not *about* him. She lied to him to make him tell lies in his turn.'

'Means to an end. From which she has never deviated. One has to admire her single-mindedness, if nothing else.'

Arnaud shook his head.

'And she would have taken over *The Hawk* as if nothing had happened.'

'The case against her is too weak. It is not susceptible even to the ordeal. Alas, Arnaud, she has committed no provable crime. Unfortunately, you can punish people only for what they do; it is God alone who can punish them for what they are.'

Arnaud swore under his breath.

'So unfair. I feel so helpless.'

'Do not blame yourself, Arnaud. You have done your duty. You are the enforcer of the law; you are not the bringer of justice.'

Arnaud growled, unconvinced. Bertrand patted him on the arm.

'You have done a great deal. You have saved a young man from a mob hanging. You have seen to it that a desperate innkeeper has had his wishes fulfilled. You have prevented his shrew of a wife and his animal of a stepson from stirring up evil. Not a bad day's work for a busy mayor.'

'What happens at the end of the lease?'

'That is up to Simon. Whatever he decides, he will have the whip hand.'

Arnaud grunted.

'Unless they find another dead body they can lay at his door.'

Bertrand grinned.

'Then we come back and stop them all over again. How is that for planning for the future? Come on, Arnaud. You can not stop up every loophole in the wall. Be content. We have done well.'

'I suppose so.'

Arnaud heaved a huge sigh. Then a thought struck him.

'What is to stop him going by himself?'

'Who?'

'Vico. What is to stop him going by himself?'

'Money. He has none.'

'What about the gold they stole from Scarface when he was hung?'

'We do not know Scarface had any gold left on him when he died. We do not know if Livia and Vico got their dirty hands on it. And even if they did, can you see Livia letting him have any of it? I tell you, she used him.'

Arnaud nodded glumly.

'I suppose you are right. God! To do all that, suffer all that, and get nothing at the end. Poor old Vico.'

'Serve him right.'

'He will surely hate his mother.'

'His worry, not ours. Or Simon's.'

'Surely it will make him all the more determined to go. Money or no money. Like all the other madmen. What about all those silly old women?'

'Arnaud, they go in company. With people who are like them, who understand them. Who is Vico's friend? What trade does he have which puts him in a fellowship? Hugh of Tournai goes to ply his trade among other things. Robert goes with him. For company he has his master and his memories of Lenore.

'What does Vico have? What is Vico? A listener at knot-holes. A cheat.'

'A block of wood. A viper.'

'If such a combination is possible. Who understands him? Who would be his travelling companion, ready to trust him? What is the only company he has had all his life? Exactly.'

'He wanted to go. He asked Albert for his share.'

'He *thought* he wanted to go. But if it had come to it… Even people like Vico need somebody. He is only half a human without his mother.'

Arnaud looked thoughtful.

'So you think he would never have actually done it – gone on crusade?'

'Since you ask – no.'

'Like you and being a cleric?'

Bertrand winced.

'Ah, a painful one, Arnaud. But, yes, like me. Maybe I have learned a little wisdom. Vico has not. He will be baffled, and he will be furious. And he will blame his mother. In his eyes, she stole not only his chance to get away, but his chance to save his immortal soul. She has robbed him of his passage to Heaven. He will hate her for the rest of his life. Deep devotion will turn overnight into the opposite – deep, inexpressible fury.'

'And she will realise that.'

'Oh, yes. Livia, like Albert, is intelligent. She will know he hates her, and he will live in the knowledge that she used him. That he does not come first any more – if he did at all.'

'And they will both have the reminder every month of how stupid old Albert outwitted them, when Brother William comes for the rent – for their own house.'

Arnaud mused for a while.

'You know? I almost feel sorry for Vico – having to live for ever with a cat that stifles and revolts him and a mother who has in effect locked him up for good. He has nobody he can take it out on any more. And he can do nothing about it.'

'As I said, serve him right. Remember what he had been trying to do. Remember he stole Lenore's food. Remember – '

Arnaud held up a hand.

'Yes, yes, all right. I know. But suppose – suppose – '

Arnaud hesitated.

'Speak up,' said Bertrand. 'Suppose what?'

Arnaud smiled wryly.

'I am about to be the philosopher again. Suppose Vico takes it into his head to try and betray his mother.'

'How?'

'By saying how she had killed the Limper.'

Bertrand shook his head emphatically.

'Never. He has not a shred of proof. She would run rings round him. Poor Vico is not very bright, but he is bright enough to know that his mother is much brighter than he is. He saw her with Albert enough times.'

'Well then, suppose *she* tries to betray *him*.'

'She would have no reason. She wants Vico as her tame horse. He is the only creature she can trust. God knows – she schemed enough to get him in that position.'

Arnaud persisted.

'Well then, suppose we come in and dig out the midden. What will they say to that?'

Bertrand shook his head again.

'We can prove nothing either. It will smell, in every sense of the word, but it will not be proof. And even if we did convict them, who would look after *The Hawk* for the coming years, while Simon is making up his mind? No – let them get on with it. It is the best protection of his property that Simon could have.'

'But the Limper. What about him?'

'He will keep. All the time he lies there, Livia knows he is there, and she knows we know he is there. And she can do nothing about it. If she and Vico move to take the midden to pieces, they convict themselves. One of your constables would know within hours.'

Arnaud savoured the thought, and grinned.

'So they are stuck with each other, they must keep their

mouths shut, and they must get on with it. Till Simon decides – when the lease runs out.'

Bertrand nodded.

'And all the time that body rots in the midden outside their back door.'

Arnaud poured some more wine.

'You know, old friend, perhaps there is some justice after all.'

*   *   *   *   *   *

'Kat. Kat! Katherine?'

A distant voice shouted something unintelligible. Nicholas raised his voice again.

'The soup… I said the soup! They are ready.'

'And the pork,' said Bertrand. 'Tell her to put the gravy on the pork. We shall get through the soup soon enough.'

Nicholas grinned.

'Greedy beggar!'

Bertrand raised innocent eyebrows, and pretended to misunderstand.

'Beggar indeed. I am paying handsomely for all this, and well you know it. Nothing but the best for my friend the Mayor.'

Arnaud laughed.

'About time too. You have eaten from my table often enough in the last three weeks.'

Bertrand tucked a kerchief round his neck and began to crumble some bread.

'Well, now I am making up for it. Besides, you will need a good meal inside you for what I am going to tell you… '

Arnaud refilled their mugs and sat back against the wall.

'Well, I am listening.'

Bertrand tugged some strips of crackling between his teeth to clean off the last of the fat.

'Is it true that Robert of Normandy is going on Crusade?'

'There are rumours. Have been for weeks. Getting stronger now. One or two Normans have drifted through already.'

'And you have no doubt picked their brains. What else is in the air?'

'Stephen of Blois is interested.'

'The one who is married to the Bastard's daughter?'

'Yes. The story has it that she is the one who is making him go. She is a dreadful character, you know. A true daughter of William.'

Bertrand licked his lips.

'Poor devil.'

'Urban has fixed an official date for departure. August. The Feast of the Assumption.'

'That is months away. It is not even spring yet.'

'No. But Raymond is gathering men already around Toulouse.'

'I know.'

Arnaud narrowed his eyes.

'Come on, come on – out with it. I know you. You are almost bursting with a secret. And you have been fending me off quite long enough.'

Bertrand wiped his fingers on the last of his bread.

'Very well. Simon will not be staying in St. Fulbert's.'

Arnaud made a small noise of surprise.

'I naturally assumed – "

'It never pays to assume anything with a young man like that. He changes his feelings with the wind.'

'No calling for it, eh?'

'I never thought he had. Not yet, anyway.'

'What is that supposed to mean?'

'He is a likely lad, Arnaud. But he has to know what he wants first. At the moment he is casting about for anything which will make his mind stop spinning. When it does, it may well be that he will have the calling. He might even make a scholar.'

'Like you?'

Bertrand shook his head.

'No, Arnaud. Not like me. This boy really could have it. At any rate he should be given the chance.'

'I should have thought the best way to do that was to leave him in St. Fulbert's.'

'No. Sooner or later he would have come to see it as captivity. Captivity is no way towards a vocation. He must come to it after trying everything else and finding it no use. The true calling is when you honestly can not think of a better way. When there is no alternative.'

'Like you?'

Bertrand smiled.

'You do not give up easily, do you? As for me, I have no idea. We shall see.'

It was Arnaud's turn to smile.

'And Bertrand de Montclos is the guardian who has shown this young man the way.'

'All I have done is to point out the obvious to him. There is nothing for him at *The Hawk*, and he does not want it anyway.'

'But he knows that Livia and Vico will keep it running.'

'Yes. But I do not think he sees the full significance of the advantage to him. He is just not interested.'

'Silly boy.'

'No, Arnaud. Not a silly boy – just a boy. He will come

to understanding one of these days. Did you have much sense at his age? I know I did not.'

Arnaud growled.

'He should appreciate properly what you have done.'

'What *we* have done. Give him time; he will. Right now he does not want *The Hawk* and he does not want anything at St. Fulbert's either. He has access to funds to enable him to do whatever he decides – '

'But if he does not know – '

' – and in my experience, when you have no idea what to do, the best solution is to go on a long journey. By the time you are half way there – wherever it is you are going – you have forgotten the problems you left behind. By the time you come back, you already know what to do next. It will have become as clear as a drop of dew.'

Arnaud widened his eyes.

'You are letting that boy go off on Crusade?'

'Why not? Robert of Tournai is going. He is about the same age – even younger.'

'Robert of Tournai has his master with him. And Hugh has done a deal with the bishop. They have – resources.'

'So has Simon – the remains of his father's loan from St. Fulbert's.'

'Suppose he spends it on masses for his father – you know, as we said.'

'He already has.'

'Well then.'

Bertrand smiled.

'I am afraid, old friend, there is something else I have not yet told you.'

Arnaud swore.

'I knew it; I knew it! That look on your face. It is still there.'

Bertrand raised a pacific hand.

'All right, all right. As always, it is a question of timing.'

Arnaud folded his arms and set his face into stone.

'Well? Is the time right now? Am I to be – privileged to know?'

Bertrand smiled again.

'Of course. Remember when I told you I had spent a while looking round the stable yard? And the midden? Just before I left?'

'Yes.'

'Well, I had a look inside Albert's barrel house too. Remember it was his private place, his retreat, his place of rest.'

'You said you had looked there before.'

'Yes. That was when I thought Albert might have hidden poison. I had a second look. And I had a second think too. Livia never went there – well, not that I could ever see. Albert talked to me there.'

'So what? We have discussed all this.'

'Patience, my friend. I saw Albert in his barrel house. He was himself there. He was not the Albert you saw with the customers. I reasoned that, if Albert kept any secrets, he would have kept them there.'

'You looked; you told me. No poison.'

'I was not looking for poison this time.'

'What did you do? Say a prayer to Albert and wait for him to come down and show you?'

'No,' said Bertrand evenly. 'I put myself in Albert's position, and asked myself – where would I keep secrets in there?'

'In the barrels – there is nothing else.'

'Possible, but unlikely. Besides, I looked before. This time I realised that it was not necessary. If Albert had hidden something inside a barrel, Vico would have noticed it sooner or later. He was always changing them over. He is a worker, remember?'

Arnaud shrugged dismissively.

'There is nowhere else.'

'Oh, yes there is. The walls.'

Arnaud stared.

'You could not pull the whole place to pieces.'

Bertrand shook his head.

'No need. You do not start with a chisel, but with imagination.'

'Well?'

'Remember – I said to myself, what would Albert do?'

'So?'

'So – I moved the cat's box.'

Arnaud's lips tightened.

'No more games, Bertrand, please.'

'I am serious. Thomas the cat slept in the barrel house. At any rate, his box was there, against a wall. Now Vico hates cats. If you wanted to keep him away, where would you hide something?'

'Aaahh!'

Bertrand smiled.

'I see light is dawning. Behind that box the largest stone was loose. After a little work with a knife, it came out quite easily. And inside – '

He paused with a story-teller's instinct for drama. Arnaud rose to the bait.

'Yes?'

' – was a box. A wooden box. And inside the box – '

'Bertrand!'

'All right. Inside the box was a bag of silver. Albert had been putting money away for what looks like quite a long time.'

They looked at each other. Arnaud at length shook his head.

'Clever old Albert.'

'Clever old Albert. Simon will have enough money to take him to Jerusalem, if he is careful – there and back.'

Arnaud returned to practicalities, where he felt safer.

'Very well – Simon has the money. But money can *bring* danger, not help you to avoid it. What other protection does he have?'

'He will have what every other crusader will have. He will have his safe conduct to Heaven, where he will find his beloved Lenore and her Blessed Saint Margaret. On his way there, he may even come across poor old Albert. Just as Albert wanted to take his Hedi with *him*.'

Arnaud gestured with impatience.

'Bertrand, be sensible. We are not talking about the road to Paradise; we are talking about the road to Jerusalem. Dreams and saints and popes' promises – even a long pocket – will not protect you half way across the Great St. Bernard. Or when a squadron of Magyar cavalry are charging towards you. Or when a Turk creeps up behind you in a dark street in Greece. What will that boy have?'

Bertrand paused as if this were the moment he had been working up to.

'Me.'

Arnaud almost dropped his empty mug.

'What?'

'Me.'

Arnaud continued staring.

'But you said it was madness.'

'No. *You* did. Perhaps it is. But where have reason and sanity got us in the last few years? Flood, famine, drought, pestilence – you said so yourself. And have reason and sanity kept the Holy Land out of the clutches of the Turks? Perhaps it is time for a little madness. It is certainly worth trying. We shall be no worse off.'

Arnaud almost spluttered.

'But – but – you are not cut out for it. You admitted it. You knew it years ago.'

Bertrand looked intently at his friend.

'Not cut out for Paradise? Anyone is cut out for that, according to Our Lord.'

'For *being* there, yes; not for *getting* there. Not this way. You are not fit for that sort of journey.'

'I am tired, Arnaud. I am getting old. I am tired of putting magic and wonders and hopes and longings into men's eyes. I want those things in my own heart. No longer do I want to point the way; I want to go on the journey myself. Whatever awaits me on that journey, I am ready for it. Look.'

Bertrand pulled back the flap of his jerkin, and revealed a small cross of red material stitched on his breast. Arnaud leaned forward and peered. It was fine cloth.

'Where did you get that? It is good stuff.'

'Hugh of Tournai. He has re-stocked.'

Arnaud grunted.

'Trust a merchant to profit from any situation.'

'A merchant is a merchant. You can not condemn a man for plying his trade. He sold a bolt of it to St. Fulbert's. Ten of the hands there are going. They made one for Simon too.'

Arnaud shook his head.

'Three weeks ago, at a word from Livia, they would have strung him up.'

'But they did not. God protected him then. Why

should He not protect us now? And later? We have a great chance. Let us take a shaft from Livia's armoury – let us use an opportunity. I have said all along – it is not about brains and evidence and sense; it is about opportunity and timing.'

Arnaud lifted his shoulders and let them fall again as if they were a great weight.

'There is nothing I can say, is there?'

'Except "Yes". Why not come with us?'

Very slowly, Arnaud poured himself yet another drink.

'Bertrand, if you had asked me to go with you into a dark street at night, a witch's cave, a battle, even an ambush, I would have done so without hesitation. But this…'

'Not even for salvation?'

'I do not see my road lying in that direction. You – so you say – are still looking for your Holy Grail. I have found mine.'

He waved a hand to embrace their surroundings.

'This – this is my lot. My ration. I can reasonably hope for no other. If I do, I am being unfair with God. I should be hoping for too much.'

Bertrand waved his hand too.

'This – Clermont – satisfies you?'

'Who can hope for satisfaction in this world? It is all that I dare hope for, after what I have done over the years. If I were to go anywhere – ' he paused a moment ' – I should go back to Normandy. I hear that Duke Robert wants to pawn it to raise funds. So things should be better there. If a lot of knights go with him and do not come back, there will be land and widows for the picking.'

'There will be here.'

'Yes, but not Norman. Once a Norman… I tried going

native in Italy, and look what happened. Never again.'

'You had a good wife and good children. It was the Saracens who took them away.'

Arnaud lowered his head.

'I do not need you to tell me that.'

'Well then.'

Arnaud lifted his head again.

'Would you have me do what Albert did? Take another wife and stepchildren? When I have no children of my own who need caring for?' His face relaxed into one or two amused creases. 'You would not wish another Livia on me, would you?'

Bertrand smiled drily.

'You seem happy enough, it is true, with your dumpy little Bertha from the kitchen.'

Arnaud grinned.

'Mind your own business.'

Bertrand changed direction.

'You mentioned Italy. What about young Richard and Aimery? They would have been grown men by now. You still suffer, and you can not make me think otherwise. I am your friend; I know. You could pay back the Saracens – get it out of your mind.'

Arnaud shook his head.

'They will never leave my mind. I see them there, every day. And I do not believe in revenge; it achieves nothing. Like making love, it is a rage only, and when it is over, you feel empty. Besides, if I were to kill a thousand infidels, it would not bring them back. If it did, I would follow you into the jaws of Hell itself. Nay, I would lead you there.'

Bertrand sat back.

'So be it. *Deus le volt.*'

Arnaud looked at him in wonder.

'I never thought I should see the day.'

'Nor I, old friend. Believe me, I am just as surprised as you are. Here, try this cheese. You might as well; I shall not be treating you to much more for a long time.'

Arnaud cleaned his knife and took a large slice.

'Be careful, eh?'

Bertrand patted his wrist.

'I shall, I shall.'

He took a slice himself and began chewing.

'What if Livia should find a way of stirring things up again? I should never underestimate that woman, you know.'

Arnaud smiled.

'I have beaten you to it. I have beaten Livia to it. I have beaten her at her own game. I have started a rumour.'

'Oh?'

'About Albert. You remember those soldiers that Vico turned away from *The Hawk* just before you arrived?'

'The ones who threatened to burn the place down.'

'Yes. The Saracens.'

Bertrand stared.

'The what?'

'The Saracens.'

'Who said?'

'I did.'

'How do you know?'

Arnaud looked mysterious.

'Oh – a mayor knows these things. I dealt with one of them, remember? The bag of gold? They may not have *looked* like Saracens, but take it from me; they were. They came back and killed Albert in revenge, with some devilish oriental poison of their own. I think it was very clever of me to find out.'

'Yes. Very.'

'Why not? Those soldiers killed their own traitor. They could easily have killed Albert. One of them swore vengeance – remember?'

'No proof.'

Arnaud shrugged.

'No proof that they did not. It comes down to the same thing. Proof has been remarkably absent from this whole business.'

Bertrand was forced to agree. Arnaud swept on.

'Timing and opportunity. Livia used the opportunity that a city gone mad would believe anything – about infidels, Jews, whatever you like. I have done the same thing with Saracens. What is important is not what is true, or what is provable, but what people *think* to be true.'

'Or can be persuaded to think is true.'

'If you like.'

Bertrand laughed.

'You stinking liar. You are as bad as Vico.'

Arnaud laid a finger beside his nose.

'Ah, but mine was in a good cause. People will believe anything about infidels because they want to believe it. The scapegoat again, you see. Livia can hardly object to my using her own methods. And it will rally support for Vico for being so brave when he saw them off in the first place. They can not deny it and say "oh, it is not true that they killed Albert because we killed one of them ourselves and hid his body in the midden", without convicting themselves. We have trapped them again.'

'Does the city believe you?'

'Of course. There are none of those soldiers left to deny it. You buried one in the woods. Vico buried another – well, most of him. The rest have long gone. By now they

288

will be in Spain – ' he chuckled ' – probably fighting the Moors.'

'You are quite shameless,' said Bertrand.

'Totally. Our little father from Rome – His Holiness himself – told us that killing – *killing* – is to be allowed if it is to remove infidels. Normally a mortal sin. But a mortal sin no longer if it means fewer Moslems. I am sure that the Almighty will allow a little venial lie if it is to blow away the last wisps of the smoke of witchcraft from the safety of an innocent man.'

They sat for a while in the silence of long friendship.

'When will you leave?'

'Tomorrow. I see no point in further delay. The roads are good. We should get to Toulouse in about a week.'

There was another silence, broken at last by Arnaud.

'Can you not hear her, Bertrand? "We shall do well, Ludi. Just you and I." '

Bertrand took up the idea.

' "Thomas will catch lots of rats, and you can burn them. In the fire in the yard. Lots of flames, Ludi." '

' "It will be all for the best, Ludi. It is God's Will." '

' " *Deus le volt.*" '

* * * * * *

It did not seem so simple – or so funny – in the middle of a cold morning. Bertrand had slept awkwardly, and one of his legs ached abominably. Tristan was in a bad mood, and was no company. Suddenly even the journey to St. Fulbert's to pick up Simon seemed a chore.

He stroked the bright new kerchief that he had bought from Hugh of Tournai, who, by some miracle, had completed the re-stocking of his new wagon. He patted the scabbard of a handsome dagger that Arnaud had given him. Bertrand recalled a favourite saying of his father's: 'If a man has one friend, he is rich.'

As he re-lived his last dinner with his friend, resolution began to return…

'I am going somewhere, Arnaud, and not just to the next town.'

Taillefer had in effect said the same thing, all those years ago when he had decided to sail with the Bastard on his reckless adventure to England…

'I am old and I am ill. All my life I have watched people do things, or told them about other people doing things. For once I want to do something myself.'

And he did. He died leading a charge at Senlac, and he became immortal. Bertrand himself had told stories about him…

It did not impress Arnaud.

'That may be well for you. I want to die in my bed.'

'You have become an old woman; I want to die an old man…'

It was unkind, and Bertrand regretted it. It was too late now to go back. If he had, Arnaud would have sworn at him and told him not to be so stupid. As it was, he had been close to tears.

Bertrand drew level with *The Hawk*. Two men were gossiping. One of them was the young constable, on his way to a tour of duty at the west gate. He nodded as he went off, picking a course between the frozen cow pats. The other was Brother William. Bertrand watched him dismounting from his sagging mule, and took some pleasure from the fact that he made even heavier weather of it than himself.

By the angels, was it time for the rent already? That brought a smile to Bertrand's lips. He pictured the Tub sitting eagerly with a huge kerchief round his neck, as a silent Livia tipped some soup into the bowl before him. No stream of conversation this time. She would simply grope in her apron for a chunk of dark bread. Would Thomas be hovering for scraps?

A familiar noise came to his ears.

On a sudden whim, he turned Tristan about under the creaking inn sign, and made his way down the alley to the stable yard. No, he was not mistaken.

There was the fire; there were the cages. One was bigger than the rest. Unearthly shrieks cut the frosty day in two. Vico crouched and gazed into the flames. The cheekbones shone red and the lips were retracted in the familiar grimace of concentration and delight.

A new noise – an agonised yowl – rent the air.

Vico bent further. Bertrand could have sworn he could see his eyes glowing even at that distance. Vico seized his pitchfork, and stabbed with savage fury.

*   *   *   *   *   *

THE END

Who is Bertrand?

Bertrand is getting on in years. He is world-weary, and no longer sees the need for rushing. If the truth be told, he is probably a mite lazy too. He is no adventurer, no soldier, no athlete, certainly no hero. Not even literate.

What is he then? He is a minstrel, a storyteller, an entertainer. A vital member of medieval society, in the distant days when there were no artificial media of diversion to take people's minds off the trouble and pain of an uncomfortable life. In crowded, shadowy evenings of shimmering logs and trembling candle flames, stories were everything.

So Bertrand was appreciated. He was accepted, like the weather. He travelled, so he saw things. He studied his fellow-man. As the outsider who was always moving on, he possessed the detachment necessary to analyse motives and mysteries. His illiteracy did not imply stupidity or lack of perception any more than literacy implied shrewdness or intelligence.

People told him things, as they did to friars, for the same reason: they did not expect to see him again. Because he was ageing and overweight, poor and solitary, nobody regarded him as a threat. He had no 'angle'. There was nothing to distrust. He listened and he observed, so he found things out. He pondered, so he worked things out. And, when the time was right, he sorted things out.

And then he moved on, with his beloved donkey, Tristan.

Why Bertrand 'de Montclos'?

The usual choice for a medieval sleuth is a cleric – because clerics are usually the only members of society who are literate. But medieval society did not assume that books were the be-all and end-all of human wisdom. Just as many in the twentieth century saw the advent of television as a threat to the art of conversation, so many in the Middle Ages saw the printing-press as a threat to the power of the human voice, to the art of oratory and advocacy, to the camaraderie of the storyteller and his fire-flickered circle of spellbound listeners.

So Bertrand is valid.

But why Bertrand 'de Montclos'? Bertrand was anything but athletic, anything but dashing. Who was the most unathletic and 'un-dashing' sleuth of all? Sherlock Holmes' brother Mycroft. Put 'Mycroft' into French, and you have, as near as dammit, 'Monclos'. Bertrand is poor – or he would not have become a minstrel in the first place. Like many poor people, he had social aspirations, and he was human. So he gave himself a name which sounded impressive, particularly to all those strangers he was always meeting. (After all, who was going to be able to check up on him?) He added the 'de' to make it sound even more impressive. And *voilà* – we have 'Bertrand de Montclos'.

Bertrand's personality matched the society in which he moved. Life proceeded at a more leisurely pace in the Middle Ages, so one must not expect breathless,

'Indiana-Jones'-style, nonstop violence and gallop. But that does mean that nothing much ever happened in the Middle Ages. Far from it. In the French town of Clermont in November, 1095, as it reeled from the visit of Pope Urban II, there was enough of family feuds, greed, religious ecstasy, mass hysteria, papal politics, and witchcraft to satisfy the most jaded palate.

And on the long journey to Jerusalem, on the three-year First Crusade which was set off by the Pope's speech in Clermont, there would be ample scope for more drama and mystery. First of all, perhaps, around the town where one of the crusading armies was to assemble – and Bertrand was not going to miss the Gathering at Toulouse...

Author's biography

Berwick Coates was educated at Kingston Grammar School, and read History at Christ's College, Cambridge.

Since then, he has been, at various times, an army officer, author, artist, lecturer, careers adviser, drama producer, games coach, and teacher of History, English, Latin, General Studies, and Swahili.

He has published eighteen books, including two historical novels with Simon and Schuster.

He lives in Devon, where he is the Archivist of West Buckland School.